With Everything At Stake….

It's been years since Sheriff Dawn Madison said goodbye to Texas Ranger Wyatt McPherson. She's closed the door on the heartache of her past. But when the sleepy town of Colton, Texas, is rocked by a series of shocking murders, Dawn has no choice but to trust the man who broke her heart if she wants to protect the ones she loves…

All Bets Are Off

Four years have passed. But Wyatt hasn't forgotten the bold, Native American beauty who stole his heart . . . and broke it. Losing her and the life they had hoped to share left him an empty shell of himself. But if he wants to stop the deranged killer terrorizing the innocent kids of Colton, he'll have to let Dawn back into his life. It's a risk he's willing to take, even if heartache is all he takes home…

Books by Sara Walter Ellwood

Colton Gamblers Series
Gambling On A Secret, Book One
Gambling On A Heart, Book Two
Gambling On A Dream, Book Three

Heartstrings

Published by Kensington Publishing Corporation

Gambling On A Dream

Colton Gamblers Series

Sara Walter Ellwood

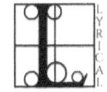

LYRICAL PRESS
Kensington Publishing Corp.
www.kensingtonbooks.com

For all of my co-workers, who have encouraged and believed in me through the years of my journey to becoming a published author. You all truly are like family.

Author's Foreword

The Colton Gamblers

In 1865, three disillusioned first cousins return from the battlefields of the defeated South to find their home in East Texas a shambles. Determined to make a new start, they head west. In the cowboy town of Dallas, Texas, they decide to pool the few silver dollars they have between them and enter into a poker game. With their gamble, they win over 100,000 acres of good grassland in Central Texas. Over the next century and a half, their descendents build a fortune in cattle and oil, but as time goes by, greed erodes their family bond.

These are the stories of the eighth generation gambling on love and bringing back the bond of family...

Chapter 1

"What the hell's going on?"

Interim Sheriff Dawn Madison closed her eyes and swallowed as she rested her hand over her lower abdomen. How would she tell him his son was dead?

She stood from where she crouched by the body of the seventeen-year-old boy, lying on the litter-strewn gravel next to the Dumpster reeking of day-old beer bottles and spilled whiskey. The rusty chain link fence trapped the body like the dirty newspapers stuck against it. She wasn't sure if the dark stain under the boy was from his blood or years of grease and liquor spilling out of the trash.

"Where's Chris?" Julie Larson's footfalls on the wood stairs from her second floor apartment to the back porch of the Longhorn Saloon she co-owned with her brother hammered through Dawn. "What's goin' on, Sam?"

"Don't know." Sam stopped to wait for his younger sister, but he never took his gaze from Dawn and her deputies. "I just got here and saw all the commotion. I can't find Chris nowhere. He ain't answering his damned phone. I started wonderin' where he is and came looking for him. He's supposed to be cleaning the bathrooms, but he ain't there. Doesn't look like he did a damned thing since closin'."

A group of curious bystanders was gathering on the side of the weathered clapboard bar near the customer parking lot. Dawn walked over to her lieutenant as he finished zipping up the body bag. She pushed down the fear and pain of telling a father he'd lost his child and pointed toward the growing crowd. "Tilly, get those peepers out of here. I don't need the grapevine going crazy over this."

With a grunt, he stood and adjusted his tan Stetson. "On it. What you gonna tell Sam and Julie?"

Wishing she could tell them anything but what happened, she glanced at the brother and sister coming closer over the weedy gravel parking lot. She fisted her hand over her lower belly, her baby hadn't been born yet when a drug dealer took him from her, and she still woke up at night from the grief. The thought of what she'd have felt if he'd been seventeen when she'd lost him made her sick. "The truth. Well, enough of it, anyway."

"Wouldn't want your job, Sheriff." Tillman "Tilly" Kennedy jacked up his gun belt and headed to do her bidding with the bystanders.

She glanced at Deputies Chet Hendricks and Doug Grant. They searched for evidence in the dry weeds, struggling for life in the greasy gravel surrounding Christopher Larson's black shrouded body.

Why did she do this to herself? Why was being sheriff of this town so important? She'd been appointed interim sheriff after Zack Cartwright hung up his shiny tin star for a branding iron last month. She was in charge, but not uncontested for the election next month in November that would decide whether the county wanted her or Chet Hendricks as sheriff. Anger twisted with grief as she looked upon the black heap of a teenager's brutally murdered body. Whether she won the election or not, she had to find the killer.

She turned away and intercepted the Larsons before they could get any closer. At least the man couldn't see what had happened to his son. The coroner was on the scene, and Lucinda Hudson, a local photographer who worked part-time for the county, had already taken pictures. Sam stared over her shoulder, not a difficult task since he towered over her five-foot, six-inch frame.

When he swung his gaze down to meet hers, she couldn't miss the fear within the brown depths. "What's goin' on, Dawn? Tell me straight."

Julie clung to her brother's big arm and bit her bottom lip. In her trembling free hand, she held a smoldering cigarette. Her hair, which was red this week, was pulled back into a ponytail. She looked as if she'd just gotten out of bed in her oversized T-shirt and nothing else.

Sam was dressed in his usual white T-shirt and jeans. The early morning sun glistened off his bald head.

The knife of anger and grief twisted in her heart. Most people had put the Larsons--Sam and his sisters, Ella and Julie--down all of their lives. Over the years, they'd crawled out of the gutter by co-owning the Longhorn Saloon and now Ella's Diner. The family had already gone through hell back in July when Ella had been murdered by her daughter's biological father--none other than the richest man in the county, oil tycoon, Leon Ferguson.

The last thing she wanted was to add to their misery only three months later, but this was her job now. The job she'd always wanted. "Sam. Julie. Let's go inside."

Glancing at the body bag, he lowered his brow. "Okay."

Once they were inside the tiny back office, she took a deep breath. Sam's ex-wife should be here for this too, but she lived down in Crawford with husband number three, or was it four?

"I think y'all should have a seat for this," she said as gently as she could.

The fear in his eyes brightened, and sweat beaded on his head as he sagged into the old leather chair behind a spotless desk. "That body out there. It's Chris, ain't it?"

Julie stood behind him and rested a hand on his trembling shoulder. Her hazel eyes filled with tears, and she took a ragged puff on the burned down death stick.

Unable to hold herself up any longer, Dawn leaned on the desk with a hip and pulled off her tan uniform Stetson.

Sam's dark eyes shimmered with unshed tears. Dawn swallowed and averted her gaze to the hat gripped in her hands as she nodded.

Julie let out a wail and hugged her brother from behind burying her face into his beefy neck. Dawn reached out and took the cigarette from her trembling hand, before she dropped the thing, and put it out in an ashtray on the desk.

Sam shook violently as tears rolled down his ruddy cheeks and emotions twisted his mouth into an ugly sneer.

He clenched his sister's fingers, and with the back of his other hand, wiped his eyes with a wicked swipe across his face. His chest heaved. "Goddamn!"

Dawn stood and fisted her hands by her side. Memories accosted her. Although her baby boy hadn't been born yet when she'd lost him, the pain was immense. She sniffed back the burn in her sinuses. "I'm sorry, Sam."

"How'd it happen?"

She cleared her throat. Dammit, she didn't want to tell him the truth. "He was beat, then stabbed."

Sam shook and grabbed onto the desk as he buried his face in the wood. Julie slid to the floor, covered her face, and sobbed, while Dawn rushed forward and rested her hand on his quaking back.

"Oh, God." Shaking his head, he sobbed. "I should've seen this coming. Especially with everything Ella went through with Annie before the Quinns took her in."

Kneeling before him, Dawn gave him all the comfort she could offer. She didn't want to ask him this now, but she had to know. "Sam, was Chris into drugs?"

He closed his eyes and nodded. The sigh escaping him came from his soul. "Yeah. That's why Peggy's latest husband kicked him out," he said, referring to his ex-wife. "But Chris... Chris was a good kid." He turned his tortured gaze to her. "Find the bastard who did this, Dawn. Or you can kiss your dream of being sheriff goodbye. I think we both know who is selling drugs to these kids. That brother of yours has always been a trouble maker."

She wouldn't believe her older brother was the dealer.

He couldn't be.

* * * *

The next morning, Dawn entered the surgical room off the morgue of Forest County General Hospital. At the stench of formaldehyde, embalming fluid, and disinfectant, the pot of coffee she'd drank that morning soured, and her belly rolled.

Stopping at the foot end of the metal table, she stared down at the autopsied body of Chris Larson. His face had been beaten to nearly unrecognizable, and he had a total of seven stab wounds.

Dr. Andy Warren, the county coroner, wiped his hands on a towel as he stood next to her. "The stab to the chest is what probably killed him. It punctured the heart and left lung."

"When do you expect to get the toxicology results back?"

He shrugged and tossed the towel onto a bloody, instrument-cluttered tray. "Should have it back in three weeks. But from the damage to his liver and heart, I'd say he's a crack cocaine user."

"Thanks, Doc." The last thing Colton needed was a crack dealer. Whatever happened to the days when the strongest drugs around were moonshine and marijuana?

Those days were lost when the Dallas dealers moved into the country to widen their net, and the Mexican drug cartels pumped more coke over the border. The answer whispered to her from the days she was a vice cop on the Dallas PD.

"Have you contacted the Texas Rangers?"

She swallowed hard. The last thing she wanted was the Rangers involved. Not because she couldn't use their help, but because of who would likely be sent to assist in the investigation.

"Yeah, I called them and the FBI too." She glanced at her watch. "I have to get back to the office. I'm meeting with the Ranger in an hour."

Back at the station, she entered the sheriff's office. The door still had Zack Cartwright's name painted in gold on the frosted glass of the window. She couldn't believe the damned fool had gone and resigned.

He'd been like a brother to her for as long as she could remember. When he first started sniffing around Tracy Quinn Parker again, she thought he was nuts. But maybe Dawn had missed her target on that one. She'd never seen Zack happier than he was now that they're back together and engaged to be married at Thanksgiving.

He'd been an amazing sheriff, but his heart had never been in the job.

Zack Cartwright would forever be a cowboy.

After setting a pot of coffee to brew in the old stained Mr. Coffee, sitting on a short metal file cabinet in the corner, she sat in the fake leather chair behind the utilitarian desk. She ran both hands over her slicked back hair and pulled out the band to shake out the bun at the back of her head. Taking a deep breath, she braided and re-wound the thick, long mess back into a knot and secured it with the black band. Playing with her hair wasn't going to make any of this go away.

Before she had a chance to mentally prepare herself for the encounter coming with Texas Ranger Wyatt McPherson in less than ten minutes, Charles "Chet" Hendricks roared through the open door like a winter storm. The deputy had been interviewing everyone living on Blackwell and Main Streets near the Longhorn.

She doubted anyone had seen anything since the time of death was estimated to be sometime around four AM, but she might get lucky because it had been a Monday morning. Someone might have been heading out to work that early. "Find out anything?"

She couldn't miss the smugness of his smile. Chet had never been counted among her friends. He and Talon had been classmates, and Chet had bullied her older brother for years over being the youngest bastard son of the notorious Jock Blackwell, until he'd had enough and pounded the hell out of Chet. The deputy hadn't made it a secret he didn't want her as interim sheriff, and threw his hat into the election and campaigned against her.

But his dislike went deeper than Talon's illegitimacy or her ability to be sheriff.

Chet disliked anyone who didn't check the Caucasian box on the census form.

Despite this, the town loved its veterans, and Chet qualified. He'd gone to the Army National Guard after high school and had done a stint in Afghanistan before getting out of the military.

While her father had been sheriff for over a decade, his tenure as the county's first Native American sheriff had not been free of scandal. His election had been bought and paid for by his adopted family-- the Cartwrights. And he'd been accused of looking the other way in more incidences than one, especially those involving the Blackwells, Cartwrights, Fergusons, and McPhersons.

An excited gleam came into his eyes. "I got a witness that puts Talon Blackwell in the vicinity of the Longhorn at the same time as the murder."

She leaned back in her chair and gripped the armrests. What the hell was Talon doing on Main Street at that time in the morning? He'd moved back to town two months ago and into the old hunting cabin on the third of the family ranch belonging to him. His big plan was to raise cattle on his part of the M bar C, their family's ranch, now that he got his share of money from the sale of the Blackwell Ranch.

At four AM, if a rancher was up, he was feeding stock, not cruising through a sleeping town, fifteen miles away.

"I'll question Talon as soon as possible. He may have seen something."

Chet's lips twisted into a sardonic grin. "Yeah, you do that, *Sheriff.*"

Determined not to let the pissant intimidate her, she stood and leaned over the desk. "I should remind you, *Deputy* Hendricks, I was appointed sheriff by the town council, and you haven't won the election. You are very close to insubordination."

"Hope I'm not interrupting anything."

Both she and Hendricks turned toward the door. Texas Ranger Wyatt McPherson stood in the opening. He pulled his hat off his head of thick chestnut brown hair. His full lips twitched up in one corner, and amusement caused small crinkles at the corners of his bluebonnet-blue eyes, as if he spent too many years squinting into the sun.

Dawn sucked in a breath and hated that her heart seemed to speed up. Damn, she hated when people snuck up on her. She refused to think about the fact that her heart hadn't started beating fast until *after* she'd conducted a full assessment and determined the interruption was harmless.

Well, as harmless as a rattlesnake.

Wyatt ambled into the room with the loose walk of a man who'd grown up riding horses.

"Lieutenant McPherson, welcome." She pasted a smile on and prayed it looked genuine. The last thing she wanted was either man to know how much Wyatt's presence affected her. She'd made that mistake last month when he showed up on duty to help catch a gang of cattle rustlers.

The Texas Ranger held out his hand. She shook it quickly and tried to ignore the way his touch caused her skin to tingle.

"Sheriff, it's good to see you again."

Yeah, right. Like working together on the rustling case had been a picnic.

"Glad the Rangers sent you, Wyatt." Chet faced Wyatt with all the self-importance of a bantam roster. "I have a witness that puts Talon Blackwell at the scene around the time of death. I think he should be brought in for questioning."

Wyatt glanced at her, but she ignored him to glare at Chet and said through gritted teeth, "Deputy Hendricks, you are dismissed."

With a glower at her, he didn't say more. He stormed out of the office, then shut the door with a bang behind him. She took a deep breath and let it out slowly.

"I almost need my hunting knife to cut the tension in here. What was that all about?"

She met his blue gaze. "You know you can't trust us Injuns. Maybe I'll ride on over to his place later and scalp him in his sleep and hang his mangy pelt on the totem pole in front of my teepee."

Wyatt chuckled and sat in the chair in front of her desk. He laid his black Resistol hat on the edge. "See, that's why you'll make a great sheriff."

She narrowed her eyes on him. "Better share that with the rest of the town. Chet has them convinced he'd be the best choice for sheriff."

He shrugged and grinned a one-sided smile, making him look like a sexy cross between a young Harrison Ford and Clint Eastwood all rolled up in one. "He won't win, and Hendricks will either come around, or else once you're elected sheriff, he'll quit. At least it won't be like when your dad was elected. Over half of his deputies up and walked out in protest."

She remembered the day her father won the election. "Yeah, and Dad wouldn't have gotten elected if the Cartwrights and your dad hadn't pulled every string out there. When I win this election, it will be because I earned it, not because someone bought it for me."

Had she imagined the shadow over his eyes as he lowered his gaze to his hands?

"You're still just as driven as you've always been."

"When someone thinks killing kids on my watch for drugs is okay, damned right I'm driven." She folded her arms over her chest. "I just hope the people in Forest County realize the fallout if they put a bigot like Chet Hendricks in the sheriff's office."

Wyatt leaned back in his chair. "I told you he won't win. Give the folks of this town some credit."

"I'll be happy when the election is finally over." She stood and headed for the coffee in the corner.

"So, what was he yapping about concerning Talon?"

She dumped fake creamer into her cup and handed Wyatt a cup of black. "Someone supposedly saw him near the murder scene."

"We'll have to question him."

She sat behind her desk again and sipped the strong, hot coffee. "Yeah, I know."

"I thought he was living out on the M bar C. How's he doing these days?"

"Yeah, he's living there." She set her favorite bright green mug on the desk and shrugged. Would he recognize it as the one he'd given to her on her thirtieth birthday? She wasn't sure if she was happy or disappointed when he glanced at it, and his face showed no signs of recognition. "You know Talon. He's always been a loner. He's more so since coming home."

"Prison will do that to a person."

Talon's life had never been easy. Their mother married Dawn's father when Talon was only a baby. Her dad had wanted to adopt him, but Talon's biological father wouldn't allow it. Jock Blackwell had insisted Talon carry his name, but he never was a father to Talon, or his other three illegitimate sons for that matter. Her dad had tried his best with Talon, but he'd rebelled early and gotten himself into trouble on a regular basis. Her father always got him out of the misdemeanor stuff--except he hadn't been able to get him out of the bogus drug charges he'd racked up two years ago in Amarillo.

The day Talon graduated high school, he'd left home to ride the rodeo circuit, until he was thrown from a bull and nearly killed six years ago. He'd moved home to recover, and this time his father wanted to spend time with him. Dawn suspected Jock had wanted to gage his youngest son's intentions. Of all his sons, Talon was the only one who hadn't ever cared about getting his hands on Blackwell Ranch. After a few months, Talon and Jock seemed to form some sort of relationship. Then one day, Talon had ridden out over the pasture of his father's ranch and discovered Jock dead. Her bother never talked of the sight, but it had to have been gruesome. Jock had died from a head injury and lain in the July heat and elements for three days.

She shook her head at the thoughts. "You don't honestly believe Talon would do or sell drugs, do you?"

Wyatt sipped his black coffee from the Styrofoam cup as if considering his response. "All I know is no one truly decides to be an addict. You know that."

She stared at the coffee in the mug clutched between her hands. "Talon swore in his trial the coke had been planted on him to keep him from competing in the rodeo. I believe my brother, Wyatt. Talon has always been a hothead and a roughneck, but he has never been an addict, dealer--or a murderer."

"We still have to talk to him."

She let out a long breath, sagging with the exhale, and nodded. Wanting to change the subject, she asked about his younger sister. "How's Rachel? I heard she came home the other day."

"Rachel's home, but having a tough time."

"I'll have to come over and visit her." She and Rachel McPherson had been friends in school. But they'd grown apart as high school friends do. Dawn went off to the police academy in Austin, while Rachel went to the University of Texas, graduating as a registered nurse. She ended up joining the Army, being commissioned, and was deployed to Afghanistan. This last deployment had been her third time over there, and it would also be her last. She'd been shot multiple times and had lost her lower leg.

The damned war. Post traumatic stress disorder had screwed up Zack in a big way. He'd all but been an alcoholic, and she believed if it hadn't been for his little girl, he would've put a bullet in his own head after his wife died. His depression, and her fear that he'd go off the deep end, had been what convinced her to talk him into running for sheriff after her father retired, instead of running for the office herself.

"I just wish there was something I could do." He sipped his coffee and shook his head. "Yesterday, after I brought her home from the Waco VA hospital, Audrey showed up. I love my twin, but I wish she would stay away for a little while. Rachel seemed more depressed after Audrey left, and of course, that upset Mom."

"Was Lance there too?" What a mess. Lance Cartwright was the last person Rachel needed to see right now.

She understood Rachel's pain. Nothing worse than being thrown away by a man you loved. Dawn had taken a bullet for Wyatt, costing her their baby's life. He left her the moment he discovered she'd been pregnant. Like she'd always feared he would, which had been exactly why she hadn't told him.

"No, he had the good sense to stay away." Wyatt rubbed the back of his neck. "But my mother thinks everything will be fine and dandy if they all make up. She's planning a huge dinner Sunday and invited Lance and Audrey over."

Dawn let out a breath and hugged her mug between her hands, hoping the warmth would take away her sudden chill. "Damn. I mean… This has to be brutal for Rachel. Doesn't your mom realize how she must feel?"

Not only was Rachel now sterile after being shot in the gut, but there was a time she loved Lance before her sister stole him away by seducing him.

"I think Mom's in denial. She wants all of us to get along."

When he looked up, the love for his sister shining in his eyes twisted her heart. He'd always been there for his sisters, but he hadn't stuck by her when she needed him.

"My baby sister can't take much more, and without her friends, I'm afraid for her."

She nodded, but her friend's welfare wasn't what had her reeling; it was the man she had once loved.

Chapter 2

Dawn paced the length of the conference room. The tapping of her boots echoing through the room only served to grate on her nerves as much as the kooky bird sounds emitting from Wyatt's phone. The familiar scents of burnt coffee and lemon furniture polish made the oppressive air somewhat tolerable.

She stopped only to start up in her restless movement again as she and Wyatt waited for Chet and his brother-in-law to show up. Wyatt leaned against the large wall map of Texas at the end of the room and stared down at his iPhone.

She ignored him, or at least tried to. But ignoring him was as easy as pretending the conference room wasn't about a hundred degrees. Sweat gathered in her hair and between her breasts causing her skin to itch and feel over-exposed.

"Damn it, where are they?" She looked out the glass window of the conference room door.

"It's only been a half hour. Gene probably had to find someone to cover at the Quick Fill." Wyatt pushed away from the wall and sat on one of the chairs at the square table in the center of the room, but continued to play his game.

She couldn't help but smile. When they were kids, he and her brother had been addicted to video games. They'd spend hours during the winter sitting on her family's couch, hogging the only TV to play on Talon's old Nintendo.

A cackling sounded from his phone, and he hissed a curse.

She took a few steps toward him and chuckled. "The pigs won?"

"This round." He glanced up, his blue eyes bright with amusement as his lips quirked in a one-sided grin. "I love this damned game as much as I hate it."

She sat beside him and folded her hands in her lap. They'd spent a lot of time together on stakeouts, playing card games and doing crosswords. "I refuse to play games on my phone. I'd be addicted in a minute and never get any work done."

"I'm not addicted." He glanced down at his phone with a pucker on his lips.

God, he looked so damn kissable.

She shifted in her seat and stood, crossing her arms over her chest. "Right. When did you start playing it?"

He set his phone on the table. "Two weeks ago. One of the guys in the Rangers got me started."

There was a knock on the door and it opened. She turned toward Chet and his brother-in-law as they entered the room.

After the greetings and formalities, Gene Murphy sat in the seat across from her and Wyatt with a tape recorder in the middle.

She pulled a notepad from her folder and smiled. "Tell us exactly what you remember from yesterday morning between four and five AM."

Gene shifted his broad shoulders and glanced at Chet, who'd taken the seat beside Wyatt; then he rubbed his hand over his dark beard. "I'd just opened up when I saw Talon Blackwell walk by in front of the Longhorn. I thought it was real odd that he'd be around at that time. The saloon had closed two hours before, and there's nothing else in that part of town other than the downtown bank branch, old lady Pratt's boarding house, and the daycare center her daughter runs two blocks down."

Wyatt leaned forward over his arms. "What was he doing when you saw him?"

"Just walking." Gene scrunched up his brows as if that would help him to remember better. "He was looking at a piece of paper or something, and he looked a little out of it. You know, like he was dazed or something. And he wiped his face on a rag."

"Do you know what time this was?" Wyatt asked.

Gene folded his hands on the table. For someone who worked in a gas station, he had extremely clean hands.

"It was exactly four twenty-five." Gene pulled his hands from the table and hid them in his lap as if Dawn's scrutiny made him nervous. "I know because I glanced at the clock."

Dawn's heart thundered in her chest. How could Talon be involved with murdering a kid? When she'd lost her baby, her brother had been one of the few people who knew about it and had been there for her. "Did you see him either go into the ally to the parking lot behind the bar or come out of it?"

She held her breath as Gene glanced at Chet and shook his head. "I didn't see him come from behind the bar, but I know he did."

"What happened that you didn't see him?" Wyatt's voice held an edge of warning. She'd heard it more than once when they'd been in vice and questioned bystanders. He never liked when a witness made conclusions that might not be true and could color their perceptions.

Gene frowned and glanced at Chet, then met her and Wyatt straight on. "I got a costumer then. A truck driver pulled up and came in for a burrito and coffee."

Sweat trickled down Dawn's neck into her collar. She wasn't sure if the heat of the room caused it or the memories of her and Wyatt. She rubbed the back of her neck. "Do you know this driver?"

"Nope. Never seen him before. A lot of them use Highway Six through town to get west of the interstate mess around Dallas and Fort Worth."

"He may have seen something." Wyatt put voice to her thoughts.

She glanced at him, and for a beat, she went back in time, before she'd lost the baby, before he'd left her. They broke the spell at the same time when they turned away. She shifted in her seat to lean over her arms, and in the process, brushed his arm. "Do you have surveillance video?"

"Yeah." Murphy leaned back in his chair.

Wyatt stood and moved to the other end of the table where he folded his arms in front of him. The meeting was over. "We'll need to see those CDs."

Gene nodded his head. "Sure. I'll bring them by later today."

* * * *

Wyatt parked his Silverado beside his mother's Ford Focus in the gravel driveway, leaned his head back against the rest, and closed his eyes.

He should have known taking this case would bring back memories he'd long ago tried to forget. Dawn was still as driven as she'd always been. Four years ago, they'd been paired together on the Dallas PD, after his partner took a job with the DEA. Wyatt had worked in vice for about two years, and Dawn had been on patrol a little over a year.

They'd been friends since they were kids, he'd even taken her to her senior prom, but working together as police partners had required a deeper relationship. Some cops claimed it bordered on a marriage, especially among vice cops who were constantly working in dangerous situations where undying trust and strong commitment to each other were important.

Dawn had been a great undercover cop. Since she was young, and all but full-blooded Native American with a little African-American and Spanish blood mixed in, she could infiltrate gangs rather easily. He'd loved to watch her work.

Then one night while they'd been on a stakeout, they'd let their mutual attraction get away with them. The moment they were off duty, they'd gone back to his place and made love for hours.

He'd just come off a bad breakup with a local TV news anchor he'd dated off and on since college, and Dawn had dumped a loser whom she caught cheating on her. There had been no regrets after that night. If anything, they'd wondered why they hadn't ever gotten together before then. For five months, they'd spent every moment together. She'd maintained her apartment for appearances, but had moved in with him.

He'd wanted more, but she wanted to become a detective. His dream had been to buy a ranch somewhere and raise a family with her. However, all she ever wanted had been to work her way up the ranks and eventually run for sheriff of Forest County. For her, settling down and family weren't even on the radar.

He'd fallen in love with her, and he'd been confident she felt the same about him, but she'd never mentioned having a future with him.

He opened his eyes and straightened in the seat, shutting down the memories before they dragged him down into the sewer of pain and betrayal. Revisiting the night his world came to an end wasn't something he willing did.

In the distance, a car alarm went off, drawing his attention to the east and beyond the old split rail fence where the pastures used to be. Now, a bunch of Dallas and Waco middle management types and soccer moms populated the housing development that had sprung up over the past three years.

Considering Leon Ferguson was in jail for his numerable crimes, who would take over building the city-slicker cookie-cutter houses?

With an ounce of luck, no one would take over. He was glad the construction had halted. Thank God, the mall was on the other side of what used to be a five-hundred-acre ranch. He grew up on the Circle M, working with his grandfather, and his younger shithead brother, Kyle.

Kyle was also staring down a long stint as a resident of the state pen for his conspiring with Leon Ferguson against Wyatt's cousin, Dylan Quinn, and his new wife, Charli Monroe Quinn.

What a waste, not only of Kyle's life, but of the land, too. Would his grandfather still have sold the place to the developer if he'd known what would have come of his home? What if he had known Wyatt had come to his senses and wanted to become a rancher?

Wyatt's father never had any interest in the ranch. So, when the time came for Granddad to hang up his branding iron, he figured it would be best to sell the place. At the time, Wyatt had been a big city vice cop, and his younger brother was about as responsible as a horsefly. While his sister Audrey already lived on a twenty-thousand-acre ranch with her fancy divorce lawyer husband, and his other sister had been working her way up the ranks in the United States Army and rarely came home.

Besides, his grandfather figured the money from the sale would be a wonderful chunk of change for all of them. Having a few million in the bank was nice, but damn, Wyatt missed the ranch.

He got out of the SUV and headed up the front porch steps to enter the home he grew up in. His parents had built the ranch-style house after their wedding. His grandparents had lived about a quarter mile down the road. Now, a bank sat where the house had been, his grandmother moved to Phoenix with her best friend, and his grandfather resided in the Ferguson family plot in the Colton cemetery.

Goddamn, he hated change.

He wanted his life the way it had been before things were all fucked up because he failed to protect what was important.

Thinking about Dawn was as crazy as remembering his life on the ranch way back when. Neither one could be changed.

Inside the foyer, Crystal Gayle's *Don't It Make My Brown Eyes Blue* drifted to him from the direction of the kitchen. His mother was frying chicken and baking homemade bread and maybe apple pie, if his nose could be trusted. He hung his hat on the rack in the corner by the door and followed the smells into the kitchen.

Jeannie Burton McPherson looked up from the electric frying pan she only used to fry chicken. A cheerful smile brightened her still-pretty face. From the tight curls her graying red hair was wound into, she'd visited their cousin's beauty salon earlier that day and gotten a perm.

He rounded the counter and bent to kiss her on the cheek, the odor of the perming solution lingering in her hair, and the delicious aroma of the foods wrinkled his nose as they mixed. He pulled away and smiled. "Ma, Dad's gonna have to keep an eye on you. You keep getting prettier. I like your hair."

She laughed and swatted at his shoulder, but he didn't miss the slight blush. "You're such a charmer."

With a grin, he looked into the frying pan at the batter dipped chicken pieces frying in what was undoubtedly lard and butter. "You're gonna make me as big as a linebacker if you keep up all this cooking."

She flipped a crispy drumstick. "You could use some more meat on your bones. You always look half-starved when you come home. I swear you don't eat when you're living on your own. I remember that time before you quit the police in Dallas, when you were so skinny, I could almost see through you."

He didn't want to think about that time in his life. After Dawn took a bullet meant for him, he stopped caring about much except going after the thugs who had almost killed the only woman he'd ever loved. But it went deeper than that, she hadn't only put her own life in jeopardy, she sacrificed the child he hadn't known she'd carried.

His son.

Goddamn, now wasn't the time to take a trip down that particular rocky memory lane.

The last thing he wanted was his mother noticing the searing pain he was sure reflected in his face. He picked up a lid on one of the pots to find boiling potatoes. "I eat. I just take after the Ferguson side of the family. I'm tall and lean, but I've never been skinny."

He carried the hundred-ninety pounds of hard muscle on his six-foot, two-inch frame to prove it.

A timer went off, and she opened the oven door to pull out a golden brown apple pie. She set it on a cooling rack. The rich apple and cinnamon scents filling the kitchen made his belly grumble with hunger.

"We'll be eating in a few minutes. Why don't you go get your sister? She hasn't been out of her room all day." He didn't miss the sadness in her voice or the pleading in her faded denim eyes. "You've always been good with her."

He left the kitchen and headed down the hall to stop before the door across from his. He'd packed up his dive of an apartment in Waco, sent his stuff to storage, and moved into his parents' home temporarily to help with Rachel, but he wanted a place of his own.

He took a deep breath as the day his parents brought Rachel home from the hospital drifted into his mind. He and Audrey were only three, but they had both been excited to have a real live baby in their midst. Audrey wanted to dress her up like her favorite doll. He'd wanted someone else to play with, but to be honest, he'd been a little disappointed she wasn't a boy. He'd never dreamed he'd become her protector. Although he loved his twin sister, and technically, was her older brother too--if you can count a whole four and a half minutes as being older--Rachel held a special place in his heart.

Sounds of his father chatting with his mother from the kitchen brought him out of his thoughts, and he knocked on his sister's door. "Rach, Ma's got dinner ready."

"I'm not hungry." Her voice sounded muffled and distracted.

He looked to the ceiling and sent a prayer to heaven to give him the strength and the knowledge to help his baby sister. "I'm coming in."

When she didn't respond, he turned the knob and entered the room. A modern-looking pine queen bed and Rachel's sophisticated styles had replaced the twin canopy beds and white girly furniture. Everything that had been Audrey's was long gone. After all, the few times Rachel came home from her stints as an Army nurse, this was where she'd come.

She sat huddled under an old crocheted blanket in a stuffed chair and stared out the window. What he could see of her face behind her short auburn hair was pale and splotched red, as if she'd been crying. Her hands were curled into fists and tucked in close to her body. Her prosthetic lower left leg sat in the corner with her crutches.

He let out a long breath and sat on the edge of her unmade bed. When he glanced up, he noticed what had her riveted outside the window. In the yard on the other side of the rail fence, two young children played on a swing set while their father and mother worked in the yard. A picture of the perfect family. He closed his eyes and hung his head low.

God, how much more can she take?

"All I ever wanted was a family of my own." Her voice rasped as if coming from her soul.

Yeah, me too. He swallowed hard, but his voice still came out sounding like a frog's croak. "Ladybug, I'm not going to lie to you. I don't know how to make this better."

She turned red-rimmed blue eyes on him. "You haven't called me that in years."

He'd given her the nickname when she was only a baby because, with her bright red hair, she reminded him of a ladybug. For years, the whole family called her by the nickname. He sniffed and swallowed again. Damn, his sinuses burned.

"Everyone thinks it's because of Audrey and Lance that I'm such a mess."

"I know it has to be hard seeing them…"

She shifted her shoulders as if she shrugged, or maybe she took a deep breath. "The lieutenant colonel who was killed in the attack wasn't just my commander."

From the report, he knew Rachel had been attacked by an Afghani national who worked on the base where she'd been deployed.

She and a doctor had been working together late when the Afghani found them. He'd shot the lieutenant colonel and Rachel while they were talking in his office. She'd taken a high-powered bullet in the pelvis area and her lower left leg, which shattered the bone beyond repair. The doctor had died from his wounds, and Rachel had been flown to Landstuhl, Germany, where her leg had been amputated, her pelvis repaired, and her uterus, where the bullet lodged, removed.

The terrorist had committed suicide. His body had been found in his room along with the weapon he'd used to kill the doctor and to shoot Rachel.

Wyatt moved off the bed and kneeled beside her. He took her icy hands and held them. "You weren't working, were you?"

She sniffled and shook her head. As she turned to look out the window again, she whispered, "Alex was my fiance. We planned to get married as soon as I could put in for promotion, but we had to keep our relationship secret since he was my commanding officer until then. No one can ever know about it. I'd never risk his name being dishonored."

Which meant she would never discuss it with her shrink at the VA hospital. The air went out of him, and he bent his head over their joined hands. "Oh, God, Rach. I'm so sorry."

"I wish I'd been killed too," she whispered in a faraway tone that sent an arctic shiver through him.

He squeezed her hand and forced her to look at him by turning her head with his thumb under her chin. "Don't you *ever* say such a thing. We love you. We need you here with us. You hear me? I need you." He swallowed hard and sniffed back the hot knot clogging his sinuses. "I understand how you feel. But *that* isn't the answer."

She shook her head and yanked her hand from his. "How could you know what I'm going through? You have no idea what happened to me. What it was like to watch the man I love die."

He glanced out the window at the happy family. The little boy was Mason, the girl Katie. He was five years old, and she was almost three. The same age his son would have been. He'd met the family on several occasions since they moved into the recently built home three months ago. "Dawn Madison and I were all but engaged while we worked vice on the PD." He met his sister's gaze. "She took a bullet that was meant for me and almost died."

She huffed. "But she's still alive. Alex is dead."

"True." He averted his gaze to his hands. "But I'll never forgive her for what she did. She was five months pregnant and lost the baby."

"Wy, I'm so sorry." She took his hand and squeezed it.

He sniffed again, but he couldn't look up. "She lost our son simply because she wouldn't take herself off the case. The captain would've never allowed her on the sting if he'd known. Hell, if I had known about the pregnancy, I would've had her taken off the case." He shook his head and wiped his nose with the back of his free hand. "I know that isn't the same as what happened to you. But there isn't a day that goes by I don't wonder what my little boy would've grown into." *Or what life with Dawn would've been like.*

"Why do bad things always happen to good people?"

The only answer he had was to take her into his arms and hold her as he closed his eyes against the tears he wouldn't dare let fall.

"I don't know, Ladybug. I don't know."

* * * *

That evening, Dawn got out of her Ford F-150, her boots hitting the dusty ground with a thump. Her brother's old Dodge pickup and a horse trailer were parked next to the old-line cabin on his third of the M bar C.

The old shack wasn't more than termites holding hands. The roof sagged on one side, and a black tarp covered the rusted tin where a leak had weakened the boards beneath. Half the porch had rotted away. The bold tanginess of deterioration mingled with the scent of creek water, horse, fresh hay, and lumber. Someone, probably Talon, had replaced the steps with a concrete block and laid a sheet of plywood over the decaying wood from the step to the door.

East of the cabin, the west branch of Oak Springs Creek meandered along slowly. As kids, she and her two brothers would fish from the bank. On the other side of the shack, a lean-to with a small corral barely contained a massive bay stallion--her brother's horse, *Ugedaliya.* Or Ugly, as the whites called him, since the Cherokee word was hard for them to pronounce. Talon never told the poor bastards that the word meant tornado. Which fit the monster of a horse perfectly.

She closed the door of her truck and walked to the correl. *Ugedaliya* came up to the railing and snorted. When she petted his velvety nose, he nickered. She'd taken care of the contrary stallion while Talon had been in prison last year. "*Fierce Ugedaliya,*" she cooed in her mother's native Cherokee. "*I've missed you.*"

Once *Ugedaliya* realized she wasn't offering carrots or apples, he tossed his big head and moved away to nibble on the short grass growing around the corral posts.

Unable to stall any longer, she took a deep breath and headed across the rutted path, serving as the driveway to the framework of a barn, rising from the ground like a giant skeleton.

Just like Talon to be living in a shack while he built a mansion for his horse.

"I wondered how long you were gonna stand there taking in the sights." Her brother's deep voice came from behind her. "What do you want?"

She turned to Talon coming out from around the lean-to, carrying a feed bucket.

The horse trotted over to him. He stroked the stallion's face. "I doubt this is a social call."

"I need to talk to you."

He dumped the contents of the dented bucket into a trough for his horse, then wiped his hands on a rag he pulled from the back pocket of his faded jeans. His plaid shirt hung open, revealing his deep tan. A bandana was tied around his neck, and his long black hair was held back in a ponytail under an old straw hat.

Hazel eyes, set in a face sharp with the hard angles he'd inherited from his white father, narrowed as he looked over her uniform. "Do I need my lawyer present?"

She straightened her back and wished she and her brother had remained as close as they'd once been. "That depends. I hoped you'd tell me the truth because I'm family and that used to matter to us."

He wiped the back of his hand over his forehead. "That was a long time ago. What the hell do you want? I'm busy."

Sighing, she fought the hurt pinching her heart. "You hear about Sam Larson's son?"

He glanced toward the cabin. "I read something in the paper. But what's it got to do with me?"

She folded her arms in front of her to ward off the sudden chill. Gene Murphy had brought in the surveillance videos from his gas station. The only incriminating thing on them was the perfect view of Talon walking in front of the Longhorn. "Chris Larson was found dead yesterday morning by a garbage man behind the Longhorn." She waited for his response, but when he only stared at her with something akin to impatience in his dark eyes, she said, "We have a witness who puts you near the scene at the time he was murdered."

He turned and headed toward the front of the cabin.

"Talon?" She hurried after him.

After a few steps, he spun and bore down on her. The contempt and harsh anger, turning his handsome features into unforgiving stone, had her stepping back. "So what?"

"Did you see anything?"

He made a disgusted sound between his teeth. "What you really want to know is if I killed that boy. I read he was probably killed over dope." Glaring at her, he asked, "Tell me, Sister, do you think I'm a drug dealer?"

"No, of course not!" She fisted her hands to the point her nails bit into her palms. She hadn't read the local paper, but she could only imagine what the article contained. "But people do, and I want to make sure the same thing doesn't happen here that happened in Amarillo. Answer my question. Why were you in town yesterday morning?"

"I was in town. But the why of it is none of your goddamned business." He turned and headed up the makeshift steps to the porch.

"You're going to force me to bring you in for formal questioning." She shook her head. "If I don't follow through--"

When he looked over his shoulder, she knew she'd destroyed whatever was left of their relationship.

He finished her sentence with a sneer. "You'll look like you're playing favorites like Tom did when he was sheriff."

She jerked back at the reference to her father.

He reached for the rusty, torn screen door. "So much for family trust. Get the hell off my land, *Sheriff*."

Chapter 3

Dawn sat on her couch and shook the colorful woven blanket over her knees. Her grandmother had made it for her when she'd graduated high school. It always reminded her of the cozy warmth that comforted her when she'd visit Nana in Oklahoma. As she picked up the remote from the end table, Taco, her beagle, waddled over from her doggy bed in the corner by the bookshelf.

Taco looked up at Dawn and barked, her tail swishing back and forth. She had more white then brown on her muzzle and face, and her old joints were slow with arthritis. Dawn leaned over and helped the aging pup up onto the couch beside her.

"You're getting too heavy, ole girl. Doc Evans is going to have a fit the next time I take you for a checkup," she said, referring to the town's veterinarian.

Taco's response was to lay her head on Dawn's lap and close her eyes.

As Dawn flipped through the channels, she stroked over the smooth fur of the dog's head. With a chuckle and a glance at Taco, Dawn turned up the volume of the TV so she could hear it over the beagle's snores.

She paused the clicking long enough to stop at the eleven o'clock news on Channel Ten out of Dallas. Dawn frowned as she stared at the anchor, Vanessa Burk, while she talked about a fatal multiple car pileup on Interstate Twenty. She was a beautiful blonde with gleaming hair, cut in the hottest Hollywood style, with straight white teeth and big green eyes. Dawn turned off the TV and set the controller on the end table.

She leaned her head back and closed her eyes. Wyatt had dated Vanessa for over ten years. They'd met in college and had even lived together for several years, but when she wanted to get married, Wyatt called off the relationship.

Two months later, Dawn had sex with him after a stakeout, and her life became everything she'd ever wanted. Had things gotten too serious between them? Had he been afraid of getting tied down with a woman? Was that why he'd left Vanessa? Had Wyatt planned to dump her too? Was that why he'd left her after she'd lost their baby?

She shook her head to dispel the litany of questions she'd asked herself for years and glanced down at the sleeping dog. Had Wyatt ever loved her at all?

As she took a deep breath, she stood, folded the blanket, and put it in its place over the arm of the couch. Taco woke up, and Dawn helped the dog to the floor. "C'mon, time for bed."

Taco lumbered back to her bed in the corner while Dawn headed for the kitchen. She put the dishes from the drying rack away in the overhead cabinet. As she dumped the last of the day's coffee down the drain, she turned off the coffee maker. After she rinsed out the sink and turned off the kitchen lights in her trailer, she made her way back through the living room to the bedroom at the end of the singlewide.

Someday she'd have a big house, but for now, the trailer she'd moved onto her third of the ranch was enough.

She turned on the lamp hanging on the wall by the full-sized bed and changed into the T-shirt and shorts she slept in. Her knees were only inches from the oak dresser when she sat on the end of her bed. She opened the top drawer to take out a pair of socks when the corner of an old photo album she had in the bottom caught her attention.

With a deep breath, she pulled out the album and laid it on her lap.

She smoothed her hand over the damask of the cover before opening it to the first page. The picture staring back at her had been taken twenty years ago and was of her, Wyatt, Audrey, Rachel, Talon, the Cartwright kids--Zack, Logan, Lance and his sister Faith, and the Quinns--Dylan and Tracy. The only ones missing were her brother, Hunter, and Wyatt's brother, Kyle. They'd been toddlers when Zack's mother had snapped the photo at a church picnic.

She smiled at the cheesy grin on Wyatt's face as he, Talon, Lance and Dylan stood behind the younger kids. Back then, they'd all been friends, cousins or siblings. Who would have thought so many of the friends would end up as lovers? She laughed and turned the page as she wiped at a stray tear.

Several more family photos passed by--Christmases, Easters and the family trips to Oklahoma to visit her mother's family. Other pictures were of Talon and Wyatt, sometimes with their other friends, and several of them were of her and Zack Cartwright at the various rodeos they'd participated in as teenagers.

She turned the page to a picture Wyatt's mother had taken the night of her senior prom. Zack and Rachel talked her into going, despite her not wanting to. She never had a boyfriend, partly because her mother had always discouraged her from dating white boys, and because the boys had been too scared of her brother, Talon, and her father to ask her out.

Wyatt had learned of her lack of a date and asked her to the prom. That night had been a dream come true for her, and the big bright smile on her eighteen-year-old self positively glowed. She wiped away another tear as she stared at the tall, lanky boy who'd stolen her heart so many years ago.

She turned to the last page in the album and touched the grainy, black and white sonogram photo. Her baby boy on his last day of life. On the morning she'd been shot in the chest, she'd gone for her checkup and had a sonogram done.

"Let's see what's going on. This might feel a little uncomfortable." Dr. Rice smiled and rubbed the transducer over Dawn's lower belly.

The cold slimy feeling tickled, and the pressure on her full bladder hurt. The static cleared, and the fast beat of a heart echoed through the room. On the monitor, the outline of her baby materialized, and she stopped breathing, forgetting about the discomfort.

"Oh, God." She gasped. Until then, her pregnancy hadn't seemed real. She hadn't been sick more than a few times and had started to get a little rounding in her belly. "It's so different from the last sonogram."

"You're further along than you were during the last one." The doctor nodded and grinned as she glanced at Dawn. "Everything looks normal. Would you like to know the sex?"

She stared at the whitish outline of the baby and fisted her hand over her heart. A hundred different emotions chased through her--love, awe, hope, fear. Would Wyatt want to know? What would he do when she told him she was pregnant? Would he want to marry her? Or would he bail like Jock Blackwell had on her mother when she found out she was pregnant with Talon?

So many questions with no answers. But she couldn't go on without telling Wyatt he was going to be a father.

She nodded and met the doctor's expectant gaze. "Yes. I'd like to know."

"You're going to have a son, Dawn. Congratulations."

Dawn touched the small face of the only photo she had of her baby. Although the world would never see his features, in her mind, he had

Wyatt's blue eyes and her dark hair. "I love you, angel baby. Please forgive me for what I've done to you."

She closed her eyes. No matter what, she had to find out who was dealing drugs and killing kids in her town. She owed it to her baby for the life he was denied.

To do so, she'd even put up with the man who broke her heart.

* * * *

Wyatt sat across from his childhood friend at the conference table in the sheriff's department. Talon Blackwell stared over Wyatt's shoulder with a hard glower at Dawn, who stood behind him against the large map of Texas on the wall.

"If you aren't formally charging me with Larson's murder, I don't have to answer your questions."

Wyatt let out a breath. He'd been questioning Talon for an hour. They didn't know any more than they did before.

Dawn moved forward and leaned over the table beside him. Her fragrance of honeysuckle and citrus filled his senses with memories of having her lying beside him, and of the pillow he'd kept long after they'd broken up just to keep her scent around.

"Talon, be reasonable here. We don't think you were involved, but we have to close this loop." Dawn sat beside Wyatt as she spoke. "Just tell us what you were doing on Main Street Monday morning at four AM and if you saw anything that can help us find the killer."

"I told you." Talon huffed out between his teeth and leaned back in the chair. "I didn't see anything. I was on Main Street, but I don't know anything about that boy."

It was useless to keep up the questioning. Talon wasn't telling them anything. Wyatt hated to admit it, even to himself, but Talon acted like a man with something to hide. He closed his notebook and glanced at Dawn. She tried to cover the tired dark circles under her eyes with makeup, but it had long ago worn away. Her shoulders sagged under the starched tan uniform blouse.

"I think we're done here." Wyatt stood to stretch his back.

Talon rolled out of his chair onto his feet and picked up his old straw cowboy hat. "Good. I've got work to do."

Before he reached the door, Wyatt stepped into his path. "I hope I don't have to remind you to let us know if you feel the need to leave the county."

Talon cocked a dark brow and tipped his head as he put on his hat in a gesture Wyatt hoped was acquiescence, but could have as easily meant *screw you.* As Talon shoved past him to head for the door, he didn't so much as look at his sister.

When the door closed with a resounding click, Dawn pounded a fist onto the table with enough force to rattle their coffee mugs. "Dammit, who is he protecting?"

He glanced back at the door. Talon had always had it rough, but no worse than his sister or younger brother. Sure, being one of Jock Blackwell's ill-begotten sons wasn't something he'd wish on a rabid coyote. However, Tom Madison had treated Talon like a son all his life, even giving him a third of his ranch when he retired.

Talon had changed, and not for the better. His problems didn't come from how he was raised, or even the occasional bullying. He was a troublemaker, and nothing would have changed him.

He sat in the chair Talon had vacated. "Or the question could be what is he hiding?"

She ran her hands over her dark hair to the tight bun at the base of her skull. With jerky movements, she pulled out the band holding the twisted braid captive. As she ran her fingers through the long mass of raven silk, heat coursed through him at the memories of all that hair covering him like a blanket while they'd made love. When she bent over the table and scratched her scalp in pure frustration, all he could think about was her hair hanging down her back to brush and tickle his thighs as she rode him--her favorite position--to orgasm.

The erection was fast and furious and nearly had him groaning. Thank God, he was sitting. He forced his numbed mind to focus on the case.

"We have to find someone else who may have seen or knows something." She glanced across the table at him and straightened. If there was ever the perfect picture of a beautiful Indian maiden, it was Dawn with her hair down. Had she ever had the stuff cut? He swallowed hard and shifted in his chair as his jeans strangled his cock. How long had it been since he'd had sex? He couldn't remember, but refused to believe he hadn't been with someone since Dawn.

With swift, practiced motions, she broke the trance he was under by daftly braiding her hair and wrapping it into a bagel-sized knot at the back of her head. She snapped the hair band over the bun.

He cleared his throat. "When are we talking to Chris's friends?" His voice came out sounding a bit husky, even to his ears.

She stood, taking their coffee cups with her, and refilled them. After she dumped that god awful crap pretending to be creamer into hers, she handed him a mug of black joe. Sipping her coffee from the extra-large, bright green mug he'd given to her for her thirtieth birthday, she returned to her chair.

"Hendricks and Kennedy are getting a list, but according to Julie, he didn't have many friends in Colton."

"How about Justin Vaughn? He's always been a known dealer. Maybe he knows something." He sipped his coffee.

She smiled, and he almost choked as he swallowed the hot, bitter brew. "Haven't thought of him. We should talk to him. They're about the same age. Vaughn's working over at his uncle's farm and garden market."

He set his mug on the table and glanced at his watch. "I can't today."

"Hot date?"

Grinning, he stood. "No. I'm buying the Estrada Ranch."

Her dark eyes widened. "Really? I heard Luis and Stella were thinking of moving to New Mexico, but I didn't know it was a done deal. I figured it would go to either Jose or Mary," she said, referring to the Estradas' son and daughter. "How long has their place been up for sale? I haven't seen a sign in their yard."

He shrugged and reached for his hat where it sat on the edge of the table. "Luis and Stella told Mom and Dad they planned to sell the place a couple of weeks ago while playing Bingo at the firehouse. When they told me, I called the Estradas and made an offer. It never officially made it on the market. I've been looking for a small ranch."

"We'll be neighbors when you settle in there." She cocked her head to the side. "I never knew you wanted to be a rancher."

"You never cared about a lot of things I wanted." His bitterness surprised even him.

She stood and picked up her mug, leaving his where it sat. As she headed for the door, she nodded toward it. "We have a policy around here. We clean up after ourselves. Something I seem to remember you have a hard time with."

* * * *

Wyatt signed his name on the last page of the contract and leaned back in the chair, the gravity of what had just transpired making him dizzy. Three hours ago, he was as rootless as tumbleweed and had more money in the bank than he'd known what to do with. As of two seconds ago, he was the proud owner of a hundred-acre ranch and had a few million dollars less to worry about getting moldy in the Cattleman's Bank and Trust.

"Congratulations." His brother-in-law, Lance Cartwright, smiled at him from across the table sitting in the middle of the massive country kitchen of what was now his new house. Or at least, it would be as soon as the Estradas moved out at the end of the week.

"Thanks for drawing up the papers." Wyatt set the pen on top of the documents as Lance reached for them. He looked at the smiling Estradas, sitting at the end of the table. "Thank you. I don't want you to think I'm rushing you out of your home."

When he'd arrived at the Estradas' ranch, Stella was waiting for him with a plate of warm chocolate chip cookies, while Luis handed him a cold Coors. Stella and his mother had been best friends since they were children. Luis and his father had been drinking buddies for years. The older couple couldn't contain their excitement that Wyatt was interested in their ranch.

Stella reached over and squeezed his hand. "Nonsense. You aren't rushing us out. Our place in Albuquerque is ready for us to move into. And now, we don't have to burden the kids with trying to get rid of the stock and the ranch. Jose has his life in San Antonio, and Mary has her hands full with teaching full-time."

"We are so happy you wanted the place, Wyatt. Let's have a drink to celebrate." Luis stood and headed for the cabinet by the refrigerator, but stopped half way there and looked around the kitchen. "This is a great house for kids. I remember when Stella babysat. Those little buggers would drive me crazy."

"Hey, I remember being one of those little buggers." Lance laughed and pointed at Wyatt. "But you're right. Wyatt could use a couple rug rats running around this place."

Wyatt's grin froze on his face, and he forced a chuckle. "Don't start sounding like my mother. I'm not ready for kids." The lie hung heavy in the air. "How about that drink?"

"Comin' right up." Luis took a tequila bottle from the cabinet. As he poured three shots, Stella grabbed a can of Coke from the fridge. She never drank anything stronger. As Luis handed one of the glasses to Lance, he asked, "Have any of those mares your cousin has pastured next to our place pop up pregnant?"

Lance took the shot and chuckled. "Two of them are."

Wyatt accepted his glass from Luis and grinned. "Is Zack still upset with old Thunderbolt?"

Back in August, the fence between the Estradas' ranch and the CW had broken down, allowing an old rodeo paint stallion by the name of Thunderbolt to get in with Zack's newly purchased thoroughbred mares. From what Wyatt recalled, Zack had been furious until Talon's older half brother, Johnnie Blackwell, and their cousins, Jake and Brent Parker, had relieved him of the mares by stealing them. Fortunately, Wyatt had contacts west of Midland who'd been investigating a ring of horse thieves, and the Texas Rangers had been able to recover the animals before they'd been sold on the black market.

"Do pigs like mud?" Lance shook his head. "But he'll get over it. Thunderbolt was a champion back in the day. Those foals will be damned good horses." He raised his glass to Wyatt. "And just think, now that stud is all yours."

Not only had Wyatt purchased the ranch, he'd also bought eighty-five head of cattle and six horses. Talk about jumping in with the alligators.

Luis held up his shot glass. "Make sure you charge him for the stud service the next time."

They all laughed and clicked glasses. "I sure will. To new beginnings."

Lance's smile broadened. "You better believe it. To new beginnings."

* * * *

Talon strode through the old beer joint and looked around the dark interior from under the brim of his hat. Unlike the Longhorn Saloon, the Hardware Bar was a dive he liked to avoid. His boots crunched on the peanut shells covering the floor as he made his way to the scuffed bar. He breathed a sigh of relief that his older half brother, Darryl Blackwell, and not his mother was at the bar. She was the number one reason he didn't like the place. Although Talon had never been close to any of his Blackwell brothers, Darryl was the one that seemed to accept Talon into the clan the most.

Darryl nodded a greeting as he stopped to take Talon's order. "Hey, what can I getcha? Haven't seen you in a coon's age."

With a shrug to Darryl's second statement, he said, "A bottle of Coors." When his brother handed it to him, he jutted his chin toward the back room. "Is Chief in the back?"

Darryl chuckled and wiped at the bar with a rag as stained and beat-up as the wood. "Of course, where else would he be Wednesday night? From what I'm hearing, he's beating the pants off the guys."

"Thanks." Talon tossed a bill on the bar to cover the cost of his beer and headed to the back room.

Several cowboys looked his way as they waited their turn on the pool tables, but he ignored them and entered the poker lounge. Although gambling was technically illegal in Texas bars, the Hardware somehow always avoided being shut down for its gaming room. His stepfather had claimed the reason was Lydia O'Donnell, Darryl's mother, knew too many secrets of too many men on the town council for them not to be afraid of her.

Smoke from cigars and cigarettes clung to the air as he looked around until he found Chief. The old Comanche picked up the cards dealt to him and tossed two away. Talon waited on the fringes of the room, drinking his beer, as the man he'd always considered his grandfather played out the game.

Tate Jackson tossed in his cards with a curse. "I'm done." The big African-American stood and rubbed a hand over his mouth. "Louise is gonna kill me if I'm not home by ten."

Chief gathered up the chips in the center of the table. "More like that wife of yours don't like you donatin' your paycheck to my retirement fund."

Several of the men standing back, watching the game, chuckled. Tate grinned, his white teeth bright against his dark face. "That too. Have a good one, Chief." He slipped on a warn denim jacket and looked around. "Hope your luck's better than mine, boys."

After Tate left, Chief glanced at Talon. He took the chair across from his grandfather. Something in his stark expression must have alerted Chief that Talon wanted to talk and didn't want an audience.

"Gentlemen, I'd like a word with my grandson."

A moment later, they were alone, and the old Comanche, who everyone in town called Chief, including his grandchildren, leaned forward over his crossed arms, resting on the table, and waited.

Talon stared at the scuffed table and took a deep breath. No use beating around the bush with Chief. He'd always admired the old man's no-bullshit personality. "I'm going to Vegas."

Chief raised a brow. "Thought your sister told you to stay put."

Talon huffed between his teeth. "I can't do that. Something's come up, and I have to go." He pulled an envelope from his jacket pocket and laid it on the table. "Please give this to Mom."

Chief glanced at the white envelope but didn't pick it up. "Son, I know you don't have anything to do with the crap that's goin' on 'round here, but if you leave, you'll only make yourself look as guilty as a half-dressed whore at a church picnic."

Talon tapped his fingers on the table. He didn't need anyone to tell him that, but if he didn't leave now, he'd never forgive himself. "Just tell Mom I'm sorry."

Chief shrugged and leaned back in his chair. "I guess you ain't gonna tell me why the sudden need for the Vegas vacation."

Looking down at the table, Talon signed and shook his head. "I can't."

"Guess it's best I don't know. Then I won't have to keep track of a bunch of lies." He shuffled the cards in his hands.

Talon let a small smile touch his lips. Chief might be bursting with curiosity, but he wouldn't press him to learn his secrets, which was the reason he'd come to his grandfather and hadn't told anyone else in his family where he was going. He didn't want to answer questions he wasn't even sure the answers to.

The door opened behind him and he turned. The smile fell right off his lips. Damn, this was the last thing he needed to deal with right now.

"Well, well, what do we have here?" Chet Hendricks ambled into the room like he was John Wayne. "Teaching the boy your bad habits, Chief?"

Talon stood and faced the son-of-a-bitch who'd made his life hell since he was a kid. Surely, Dawn wouldn't have sent Chet after him. "What do you want, Hendricks?"

Chet shrugged and moved around the outside of the dingy room. "Nothing but finding a murderer and drug dealer." He faced Talon with a tight-lipped grin that never reached his hard eyes. "You wouldn't know anything about that, would you, Blackwell?"

Talon had more than his share of assholes as arrogant and mean as Hendricks in his life. He glanced at his grandfather. "See you later, Chief."

Hendricks stepped in front of him as he headed for the door. "Not so fast. I want to know what you and Justin Vaughn were so chummy about. Heard you and he were talking yesterday. We all know he's a two-bit dealer."

What the hell was he talking about? Vaughn was the kid he'd bought apples for his horse from. Talon had gone to school with his mother and had always had a soft spot for him because the kid had dealt with the same shit he had to put up with while growing up.

The chair Chief sat on scrapped the floor as if he stood, but Talon didn't look away from the deputy.

"Unless you are here on official business, Deputy Hendricks, I suggest you leave now, because police harassment is still illegal from what I understand. And I do believe the Constitution guarantees due process and innocence until proven guilty. Besides, you wouldn't want it said you don't follow the law to the letter, now would you? That might look bad in your campaign for sheriff."

It never failed to amaze Talon when his dear ole granddad put away the vernacular of the illiterate Indian cowboy, which most folks in town believed him to be, and reverted to the speech of the college-educated man he was. Of course, when Chief pulled out the big words, it was his way of saying *fuck off.*

Hendricks backed up and smirked in a self-satisfied way. "Nice to know you got your whole family protecting you, huh?"

Talon fisted his hands, but common sense kicked him in the ass before he let a punch fly. He glanced back at the envelope still on the table. He had more important things to consider than knocking the head off Chet Hendricks, no matter how damned satisfying that might have been.

"If you're arresting me, do it. If not, get the hell out of my way." When Hendricks stepped to the side, he stalked past the deputy and out the door.

* * * *

Dawn pounded on the door of the apartment above a weathered tractor shed at Vaughn's Farm and Garden Market. "Justin, this is Sheriff Dawn Madison, open up!"

When no response came, she looked over her shoulder at Wyatt. He moved his leather vest away from his shoulder holster and gripped the Colt 45. She took his cue and drew the Glock from her hip holster. With it pointed to the bright morning sky in her right hand, she tried the knob with her left.

The door opened slowly, and Wyatt moved into the dark, rank-smelling interior after he determined the place was clear. He went right into the tiny bedroom; she headed left toward the living space. The action so natural her heart stopped for a split second.

When the stench caused her stomach to churn, Dawn switched to breathing through her mouth. Her eyes adjusted to the dimness, and she scanned the messy room. Beer cans cluttered the tops of an old-fashioned iron sink and an ancient gas stove. Rust splotches pitted the dull white enamel of both.

The door of the 1970s Frigidaire stood open. The light inside flickering over shelves littered with takeout containers and a partial six-pack of Budweiser. A blackened tablespoon, two insulin syringes, and a burned down candle sat on the 1960s era aluminum table. One of the two miss-matched chairs was overturned, and yellowish stuffing poked out of the tears in the sagging greasy couch.

"Aw hell."

Wyatt's frustrated voice drew her attention to the doorway into the bedroom. He shoved his Colt into the holster. She rounded the unmade mattress to see what he'd found to make him feel safe enough to put away his gun.

He looked over his shoulder. "Well, we found Vaughn, but I don't think he'll be doing any talking."

The eighteen-year-old lay flat on his back on the putrid carpet, surrounded by dirty clothes. He wore only a pair of filthy boxers. Inches from the bluish fingertips of his right hand lay a wide black piece of rubber and a syringe. Infected track marks darkened the inside of his elbows. But what probably killed him were the three blood-crusted stab wounds in his chest.

His sightless eyes stared at the ceiling, and his normally pale face and the bare skin of his chest had taken on the gray pallor of someone who'd been dead for a while.

She shoved her gun back into her side holster and knelt beside Wyatt. With a long exhale, she said, "You know, the stink when I opened the door should've been our first clue. Goddamn."

Wyatt shook his head and stood. "Looks like the same MO as Larson's murder."

"Yeah. Probably killed for the same reason as Chris too. Shouldn't surprise me. Vaughn's been a petty dealer and user for years. I thought he was turning his life around after we arrested him in the spring." She followed Wyatt to his feet, but the action was harder than it should have been. The weight of finding the killer settled squarely on her shoulders. Their only possible lead was literally a dead end. The only suspect was her brother, and she refused to think he had anything to do with this. She unclipped her iPhone from her service belt. "I'll call it in."

* * * *

Wyatt was ready to call it a night, and at nine PM, after speaking with Justin's uncle and aunt, he was finally heading home. He was anxious to find out how Rachel made out at her VA appointment earlier that day.

Yesterday, he'd called her therapist and mentioned that he was afraid she might be having thoughts of hurting herself. He hated doing it, feeling like he was somehow tattling on his baby sister, but damn it all to hell, if she committed suicide, he'd never forgive himself.

"Wyatt, wait up."

Turning at the voice, he stopped.

Chet Hendricks came out from behind his desk in the communal area of the station and headed toward Wyatt. "I hoped you'd be up for a beer over at the Hardware Bar. I wanted to talk to you."

"I'm headed home." Wyatt dug his truck keys from his jeans pocket. "Can it wait until tomorrow?"

Chet shifted his feet and hiked up his service belt. "Actually, no it can't. It's about Talon Blackwell."

Wyatt glanced toward the glowing glass panel of the office door on the other side of the room. The gold painting and block letters still proclaimed his friend, Zack Cartwright, sheriff, but that office was Dawn's domain.

"What about Talon?" Wyatt faced Chet.

The deputy's dark eyes brightened, and his lips twitched as if he was fighting off a smile. "Not here. I'll tell you at the saloon." He patted Wyatt's shoulder with a bony hand. "I think you'll find this interesting."

As they moved down the aisle to the back door, with Chet waving and tossing out "good nights" to the other deputies still at work, Wyatt got the feeling he was being herded. He stopped. No one herded him. "I'm not interested in a drink, Chet. If this is about the murders, out with it. Otherwise, I'm going home."

Chet flattened his lips into a tight line and rubbed the back of his neck. But the displeasure lasted only a second. His half smile was back. "Okay. Here's what I think. Talon Blackwell is guilty as sin and Dawn knows it. We all know she testified that her brother wasn't an addict when he was caught and thrown in jail in Amarillo. Well, the evidence suggested otherwise. I looked up the reports. Talon not only was charged with using and possession of cocaine, but three witnesses testified they saw him dealing as well."

Wyatt needed to look at those reports, but something about considering Talon didn't sit right with him. "We have no evidence implicating him in either one of these murders."

Circumstantial evidence was all they had. He'd been a cop too long to fall for the circumstantial. Occasionally, it provided the breadcrumbs through the forest to the real McCoy, but not often enough. Mostly, those breadcrumbs lead to dead ends or nothing at all.

He thought about the responses made by Justin's uncle during his questioning. Kenny Vaughn mentioned Talon stopping by his farmer's market on several occasions to buy apples for his stallion, and he would often talk at length with Justin, the last time being Tuesday morning. But Kenny had no idea what those conversations entailed.

Wyatt also knew Talon had always had a soft spot for the underdog. Despite the changes in his old friend, he still believed that part of Talon was there. Justin definitely qualified as someone stuck on the fringes of society, much as Talon himself always had been. Justin's mother had been a classmate of his and Talon's and got pregnant when she was seventeen. No one ever knew who his father was and the rumor had been that it was their high school band instructor. She ended up raising the kid on her own until breast cancer had taken her life four years ago, which had been when Justin's addiction problems started.

Wyatt wouldn't have been at all surprised if Talon saw Justin as something of a kindred spirit and wanted to help the kid out.

Chet rubbed his neck again. "Look. I know you and Talon were friends, but he's into some bad shit these days. I think he's getting rid of his competition."

"What do you want, Chet?"

Shifting his feet, Chet cleared his throat. "I would like you to campaign for me. We all know Dawn isn't the right person for sheriff. She'll run this office as crooked as her father did."

He narrowed his eyes at the deputy, then slipped his gaze to the others shifting in their chairs, pretending they hadn't heard. The last thing he wanted was someone like Chet Hendricks in the sheriff's office. The glow from Dawn's office door window caught his attention again. Despite all of his bad feelings for her, and hatred of what she had done to him, she was the right choice for sheriff.

As he set his hat on his head, he met Chet's expectant brown eyes again. "Tom is and was a good man. Yeah, he got a few kids out of trouble now and again, but when it mattered, he shot straight and true. Dawn will make a good sheriff for this town."

Chet's too-thin, boney face melted a bit. His was a day past a five o'clock shadow, and some of the scruff was coming in gray to match the patches of nearly white in his dark hair. The man was aging fast and not in a good way. Hard to believe Wyatt and Chet were the same age.

"Are you going to question Blackwell?" Chet put his hands on his skinny hips.

Wyatt reached for the knob of the back door to the parking lot. "Yes, but tomorrow is another day."

Chapter 4

"Is he crazy?" Dawn stood on her parents' porch and stared at Chief. "Damn it! Is he trying to make himself look as guilty as possible?"

"You know your brother hasn't done anything wrong." Her grandfather's easy tone only served to grate on her nerves as much as the slow motions of his gnarled and age-spotted hands with the paring knife as he skinned an apple. He set the peeled Macintosh into a bowl beside him and picked up another from the basket at his feet. "Why do you think Talon had anything to do with these murders?"

Her mother's mums splashed reds and golds against the white clapboard of the house, and the whicker rockers scattered over the expanse invited her to take a seat as she had so many times before. She leaned against the thick railing and crossed her arms. The deep porch where she and her brothers played as kids shaded them from the late-morning sun.

A board creaked as Wyatt shifted his weight. From the hard line of his jaw, he was gritting his teeth. "Chief, we don't think he's guilty, but the evidence isn't looking good in his favor. And leaving town now, only serves to make matters worse."

Chief squinted his eyes as he looked at Wyatt. "I'll tell you this much. Yes, I know where Talon is, but I ain't free to tell you. I can tell you it's a personal matter and got nothing at all to do with these dead kids or the drugs they've been dealin'." He glanced at Dawn and winked. "I think he took a plane out of Dallas." He set to peeling the apple again. "Now, get out of here. Your momma can be a real slave driver. She wants these apples peeled before noon."

Her mother wouldn't have expected Chief to do any such thing. He no doubt offered to peel the apples for her. With a smile tugging at her lips, Dawn pushed off the railing and kissed her grandfather on the cheek. "I love you, Chief."

He pulled back and frowned, but she saw the grin that blossomed before it first. "What's this? I didn't say nothin'. But I guess I love you too." He shook the apple and knife. "Now, I mean it, get goin' with ya and stop botherin' old men like me."

Shaking her head with a smile, she patted Wyatt on the arm. "C'mon. Let's go."

When they arrived at her sheriff's Tahoe, Wyatt climbed into the passenger's side and watched as she buckled herself in. "I'll check out the Dallas flights."

She nodded and turned the key. "Good. Chief gave me more than I'd expected he would." As she turned the SUV around in front of her parents' garage, she glanced at Wyatt. "We both know Talon isn't the killer, and chasing him is taking the focus off the real murderer."

"That's what I think too." Wyatt latched his seatbelt and looked out the side window. "I'll check out the lead with the airport. You continue to see what else you can find out about who might be involved with the drug culture of Colton."

Turning onto Blackwell Road to head back to town, she looked out over the pastures and trees that lined the narrow country road. She huffed and shook her head. "Who would have ever thought a tiny town like Colton, Texas, would have a drug culture?"

* * * *

Dinner at the McPhersons' house on Sunday afternoon was quickly becoming the crowning jewel in a shitty week.

Yesterday, the coroner's report came in for the time of death for Vaughn--sometime between nine and eleven o'clock Tuesday night. No witnesses put Talon, or anyone else for that matter, at the scene. As for the lead Chief gave them, Wyatt discovered Talon boarded a redeye for Las Vegas late Wednesday night. A murderer would have covered his tracks better than that.

"So, Wy, when are you moving out to the ranch?" his twin sister asked him over the autumn daisies, sitting in the middle of his mother's antique oak table.

He shook off his thoughts from yesterday and reached for his glass of sweet tea. So far, dinner had been anything but pleasant. Rachel sat to his left and picked at her roast beef and garlic mashed potatoes. Lance sat next to his wife across from Rachel and kept his gaze on the plate of food he wasn't doing a good job of pretending to eat. Only his parents seemed excited to have their family gathered. Of course, no one mentioned the conspicuously empty chair tucked in the corner by the door. Kyle's name and what he'd done to Charli Quinn weren't brought up.

He sipped his tea. "I'm hoping to start moving tomorrow. I'm off, since it's Columbus Day and the Estradas moved out over the weekend."

"We'd be glad to help." Lance glanced at Audrey who nodded.

His mother sipped her sweet tea. "Of course we'll help you move too."

"I'll have to check in at the firehouse, but I'll be around." His father cut into his roast. "Now, you need to find a wife and start filling up that big old house with my grandkids."

Marlin Ferguson McPherson had always been something of the black sheep of his family. He'd joined the Navy when he was seventeen to get away from the ranch that had been in his father's family for three generations. But Wyatt suspected his father had also left Colton to get away from a family legacy he never quite lived up to. After all, he wasn't a Ferguson by name, but everyone in the county considered him one since his mother was part of the famous clan that helped build Colton, along with the Cartwrights and Blackwells.

In the Navy, his father had become a firefighter and spent the Vietnam War on a ship in the Pacific. When he'd gotten out, he'd come back to Colton and married his high school sweetheart. But he'd refused to be just a rancher. He'd volunteered at the local fire department and lobbied for them to organize into a paid entity. He'd been the first and only fire chief to have ever been a Forest County employee.

However, for as much as his dad yanked against his roots in the hard, dusty soil of Central Texas, he'd lived as God wanted every good Texan to--married to a good woman, an even better cook, and had at least one child to pass along the family bible to.

So far, all four of his father's children have been a disappointment in that last area. Wyatt didn't miss the look that passed between Audrey and Lance. They'd been trying to have a child for twelve years, ever since Audrey lost her first pregnancy after a riding accident. The only other time Audrey was pregnant since, she'd miscarried early.

Rachel shifted in her seat, and he frowned. His father was one of the most genuine and nicest men he'd ever known, but sometimes he was as uncouth as a bull in rutting season. Hadn't he considered how his words would have hurt his daughters? Rachel had never been pregnant, and now she would never have a child of her own.

Wyatt shoveled a fork full of the mashed potatoes smothered in rich gravy into his mouth to keep from responding.

"At least, you had the good sense not to marry Vanessa." His mother forked some green beans into her mouth.

Marrying Vanessa would have been the biggest mistake of his life. When she confronted him about marriage for the last time, she gave him an ultimatum--he had to either marry her or breakup with her. He walked away and never looked back.

"You need to find a local girl," his mother said.

"Amen to that." His father took a bite of the roast. "Jeannie, this is one damned good roast."

"Thank you, Marlin." His mother actually blushed. "It's your momma's secret recipe."

How could a recipe be secret if his mother knew it? He didn't know, but he was glad the talk of grandkids was dropped.

"Lance and I have good news," Audrey said.

"What's that, sweetheart?" His mother took one of her homemade rolls out of the basket beside her. "Rachel, dear, could you please pass the butter."

Lance and Audrey exchanged a secret smile, and Wyatt had the feeling of sinking in quicksand as he shoved another bite of potatoes into his mouth.

"I'm having a baby!"

Wyatt choked on the potatoes and stared across the table at his sister and the man sitting next to her. His stomach twisted and flopped over. So much for the topic of kids being over.

He jerked his gaze to Rachel when her fork clattered on the china plate in front of her. Her shoulders curved inward, and she folded her hands in her lap so tightly her knuckles were white. Wyatt could have wrung his twin sister's neck right then and there. Goddamn, didn't she have any idea what this was doing to their baby sister?

As his mother jumped out of her chair at the far end, she dropped her butter knife. It clanged against her plate and fell to the oak floor with a soft thud. Ignoring the utensil, leaving a grease stain on the ancient braided rug, his mother rounded the table. Audrey stood and hugged her mother.

"Oh, God, that's fantastic news, sweetheart!" His mother moved from his sister's embrace and into Lance's arms. She kissed his cheek. "I'm so happy for you both." She took Audrey's hand. "When are you due?"

"April tenth." Audrey laid her free hand over the flared blouse covering her belly. Her smile was bright enough to short out a power plant. "We waited until we were sure things were okay before saying anything. I had a doctor appointment on Friday, and he's convinced this pregnancy is healthy and perfect. I couldn't wait to tell you, Momma."

"The funny thing is we found out she was pregnant during our appointment with the fertility specialist last month." Lance chuckled, wrapped his arm around Audrey's waist, and pulled her close. "Shocked the hell out of us both," he drawled, in that deep Texas cowboy twang he'd seemed to have perfected despite the law degree hanging in his Dallas office and his thousand-dollar designer suits.

"Congratulations, Tinkerbell." His father kissed Audrey on her forehead and chuckled as he shook Lance's hand. "About time you get the job done right, buddy."

His parents were thrilled, but Rachel shook as if cold, as if she were only holding herself together by the thin stitches of her pride. She grabbed her cane from the back of her chair and teetered to her feet.

Wyatt stood, taking her freezing hand. "Where're you going?"

"I'm not feeling well." She pulled her cold fingers from his hand as she looked up at him. The pain in her eyes broke his heart.

With the cane for balance, she turned and set her prosthetic foot on the floor before her. She moved her good foot forward, then the fake one. The going was slow, but the result was the same. She was running away. And that scared him. Rachel had been running away for most of her life.

Audrey moved away from her husband and parents and easily caught their sister at the door. "Rachel?"

She jumped at her sister's soft touch on her shoulder. She'd been so intent on running she must not have heard Audrey behind her.

"Are you okay?"

Wyatt couldn't see Audrey's face, but the concern in her voice seemed genuine.

Rachel sucked in a breath so deep her shoulders moved up, then down as she exhaled.

Audrey pushed her long sandy blond hair behind her ears. "I guess I should have been thinking when we made the announcement. It's just that after so many years of trying... and Dad's talk... I'm so sorry."

"No, you should be happy. Congratulations. But now I need to lie down." She limped out of the dining room.

Wyatt stared after Rachel until the closing of her bedroom door sounded like a thunderclap in the quiet room.

He whirled on Audrey with the fury of a tornado brewing inside him. "Are you really this much of a heartless bitch? Or are you blind to what has happened to our baby sister?"

"Whoa, buddy. Audrey might be your sister"--Lance stepped up beside Audrey and put his arm around her shoulders--"but she's my wife, and I won't let anyone, including you, talk to her that way."

Audrey swallowed again, blinked her eyes, and wrapped her arms around herself. The silence was deafening as he stared at his sister. "Is that what you think of me?" Her voice cracked.

"No." Wyatt took a deep breath and ran his hands through his hair. "I'm sorry… But damn it. This is killing her. Don't you see it? You and Lance, and what you did, is not making any of this easier on her."

Audrey closed her eyes and shook her head. "I'll admit I was wrong all those years ago. Dear God, I know I shouldn't have done what I did to her. But she's the one who's been pining after my husband for twelve years."

"I've never *pined* after Lance."

Wyatt turned to Rachel, standing in the doorway. His parents went to her side, but she stepped away from them.

"Then what do you call not ever coming home? Never once even acknowledging me? You were home in May and didn't speak to me or Lance even once." Audrey lowered her arms to her sides.

Rachel moved into the room and winced as her father helped her into a chair.

"Are you sure you don't want to go to your room?" Dad asked.

Rachel shook her head. "No, Daddy. This has to come out. This needs to be said." She tucked her cane in beside her, and he moved away.

Wyatt glanced at the stricken faces of his parents, standing next to each other in the doorway between the kitchen and the dining room.

Rachel wiped over her mouth with her left hand. For the first time, Wyatt noticed the diamond ring. She must have gone to her room to get it. "At first, I hated you both." She looked at Lance, and he squared his shoulders. "Yes, I loved you. But soon, I realized you were not the only goldfish in the bowl. In fact, you were a tadpole to my Alex's whale."

"Who's Alex?" their mother asked.

Rachel bowed her head and fisted her left hand. "Alex and I met four years ago in Afghanistan after the Battle of Wanat. I flew into his MASH in the belly of a helicopter with three wounded soldiers on board, one of them critical. He was only a private. Right out of basic and hadn't a clue. He was shot in the leg. Here." She rubbed her upper thigh over her jeans and her eyes looked beyond them, as if she were back there in the battle. "The bullet severed his femoral artery, and he was bleeding out. I couldn't apply a tourniquet on the battlefield because it was too close to his groin. All that was keeping that boy alive was the hemostat I'd clamped on the heart side of the artery and the pressure I held on the wound." She shook her head again and swallowed.

Her mother put her hands on her shoulders. "Rachel, sweetheart, you don't have to do this."

Rachel tilted her head to look at her mother. "Yes, Momma, I do. Or y'all will continue thinking I've spent my life as some pathetic, jilted old maid because my older sister stole my boyfriend." She pushed her mother's hands away and stood.

When she wobbled, Wyatt rushed forward and caught her before she fell.

Rachel glared at him, but she didn't push him away. She held onto him as she faced their sister and brother-in-law. "As the other two wounded were helped out by the medics, Alex climbed into the Hewie, and together we saved that boy's life. The kid had long ago passed out, so we did what we had to. Once we got him inside for surgery, we cleaned the wound, removed the bullet, and repaired the artery."

She lifted her left hand. "Alex Webster and I saved that kid's life. We found out later he'd named his daughter after me and his baby boy is named after Alex." She smiled, but the tears on her cheeks spoke of the pain the memory brought her. "But for me and Alex, the real joy was that we'd met. We hit it off immediately, and I think we both fell in love saving that private's life. But we had to keep our romantic relationship between us. Alex outranked me, but we'd never served in the same unit, so it was easy to keep things secret." She sniffed and wiped at the tears on her face. "Then we got our assignments for this last deployment and had the shock of our lives. He and I were not only serving in the same unit, but he was my commander."

Wyatt wanted to stop her, to keep her from her pain, but Rachel needed this. They all did. Then maybe, she could finally grieve in open, and his family would at long last understand her.

Lance narrowed his eyes and pointed to the large diamond on Rachel's ring finger. "This Alex. He gave you the ring?"

She met his gaze and nodded. "He asked me to marry him last Christmas. That's why I didn't come home. I went to Maine to meet his family." She laughed but it came out choppy. "His dad made fun of my saying *y'all*, and I joked about his hard *Rs*. They're great people. Alex asked me to marry him after we'd gone skiing two days before Christmas." She choked out that jerky laugh again. "He was so nervous he dropped the ring in the snow." She broke down and dropped onto the chair. As she covered her face and sobbed, she whispered, "God, I loved him. Why did that bastard have to kill him?"

Wyatt didn't know what to do. Her secret was out, but his heart broke for her all over again.

Lance stepped forward, kneeled before her, and gently brushed her hair from her face. As his fingers lingered on her pale, wet cheek, she turned her gaze on him. "I'm sorry, Rach, for all you've gone through." His voice vibrated deep and raw.

Wyatt rubbed his jaw line. Was Lance talking about the loss of her Alex, or everything he'd put her through when he'd slept with her sister all those years ago?

"Let's get you to bed. Okay?" Lance said.

When she sniffled, Lance reached into his back pocket and pulled out a folded white handkerchief. She stared at it when he held it out to her. "It's not used, I promise."

"You still carry a handkerchief with you?"

"I seem to remember you always ended up crying all over me at the movies. Carrying one became a habit I never broke."

She wiped her nose and a ghost of a smile tilted the corners of her pale lips. "You always took me to sad movies."

"I had my reasons." He stood and held out his palm. She stared at it for a moment before placing her shaky hand into his.

Lance surprised Wyatt, and probably everyone else, when he helped her to her feet, swung her up into his arms, and carried her out of the room.

Wyatt turned to face the rest of his family. His father had pulled his sobbing mother into his arms, while Audrey stared out the door Lance had carried their sister through with an expression on her tear streaked face he'd never seen before.

* * * *

Whistling softly between her teeth, Dawn slowed her F-150 to take in the view in front of her. "Sweet mercy, isn't that the sexiest thing on two legs."

Wyatt pushed his vintage Harley on the side of the dusty country road, the action showing off his muscular shoulders and forearms below his rolled up sleeves. His light blue shirttails fluttered on either side of him indicating his shirt was open. His jeans hugged his ass and legs like a good pair of Levis should. The late afternoon sun glowed through his chestnut hair, setting the red highlights on fire. A black helmet hung from the handlebar, and a black leather jacket was folded over the worn leather seat of the bike.

He glanced over his shoulder as she approached and slowed. She wasn't ready for the lusty clenching in her lower belly at the memories of Wyatt driving her crazy when they'd made love.

She bit the inside of her lip and tightened her grip on the steering wheel as primal need raked through her.

A pair of Aviator sunglasses covered his eyes. She pulled the truck off the side of the road next to one of the CW Ranch pastures. Massive Santa Gertrudis cattle munched on the fall grasses. One of the cows lifted her head from the grass and seemed to eye the truck curiously, as she chewed a wad of grass.

Dawn had never understood what Zack and Lance Cartwright saw in the big, ugly animals. She preferred the sleek sturdiness of a Herford or an Angus to the more exotic breeds.

Wyatt propped the bike on its kickstand and ambled to the driver's side window. Dust covered his boots and the bottoms of his jeans as if he'd been walking a great distance. But then, out here, where miles and miles could separate one ranch house from another, and the only living things around were cattle and horses, getting stranded and hoofing it for miles before a person came along wasn't uncommon.

"Aren't you a sight for a weary man?" Wyatt smiled as he lifted his sunglasses to the top of his head and revealed eyes as blue as the endless October sky above them.

Her heart sputtered a beat. She pulled her gaze away from his and looked out the windshield at the old motorcycle sitting in front of her truck. He'd had the thing since graduating from college. They'd spent many warm days racing along the country roads north of Dallas when they'd dated, and she'd tormented him relentlessly because she'd always beat him. "What's wrong with the hunk of junk?"

A corner of his lips kicked up in a lopsided smirk. "Carburetor. I think. It stalled in the intersection at Gambler's Folly and Cattle Trail, and I couldn't get it started again." He rubbed his forehead with the back of his hand, and squinted toward the west.

She had a hard time keeping her eyes off him. The undershirt stretched over his muscular chest under his open shirt.

"I figured it was a tossup between heading for Paul Cartwright's house or the Kennedy place."

Why hadn't he gone back to Highway Six? Hell, why hadn't he called someone? But Dawn didn't ask. "Want to load up the bike, and I'll take you home?"

He drummed his fingers on the edge of the door near the open window. His nails were trimmed, and his fingers were long and slender on strong hands. She knew how skillful they'd been at playing her body, and sucked in a breath. He turned his gaze on her.

"I don't want to go home." His husky voice washed over her, and the familiar fire in his eyes heated her insides. "That's why I didn't call Dad. I was heading for my ranch when the bike broke down."

She wouldn't give into the lust boiling between them. Too much water passed under that bridge, and she'd burned the damned thing down. Wyatt McPherson would always hold the particles of her heart--one he'd shattered to a million-zillion pieces, then trampled to dust when he walked out of her life. She wasn't stupid enough to give him another chance.

Damn the need coursing through her body.

She cleared her throat and got her raging hormones under control. "Okay. I'll take you back to my place. I have to feed my horses and let my dog out. If you'd like, I might even have a spare carburetor lying around."

He chuckled. "Thought those new hogs didn't need any maintenance?"

She smiled and shrugged.

"You still have Taco?"

The beagle had hated Wyatt. "Yeah, so I suggest you don't try anything."

He stepped away from the door as she opened it. "Wouldn't think of it."

Together they wrestled the Harley onto the back of the truck and secured it with some twine and a bungee cord. Wyatt got into the passenger side and ran his hand through his hair, which curled around his ears and fell over his tan forehead.

She turned the key in the ignition. "Missing your hat?"

He laughed and rested his hands on top of his black helmet. "Yeah. Since becoming a Ranger, I've gotten used to wearing it again."

The heat of his gaze warmed her.

"You look good with your hair down," he said.

She sucked in a breath and concentrated on driving into the evening sun rather than reading too much into the compliment. "Thanks. I hate wearing it up all the time for work, but I can't bear the thought of ever cutting it."

"Don't…"

She glanced at him when he cut himself off.

He rubbed his mouth as if he hoped it would stuff the word back in. "Don't what?"

He didn't look at her. "Nothing."

Her stomach flipped over. Wyatt had spent hours playing with it after they'd made love.

Clearing her throat, she stared at the road ahead of them. "So, you're moving in tomorrow?"

"That's the plan."

Not knowing what to say when he grew quiet, she tuned into the song playing on the classic rock station. As Lynyrd Synyrd sang about their being a free bird, she wished she could turn it up to fill the void between them with something other than the growing tension.

They passed the gate to the Kennedy spread, then the first gate to the CW, which led to Paul and Winnie Cartwright's home. Dear God, they had another fifteen minutes of this deafening silence before...

"Audrey's pregnant."

His quiet voice had her risking a glance at him. "Wow. When did Audrey announce that news?"

He huffed. "The worse possible moment today at the dinner table. But it got Rachel to finally open up."

"I just visited Rachel yesterday afternoon. I had no idea what to say to her."

With his head bent, he nodded. "Well, it's not only Lance and Audrey or even her injuries she's so depressed over. She's grieving."

"What do you mean?"

"Rachel was engaged to the doctor who was killed when she was shot in the attack."

Dawn let out her breath and looked at Wyatt again. He met her gaze for as long as she could safely hold it. "I take it that no one knew she was engaged."

"No."

"Man. This has to be brutal on your parents." She remembered how close Wyatt was to his younger sister and swallowed. "And on you, too."

"I just don't understand why she kept it such a secret. She met his family last Christmas, but we didn't even know he existed."

Dawn glanced at him again. His wince and the huskiness of his voice bespoke of his sense of betrayal.

"Hell, I understand why she might not have told the others, but I don't get why she hasn't said anything to me."

I bet she doesn't know how you dumped me after I took a bullet for you, costing my baby's life.

But she kept the bitterness locked deep inside and stared out at the long, deserted, two-lane county road. "I know it's different, but when Talon was charged for dealing and possession two years ago, I didn't know about it until I was served with a subpoena to testify. I'm sure if it hadn't been for the defense lawyer wanting to show the jury Talon's cop sister and retired sheriff stepfather, neither one of us would've been there. And we wouldn't have known about Talon's conviction until he was sent to prison." She snorted and shook her head. "Hell, we probably wouldn't have known until after he'd served his fifteen months."

"I'm surprised he wasn't paroled for good behavior."

She snapped her gaze to him. "You've got to be kidding, right? This is Talon we're talking about. He could find trouble at a church revival meeting."

He shrugged and drummed his hands on his helmet. "Yet, you totally believe in his innocence."

She hit the brake a little harder than she'd intended and snapped on the signal to turn into the long drive onto her family's ranch. "I thought you did too. I know my brother would never kill someone, Wyatt." The *tick-click* of the signal punctuated every word. "He has a temper that's hot as hell, but he's not a thug." She slowed on the rutted gravel lane and narrowed her eyes at him.

Wyatt's jaw twitched, and his eyes hardened. Was it her faith in her brother that he didn't believe in, or was it the whole stinking pile of crap he was angry at? Maybe he didn't believe in her ability to find the killer.

Well, screw you, Wyatt McPherson.

Wouldn't you just love to be the one to do it? Her body heated at the taunt, and she took a deep breath filled with his musky scent.

"Look, let's not drop the gavel on Talon's innocence before we prove he's guilty." She slowed to a stop in front of her trailer and looked at him. "Okay?"

His jaw tightened, but he nodded. "All right."

She forced a smile and opened her door. "Let's get that piece of crap fixed so you can get the hell out of my hair."

The graveness of his gaze turned humorous as the corners of his eyes tilted upward and he grinned. "I've never felt more welcome."

Chapter 5

Wyatt tightened the last bolt on the new carburetor, wiped his hands on an old rag, then climbed onto the Sportster and cranked the engine.

Like a dream, the rebuilt engine roared to life and rumbled like an approaching storm. He looked over at Dawn, leaning against the doorframe of the garage, where she tapped the toe of her cowboy boot on the spotless concrete floor. As he dragged his gaze over her tight faded jeans and crazy print sweater, she folded her arms over her chest and curled her full lips into a smirk.

He fought the tightening in his lower belly, but it was useless to fight his attraction to her, especially when she moved away from the doorframe and her hair swayed. The silky black mane hung to the top of her ass. How she managed to get all the stuff tamed into a prim bun for work never failed to amaze him.

He cut the engine. "Well, I'll get the mess cleaned up and head home. You sure I don't owe you anything for the part?"

She laughed and stopped beside him. "No. I'm just glad it worked. Hunter left it over here last year when he got it in his mind he wanted to rebuild a motorcycle."

Raising a brow, he swung his leg over the bike. "Glad to see your little brother has some sense."

"Not much."

They stood face to face for a few moments staring at each other. He couldn't miss the heat burning deep in the depths of her rich brown eyes, but he wasn't fool enough to get caught up in the lust, smoldering between them again. He broke the trance by looking away and wrestled with the urge to pull her to him and taste her lips.

A soft sigh drifted to him, and she gestured toward the open door. "It's late, and I've made some coffee. Mom sent over some of her bean bread, and I made a pot of corn soup before I went to Waco this afternoon."

"You inviting me to supper?"

She shrugged a shoulder. "Yeah. But I do have a condition."

"What is it?"

"We don't talk about the case."

What else did they have to discuss? Their past wasn't an option, and they had nothing else in common anymore. He nodded. "All right. I always loved your mom's Cherokee cooking."

The knot in his lower belly tightened when she smiled. "Hey! How about mine? Besides I also know a few Comanche recipes, that if I remember correctly, you like."

He glanced down at his hands. "You aren't too bad. But nothing beats your momma's cooking."

She swatted him on his upper arm and laughed. "You're a jerk."

Tucking his hands into his pockets, he shrugged and grinned. "I try."

Her smile slipped, and again their gazes caught and held. He was playing with fire. Despite all the pain of their past, he never stopped wanting Dawn. Working with her in September on the rustling case hadn't been fun. He'd lain awake more than one night with a hard-on as he thought about her. This case was even worse, because he saw her desire for him shinning in her eyes.

She shattered the moment before he reached for her by stepping away toward the door. "Well..." The word came out husky and she cleared her throat. "C'mon. I'm hungry."

Yeah, me too, but food isn't what I want.

As he followed her, he hoped he wasn't making the biggest mistake of his life.

They entered her trailer into the small living room. Homey scents of Dawn's Cherokee corn soup filled the air with sweetness. Rich, earthy colors decorated the windows, walls, and creamy tan furniture. The eat-in kitchen was as neat and clean as the living room, but here, splotches of bright red joined the golds, browns, greens, and blues.

A deep bark had him looking toward the hallway, leading to the rest of the single-wide. The beagle lumbered toward him and bared her teeth as she growled. "Taco, you old hound dog, I see you still love me."

The dog snarled in reply, and Wyatt laughed. She'd had the old beagle since high school. Amazing the old girl could still get around.

"Stop it, Taco. Go lay down." Dawn pointed to the dog bed on the floor in the corner beside a bookshelf loaded with James Patterson and Clive Cussler novels. The dog gave one more disapproving bark and waddled over to the bed, circled around the soft fleece inside, then settled. "Sorry about that."

He patted his hand against his thigh. "No problem. She's just looking out for her mistress. Who knows, I could be a bad guy."

Snorting, she headed into the kitchen.

"What?" He followed and came to a stop behind her in the tiny space. "You don't agree?"

From a cabinet, she pulled down two bright red bowls and set them on the counter beside a Crockpot. Turning, she took a deep breath.

Only inches separated them, and her scent surrounded him. Her eyes dilated and heated his blood. He was lost. The ache in his cock shorted out his good sense, and he reached for her. She didn't fight as she stepped into his arms, tilting her head back. With a swipe of her pink tongue, she moistened her lips. "I know you're a bad boy."

The husky words were like a mean sucker punch in the gut. He had to have her. Pulling her closer and backing her up to the edge of the counter, he pressed the evidence of his desire against her. A soft moan escaped her moist lips as he lifted her to settle his cock into the cradle of her hips, and she rubbed her thigh against his. He wasn't sure if he damned the clothing between them or was thankful for the barrier.

He came down hard on her pliable lips, demanding to be fed. She resisted his entry for a moment, but then relaxed into him and opened her mouth under his. As he buried his fingers into her hair and held her to him, he plunged in, needing to conquer her. She tasted of sweet mint, coffee, and the nirvana of a woman's desire.

Gripping the shirt over his chest, she moaned her surrender. But she demanded as much from him. As she slid her tongue against his, her body moved with each stroke against him.

He grabbed the bottom of her sweater and slipped his hand under to find the satin of her bra. Her breast was hot and heavy beneath the cloth. When he rolled his thumb over her nipple, it puckered instantly. She gasped and her hands flattened on his chest, trapped between their bodies.

Breaking the kiss, he nibbled his way along her jaw to her ear. "I want you," he rasped between nips on her earlobe.

She shuddered and her breathing came in sharp, short spurts as she tilted her head, allowing him better access to the sweet spot under her ear. As he breathed in the musky scent of her desire, he sucked in her skin. Her salty-sweetness intoxicated him.

He took her moaning his name as his cue and flicked open the front clasp of her bra. As he reached for the bottom of her sweater, she shook her head and pushed on his chest.

"Wyatt." This time his name came as a strangled pant. "Stop."

Somehow, he found the sanity to back off. He looked into her eyes and the burn of her desire drained away, out-right fear replaced it.

She shook her head again as if to clear a fog from it, slipped away from him and entered the living room. As if she fought to catch her breath, she heaved her shoulders up and down. Hugging herself, she faced away from him. "I can't do this. Not again."

He ran his hand over his face. Goddamn, was he a total idiot? Was he that hard up? Having Dawn again would be like taking a hot knife in the gut and giving it a good twist. "I should go."

At the door, he stopped but didn't look at her. The best solution was to get the hell away from temptation. "I'm requesting to be taken off the case."

"What?"

The strength in the word surprised him, but he didn't turn. "I'm taking some time off. With my moving and…"

"I need you on the case."

He hadn't expected her to ask him to stay. Closing his eyes, he sucked in a breath and prayed for the strength to walk away. He faced her.

Her hair was messed from his fingers, and her lips puffy and bruised from his kiss. A small red mark discolored her neck over the sensitive spot under her ear where he'd sucked on her tan skin. She never looked more beautiful. Thank God she'd pushed him away. At the rate he was moving, he would have stripped her and been ready to bury himself deep inside about now. What the hell had he been thinking? He didn't even have a condom. The last thing he wanted was to get her pregnant again. His heart couldn't bear losing another child he'd never know about until it was too late.

"No. You'll do fine. I can't *just* work with you, Dawn. I never could." With those words, he hurried out her door and off the small porch.

Ten minutes later, he had her garage cleaned up and was racing toward town. He needed a drink.

* * * *

Dawn stared at the closed door. Taco whimpered at her side, nudging Dawn's leg with her muzzle as if she understood her mistress's upset and wanted to comfort her. The dog obviously didn't know she didn't need comfort. She needed a damned good swift kick in the ass. How could she have let this happen? How stupid was she? She almost had sex with Wyatt McPherson!

Something she could never let happen. There could never be *just sex* between them--not for her anyway. And no amount of mind-blowing sex was worth the pain she'd feel in the morning.

The roar of his Harley, ripping out of her driveway, startled her. Taco barked and looked up at her. She knelt and rubbed over the dog's floppy ears. "You're such a smart puppy. You never fell for his charm. Lord knows I sure as hell have."

She choked on a sob and bit down on her bottom lip, refusing to cry over Wyatt. Another strangled sob snuck out, and she lost it. Sliding to the floor and hugging the furry constant in her life, she cried like a baby. Hating herself for loving a man she would never be good enough for. And hating him for not loving her in return.

Chapter 6

Dawn read the report. Hendricks and Tilly Kennedy had arrested two kids loitering outside the mall Monday night and found drugs on both of them. She looked at Hendricks pacing the length of her office, then turned to Kennedy who sat in front of her desk. "Are they still in lock-up?"

"Hell, no." The older deputy crossed his arms over his paunch. "They're a pair of those rich brats from Dallas who moved into those mansions Ferguson built over there on the Circle M. Parents got 'em out last night, spouting that bullshit about them being minors and can't be locked up in an adult prison."

"Figures." She shook her head and tossed the sheet of paper onto her desk. "Did they confess any of their sins before their parents showed up?"

"Nope. Neither one of them knows how they got the drugs."

"And I'm the queen of Sheba." Needing coffee like an addict, she poured a cup from the pot in the corner. She dumped powdered creamer into it and stirred, then looked over her shoulder at the deputies. "The new Ranger hasn't shown up yet?"

Chet scrunched his bloodshot eyes together and rested his hands above his service belt at his sides. "What about Wyatt?"

"He's taking some vacation time." She sat in her chair and sipped the strong brew. Just the way she liked it.

"That doesn't sound like Wyatt." Tilly shifted in his seat.

"He's got other things on his mind." *Like avoiding me.* Dawn picked up the report and leaned back in her chair. "Let's get back to business. We need to talk to these two kids. Tyler Demello and Jordan Arthur."

"Neither of them have been in trouble before," Tilly chimed in. "At least not with us."

She looked up at him. "That may be true, but Arthur had point five ounces of coke on him, and Demello had six ounces. That's possession with the intent to sell, Tilly. And I won't tolerate it in my county. Someone out there knows something."

Chet sniffed and started pacing again. "What about Ella Larson's girl? I have a witness who says the day before he was killed, she talked to Chris Larson."

"They were cousins. I'm sure they talked all the time." She didn't think Annie Larson had anything to do with the killings, and she prayed the girl wasn't using again. But Chris may have told her something. Damn, why hadn't she thought of talking to her sooner?

Chet shrugged his shoulders. "She's always been a troublemaker and a dopehead. I don't believe for a second Quinn and that heiress he married can change her overnight. She's still doing drugs if you ask me."

Staring at the report, she remembered how much she hated the constant parade of kids strung out on drugs and hard living while on the vice squad. "I'll call over to Butterfly Ranch and set something up for this afternoon after school. Tilly, I want you to talk to Jordan. His parents might own Super Shopper Market, but he's not above the law. This Tyler Demello. I don't recognize the name."

"He's from Dallas." Chet leaned against a file cabinet by the door. "His father's some bigwig doctor at the med center. His mother is remarried to a man damn near half her age."

Raising a brow, she stared at the deputy. "You seem to know a lot about him."

He shifted to his full height. "Not that much. My sister is friends with Audrey Cartwright. Demello is her doctor. I only know what Kristin has told me." He ambled over toward the desk and sat in the chair beside Tilly. "But I did discover he's in Colton because he was thrown out of the private school he went to in the Big D and refused to live with his father."

She folded her arms and leaned back in her chair. "Let me guess. He was caught with drugs on school grounds."

"Marijuana possession charges. But his mommy hired a hotshot lawyer and got the charges dropped on a technicality."

"Looks like he's graduated up a few notches." Tilly leaned over his long legs and studied his steepled fingers. "Who the hell is the supplier? We have to cut the head off the snake if we want a snowball's chance in Hades of curtailing the problem."

"Damn, I'd do just about anything to get these punks off the street." She'd taken a bullet in the chest over these shitheads. And lost everything in the process.

"You know who the dealer is," Chet said.

She shifted forward and narrowed her eyes on Chet. "My brother may or may not be guilty, but let's find the evidence that proves his guilt before we sign his death warrant. We need to do our job and stop playing jury and judge."

Tilly glanced at Chet. "I agree with the sheriff. We don't have any evidence that points to Talon Blackwell, except your brother-in-law's statement.

Chet's slender lips twisted and his dull eyes became indignant. "And the fact he flew the coop when he was told not to. We can't ignore his past."

Dawn stood and leaned over her desk. If she didn't have her palms firmly planted on the papers strewn over the top, she would have closed her hands around his skinny chicken neck. "Interesting that you'd bring up the past, Hendricks." Without taking her eyes off the pissant, she said, "Tilly, would you please call the Quinns for me and ask if I could speak with Annie this afternoon?"

From her peripheral vision, she saw him nod and leave his chair to do her bidding. When the door closed, she swallowed hard and let the bastard have both guns. "You know, Chet, if I didn't know better, I'd think you where against my brother because he's a Native American."

He held her gaze and pursed his lips. "Not at all. We never had trouble until last spring when he moved back to town."

She nodded once. "But a lot of new people have moved to town since spring. About fifty *families*, if I'm allowed to guess. Most of them from Dallas, Fort Worth, or Waco. So many that the school had to add four new teachers, and the school board is afraid they'll have to add to the school buildings. Besides we've had a lot of trouble since spring that had nothing to do with my brother." She stood and folded her arms in front of her. "No, I think this insistence that my brother is guilty has more to do with the very same reason you were thrown out of the Army." When his buggy eyes got even bigger, she fought the smile. "I have to wonder how you would fair in the election if your dirty laundry were aired where everyone could see it. Sure, this town has a lot of whites, but about half the population consists of Hispanic and African-American citizens. Not to mention those few Native Americans who've lived here longer than your family has."

Chet stood and a nasty scowl twisted his face. "So, you did some digging."

She nodded. "Yep. I know about the fight with the black sergeant and the reason for it." Picking up a file, she held it out to him. "You're off this case, Hendricks."

"You can't do that. I'm the best deputy for this…"

"Actually, I don't think so. Your bigotry has clouded your judgment. So, I need you back on patrol. Ethel and Helen Cartwright have called in a complaint that their neighbor's pigs are rooting through their champion rose garden. Again. I want you to go over there, check it out, and make sure old Ethel doesn't put a bullet into Joe Farley or one of his hogs."

He glared at her as he left, but had enough sense to keep his mouth shut. Too bad. She would have loved firing his ass. She dropped into her chair, took a deep breath, and buried her face in her hands. Her brother still wasn't home, and his disappearing act wasn't convincing anyone of his innocence.

Damn it, Talon, what the hell are you doing in Vegas?

* * * *

Dawn found her mother taking down laundry in the backyard of the big old two-story house Chief had built after inheriting the five-thousand-acre ranch from the man who had practically raised him--Marshall Cartwright.

Her mother folded the last towel and set it in the basket by her feet, then turned to meet Dawn. She hoped that when she hit middle age, she'd be in as good of shape as her mother. Frannie's short black hair held little gray, and her jeans fit her in a way women half her age would wish for. Her mother worked as a fitness instructor at the local YMCA and looked at least ten years younger than her fifty-five years.

"Hey, honey, I'm surprised to see you at this time of day. Would you like some lunch? Your dad made hamburgers on the grill before he took your grandfather to his doctor's appointment. I could warm one up for you."

Glad that her dad and his father weren't home, Dawn swallowed and shook her head. "I'm here to ask you some questions. But I'll take some coffee if you have some."

Her mother lost the smile and picked up the laundry basket. "Okay, let's go inside."

She followed her mom into the kitchen where she set the basket on the floor by the door. The kitchen of the old house was big and spacious, painted a warm pale yellow with white cabinets, and always smelled sweet and delicious with the scents of homemade breads and her mother's traditional cooking.

As her mother poured coffee, Dawn took a seat at the big oak table. Her grandfather's two old beagles lay in the corner on their beds. They were both siblings of her Taco but never had their sister's friendly personality. Except for her dislike for Wyatt, Taco loved people. They lifted their heads and barked a belated greeting, but didn't see the need to get up.

Her mother set the steaming mug on the table and took the chair across from her. Dawn fetched the milk out of the fridge and added some to her cup. She put the jug back and returned to her seat.

"What do you want to talk about?" Mom sipped her cup and watched Dawn stir her coffee.

"Why is Talon in Las Vegas?" Dawn set the spoon beside her mug and folded her arms on the table.

Her mother set her mug down and stared into the contents. "How do you know that's where he is?

Dawn shrugged and met her mother's gaze straight on. "Wyatt checked the Dallas airports and found out Talon took a flight to Vegas last Wednesday night."

Her mother sighed and looked down at the table. "I don't know what he's doing there."

She was lying.

Dawn tried not to let her disappointment show as she leaned over the table. "I don't believe you." She waited for her mother to look up before going on. "I have to talk to him. Doesn't he have any idea how bad this looks? He left the night after Justin Vaughn was killed."

A frown turned the corners of her mother's full lips as she sat straighter in her chair. "You think he's involved in the murders of those two boys?"

Dawn let out a breath, and her gaze slipped to the table. "No, I don't think he's involved. But his behavior isn't convincing people."

"What people?"

She met her mother's narrowed gaze. "My deputies. The Texas Rangers. Everyone who knows Talon's record."

Mom stood and stared out the window. Her shoulders dropped a little. "Dawn, I swear on all that's holy that Talon had nothing to do with those killings. He's got some personal stuff going on, and he's asked me to keep it under my hat for now."

"What could be so important that he'd leave town now?"

Mom turned and sighed so deeply Dawn heard the exhale across the room. "You'll find out soon enough. He should be home in a few days." She turned toward Dawn. "I really can't say more than that." Looking down at her clasped hands, she shook her head. "I'm worried about him.

He's not the same boy anymore. He hasn't been since he found Jock's body, and his time in jail made it worse."

Dawn glanced away. She couldn't stand the pain in her mother's eyes. Talon had always been her favorite child. But the pain went deeper. Her mother never stopped loving the man who had stolen her heart when she was nineteen. Jock Blackwell had been in his thirties, but it hadn't mattered. They'd had a whirlwind affair, and in the end, her mother was pregnant and Jock refused to marry her.

Dawn's father, also an older man who was looking for a wife, took the young mother and her baby in and married her. But none of it erased the fact Jock Blackwell never let go of his hold on her mother or Talon.

As if her mother could read her mind, she sat back down and picked up her mug. "Chief said he saw you and Wyatt McPherson drive by the house Sunday night."

The memory of Wyatt's kiss burned on her lips. She sipped her soothing coffee with the hope of dispelling the sensation. "I found him broke down out on Gambler's Folly. I had a spare carburetor. He fixed his motorcycle and was on his way."

"I can imagine working with him is hard. Dawn, you aren't getting tangled up with him again, are you?"

She flicked her gaze up to meet her mother's deep brown eyes. "No. I learned my lesson the last time."

Her mother nodded and set her cup down. "Good. I'd hate for you to go through what I have. Your father is a good man, and I'll never regret him taking me and Talon in. I will always love him for it."

God, she didn't want to talk about this. "Mom…"

Her mother ignored her plea. "But I loved Jock Blackwell. I can't deny that. He never loved me, and I was a fool not to see it. Some white men still think all we are good for is lying on our backs with our legs open."

"It's not just Native American women men feel that way about, Mom. Some men think that of all women." Glancing at the wall clock, Dawn stood. "I've got to go. I have a meeting with the Quinns and Ella Larson's girl in less than an hour. Please, if you hear from Talon, tell him I need to talk to him."

"I will." She hugged Dawn, kissed her cheek, and spoke softly in Cherokee. *"Take care, sweetheart. I love you."*

She kissed her mother back. "Love you too, Momma."

* * * *

"Thank you for letting me talk with Annie." Dawn entered the foyer of the massive Victorian mansion of Butterfly Ranch. A gleaming oak spiral staircase curved up to the second floor balcony on the right. To the left, a pair of richly paneled pocket doors closed off the living room, if her memory served her correctly about the layout of the house. The last time she'd been here was months ago when Kyle McPherson had taken a shot at Dylan Quinn. Then the walls had been covered with faded, dirty wallpaper, and the staircase barely looked safe to climb. She smiled at the thought of how Dylan not only rebuilt Charli's house, but his life too.

Charli Monroe Quinn closed the door behind Dawn and faced her. "I want this thug caught, and if Annie knows something that can lead you to the murderer, I'm happy to help." The heiress, who'd taken in Annie after her mother had been killed, and was instrumental in getting the girl off drugs, smiled, but it never reached the sadness in her eyes. She rested a hand on her pregnant belly. According to the grapevine, she was due in February with twins. "I just ask you to remember Annie lost her mother five months ago and now her cousin. She's trying to get her life turned around."

Dawn nodded. Charli was something of an anomaly. A former drug addict and teenage prostitute who had a heart of gold, and a way of seeing the good in things when most people only saw the worst. "I don't want to hurt her, Mrs. Quinn."

The smile spread across her pretty freckled face, brightening her blue-green eyes. "Good. Dylan and Annie are in here."

Charli opened the pocket doors and entered the living room. Dawn followed and her stomach flipped at the sight of sixteen-year-old Annie Larson sitting on the sofa. The girl had once fashioned herself a Goth. Her spiky hair had been bleached white and her eyes obscured with too much black makeup. Dawn had been the deputy who'd arrested her back in March when Charli had turned her in for buying drugs outside of the mall.

She wouldn't have recognized the girl if she'd passed her on the street. She wore faded blue jeans and a pink T-shirt. Her short dark brown hair was styled in a cute pixie. The excessive makeup was gone, and her brown eyes, lined with long, thick lashes, stared out of an angular face. She resembled Ella, but there was also something familiar about her features. Dawn tried to see Leon Ferguson, Annie's biological father, in her, but the only trace seemed to be her dark hair and eyes. Then she saw the resemblance. Dear God, she had Talon's nose--the Blackwell aristocratic nose. She almost smiled.

"Thanks for meeting with me." Dawn took Dylan's outstretched hand. He stood behind his adopted daughter with a hand on her shoulder.

His grip was firm as he shook her hand. "Anything we can do to help, Sheriff."

Dawn sat in the chair across from the girl and decided to capitalize on what connected them--the Blackwells. "I suppose my brother Talon is your uncle."

Annie's eyes widened slightly. "No way. You're name's Madison and you're an Ind--I mean--a Native American."

Dawn smiled. "Indian's fine. But Talon's last name is Blackwell. He's my half brother." She tilted her head. "But it goes further than that. You and I are distant cousins on the Madison side."

Annie fisted her hands in her lap and narrowed her eyes. Her gaze was steady and belied her age. "You can cut the crap, Sheriff. I know what you want. You're wondering if I know anything about Chris and Justin's deaths." She swallowed and looked at her fists.

Dawn sighed and leaned over her legs. "Yes, I'm here to ask you some questions about them." She glanced at Dylan, who stood right behind Annie, and at Charli, who sat next to Annie on the sofa. Charli nodded and reached over to hold Annie's hand. Taking out her notebook and a pen, Dawn asked, "Do you know where Chris and Justin Vaughn may have gotten the drugs they sold?"

Annie had once been a regular customer of Vaughn's, until Charli witnessed a deal between them and called the cops. The woman probably saved the girl's life that day. Annie glanced at Charli.

"Tell her everything you know, Annie. It might catch the guy who killed him and Chris," Charli said.

"I'm not completely certain, but I think someone local." She winced and rubbed the side of her face. "God, I hate rattin' on people who were once my friends."

"We know, kiddo." Dylan patted her shoulder and came around the end of the couch to sit next to her. He wrapped his arm around her shoulders and pulled her to him. "But you might save someone's life."

The endearing gleam in Annie's eyes as she looked upon the man who had become her adoptive father took Dawn's breath away. "I'm scared, Dad."

Dylan nodded and rubbed the back of his neck. "That's why it's important to be honest here."

"Annie."

Annie turned to face Charli.

Charli reached up and brushed her fingers over the girl's cheek. "When I was arrested in Las Vegas, I knew it was time for me to come clean. I told the police everything that happened to me. In the end, I still served a year in prison, but I will never regret telling the cops everything I knew about the man I thought I loved and who I believed loved me. It was the right thing to do."

Dawn couldn't believe how honest Charli was with Annie about her own past. But then, maybe that was why she was able to help Annie turn her life around. Charli had been to the dark side and back again.

Annie swallowed again and nodded. "Okay. I overheard Chris and Tyler Demello talking about something big going down. That there was a new dealer in town." She shrugged and rubbed her face again. "They weren't too happy about it."

"Do you know what this dealer wanted?"

"He wanted them to only deal for him and give him ninety-five percent of all profits."

That made sense. The big fish always swallowed the small ones. "What happened if they didn't?"

Annie's dark eyes glimmered with unshed tears. "They'd pay the consequences."

Dawn didn't need to be a rocket scientist to figure out what those were.

"I'm afraid for Tyler. He's not a bad kid. He just hates his life."

"I'm going to talk to him soon. We'll do what we have to in order to keep him safe. Was Justin Vaughn also in on this?"

Annie glanced at Charli. "Yeah. But I didn't really talk to him. He was still mad about me cleaning up and staying here with Charli and Dylan. Besides, he was into some hard shit... I mean..."

"It's okay." Dawn wanted a name. Even if it was one that would break her heart to hear. "Do you have any idea who the dealer is?"

Annie looked down at her hands. "Not by name. Chris called him Outlaw, but I'm not sure if he ever knew his name."

Dawn reached over and rested her hand on Annie's arm. "Thank you, Annie. What you've done here will help me a lot."

The girl nodded and wiped at the tear sliding down her pale cheek.

Dylan led Dawn out the door onto the wide front porch. "Dawn, do you think Annie's in any danger?"

Lying to the former Special Forces commander was futile. "Yes. She's cleaned up well, but she's hanging around a dangerous crowd."

"Yeah, I know." He glanced toward the door. "Charli won't leave until after the roundup, but I'm trying to convince her to go to Nashville and visit with her brother for a little while."

Charli's half brother was country superstar Nate McConnell. "That would probably be a wise thing to do. Logan Cartwright signed a record deal and is touring in the spring with McConnell. He's good with kids, and he's someone Annie knows."

"I didn't even think about Logan being there too. Thanks, Dawn."

She put her Stetson on her head. "All in a day's work. Take care, Dylan."

"You too."

She turned to head down the stairs, but his voice stopped her.

"I want you to know I'm glad you're running for sheriff, and that you have my vote."

"Thanks." Smiling, she gave him a sloppy imitation of a military salute, then headed for her department Tahoe.

Who the hell is Outlaw?

Chapter 7

Talon stared at the little girl. She had wheat-colored hair and creamy skin. But she peered back at him with his hazel eyes out of a face that resembled his own in structure. She lay on the garish carpeting beside her mother's stool as Maggie put the final touches to her stage makeup. In the girl's arms was a raggedy stuffed bear. Her clothes looked as if they'd come from a trashcan. The bottoms of her faded jeans were folded up several times, and her too-small T-shirt had a faded cartoon character on the front. At least Maggie kept them clean.

"Good to see you, Talon. Beth was certain you'd show," Maggie said, referring to her younger sister. She stood from the dressing table, turned, and glared at him. The bright light from the bare bulbs over the large mirrors glittered on the gold and silver sequins of her skimpy costume. Ostrich feathers stuck out of a hideous headdress atop her blond hairdo. "I had my doubts."

Several other showgirls in various states of dress watched him, but he ignored them and focused on his former fling.

"If you knew anything about me at all, you'd know better than that." He looked back at the little girl on the floor.

Maggie Pratt was the same age as his sister, and she'd grown up in Colton. She knew who his birth father was and what a prick he'd been to him and his half brothers.

"You should've told me about her." He clenched his fists and looked back at Maggie. "I would've been in her life."

The little girl sat up and scooted closer to her mother's bare legs. Bitterness filled him, fueling his anger and resolve. He wasn't his father, and he wouldn't abandon his child.

Maggie took a cigarette out of a pack and lit it. "Sure, I know you would've been around. Except for your little vacay. How was the state pen, by the way?"

He let the remark slide and glanced at the toddler again. Beth had been right. He hadn't wanted to believe her when she told him her sister had a three-year-old and claimed he was the father.

A child he'd sired when he and Maggie had hooked up after his one and only time riding in the National Finals Rodeo.

"You shouldn't have her here." He looked around at the other showgirls. Nothing about them was PG rated, from their dress, to their actions, to their conversations. "You shouldn't have a kid here."

"I normally don't. But Beth told me you were coming today." She tossed her lighter on the dressing table behind her and turned. "I didn't want you coming by my place. Alonzo doesn't like that I have a kid with another guy. Meeting you wouldn't be a good idea."

Her sister had told him Maggie had shacked up with a loser that hated her daughter. Acid boiled in his veins at the thought of another man mistreating his baby girl. Probably the reason she wore castoffs; he wouldn't allow her to have new clothes. "You told Beth you didn't want anyone in Colton to know you had a kid."

She took a drag on the cigarette. "They don't have to know I'm her mother."

In other words, no one needed to know she had a baby with him.

"Ten minutes till show time, ladies!" A tall man rushed toward them in the isle between dressing tables. His flashy blazer hung open to show off a smooth chest. Stopping, he looked Talon up and down with an appreciative smile. "Haven't seen you around, handsome."

"You're barking up the wrong tree, buddy. Get lost." Talon scowled, and the man's eyes got big as he rushed past.

She blew smoke in Talon's face. "Are you done scaring my stage manager?" Maggie stepped away from the stool and tripped over the girl sitting on the floor. She caught the counter to keep from falling, but she undoubtedly twisted her ankle when her high heel caught on the girl's right arm. "Damn it, Jessie, get out from under my feet."

The little girl let out a squawk of pain and big tears ran down her cheeks. Rubbing her arm where the heel had hit her, she backed away, fear and pain shining in her bright hazel eyes.

Disgust and hatred rolled through him as he knelt in front of the little girl and noticed she had a black and blue bruise on her wrist as if someone had grabbed her too tightly. Swallowing the acidy desire to do the same damage to the woman who allowed such a thing to happen, he picked up the stuffed bear, which the girl had dropped when Maggie kicked into her. "Hey there, who's this?"

She sniffled and swallowed hard. "Bear-boo."

Talon smiled and glanced at the old thing. It was missing an eye and the left ear was torn, as if a dog had gotten a hold of it. "Well, hi, Bear-boo. Nice to meet you. You look like a very good friend." He placed it into her arms. His heart squeezed as his hands ached to draw her to him and never let her go.

She hugged the bear close and glanced up at her mother as if looking for reassurance.

Appearing bored, Maggie put out her cigarette. "It's okay. Talon's a friend and is gonna take care of you while Mommy goes on her new job. Remember we talked about this?"

Talon met Maggie's blue eyes, hoping to see remorse. But only coldness and impatience radiated from her. Bitterness bubbled in his stomach, causing it to churn. He'd seen the same emotion in Jock Blackwell's eyes too many times when his mother would take him to his place. Could she be this heartless? Didn't she have any feelings for her child at all? How can she give her baby away while she goes off on some cruise ship with her latest fling?

At least she contacted him and hadn't given his daughter away to strangers. Or had an abortion when she'd discovered she was knocked up. Beth had asked him if he doubted he was the girl's father. His doubts vanished the moment he set eyes on her.

What was he going to do with a three-year-old little girl? Hell, he wasn't so sure he'd get out of whatever charges Hendricks dreamed up regarding the murders of those two kids back home. He didn't want to think about the possibility of going back to prison or what would happen to his kid if he did.

But he was damned sure not letting his little girl stay here for a moment longer.

She sniffled again and smiled just a little. "Hi. I'm Jessie Mae."

He swallowed hard and his heart raced. "I'm your daddy, Jessie Mae."

Scooting closer on the worn, filthy carpeting, she reached out and touched his cheek. "Daddy?"

His heart flipped over in his chest. "Yeah, sweet baby." His voice all but cracked on the words. "You're gonna live with me."

* * * *

"Rachel?" Wyatt banged on the bedroom door and glanced at his mother. "Go find the key. I don't like this."

His mother bit her lip and nodded. Fear blanched her face until the freckles over her cheeks and nose stood out in stark contrast to her pale skin. She turned and headed down the hall to the kitchen.

He tried the knob again, hoping it was stuck and not locked. Closing his eyes, he fisted his hand against the white raised panel of the door and prayed. *Dear God in heaven, please let my baby sister be okay.*

He repeated the mantra as his mother ran toward him, holding out the skeleton key that opened all of the bedroom doors. "She seemed off this morning when I helped her with her shower, but she kept telling me she was okay." Her hand shook as he took the key from her. "I wouldn't have gone to the grocery store, but she asked if I could make lasagna tonight, and I had to get the ingredients."

His mother's voice rose with growing hysteria as he shoved the key into Rachel's door. The door swung open, revealing a dark, musty room. Icy dread blew through him like an arctic blizzard, freezing his guts.

He shoved more into the room and zeroed in on the rumpled bed. Rachel lay face down with an open pill bottle by her outstretched hand. His mother's muffled scream shot though him as adrenalin and fear chased the sound around his nervous system. He hurried to the bed and kicked an object he vaguely recognized as an empty brandy bottle. Leaning over Rachel's still form, he touched her clammy skin over the pulse point at her throat. He closed his eyes as the erratic slow beats moved under his fingers. The pulse was too slow and weak to be effective.

"Wyatt, is she…" his mother choked.

"No, but she's not okay. Call for an ambulance." He lifted his sisters limp body off the bed, amazed at how light she was, and laid her on the floor on her back. As he knelt beside her, he noticed she wasn't breathing, then checked the side of her throat again. The flutter of her pulse was gone. "Tell them I'm starting CPR."

His mother sobbed, but he ignored her, placing his hands over the center of Rachel's chest, and began compressions, counting out loud to thirty. "C'mon, Ladybug, don't you do this," he said as he tilted her head to give her two breaths.

As he put his hands on her chest again, his mother knelt beside Rachel across from him with her cell phone in hand. "No, she's not breathing." Her voice cracked and she sobbed again, but somehow managed to say, "My son's doing CPR right now. Oh, God, please hurry."

She tossed the phone to the floor and took Rachel's hand. "Please, please be okay."

Wyatt fell into a rhythm--thirty compressions, then two breaths. The memory of the night Dawn was shot stabbed at his conscience. After she'd been hit, and he'd killed the kid holding him, the thug who'd shot Dawn had run off. He couldn't go after him and leave Dawn. Blood, so much blood, had soaked through her white tank top over her heart that he'd feared the worse. He'd pulled his phone, called for backup, and begun CPR. But he hadn't been able to save their baby.

"Damn it." He wasn't sure at whom or what the curse was directed--Rachel for trying to take her life, at the memories of Dawn, or the ambulance for taking so long to get there.

An eternity passed before the blast of a siren sounded from the ambulance heading to them. He glanced up as his mother hurried to her feet to open the door.

A few minutes later, his father rushed in with an automated external defibrillator.

He set it by Rachel's head and opened the red lid. The fire chief met Wyatt's eyes, and the pain and fear for his daughter shined through, but his dad kept it together and cut off Rachel's T-shirt and bra. Wyatt continued to press on her bare chest as his father connected the pads for the AED.

Wyatt leaned back and took a ragged breath as two paramedics and two EMTs came in carrying equipment bags. A female EMT put the mask of an Ambu bag attached to an oxygen tank over Rachel's face. One of the paramedics knelt beside him. "I'll take over from here."

Wyatt nodded and moved back as the AED indicated a shock was needed. His father looked around and gruffly shouted, "Clear!" Dad pressed the flashing orange button, and Rachel's lifeless body jerked as electricity entered her heart. His father leaned over and started compressing her chest, ignoring Wyatt and the paramedic on the other side of her. "C'mon, c'mon."

Wyatt stood, went to his mother, and wrapped her up in his arms. She buried her face in his chest and cried.

An EMT knelt beside his father and rested his hand on his shoulder. "Chief? Let me take over."

When his father turned to look at the man, tears soaked his weathered cheeks. He nodded and leaned back on his haunches as the medics worked on Rachel. The second paramedic pulled out a bag of IV solution and a needle kit from an equipment bag, then began prepping Rachel's arm.

The tinny voice from the AED announced that no shock was advised, and the EMT administering breaths checked Rachel's pulse at her neck.

Sara Walter Ellwood

She sucked in a breath that made her shoulders raise and fall. "She has a pulse!"

The paramedic working with the IV stood with the bag in hand and gently squeezed it. "Let's roll."

Wyatt moved his mother and father out of the crowded bedroom as the medics got Rachel loaded onto a gurney and rushed her out of the house. Dad took Mom's hand, pulling her to his side, and glanced at Wyatt. "We'll ride along in the ambulance. Meet us at the hospital?"

He numbly nodded. "Yeah."

Mom wiped tears from her face. "Call Audrey. She'll want to know."

He nodded again, but wasn't so sure having Audrey around was a good idea. Something pushed Rachel to attempt suicide. But he also knew Audrey loved Rachel as much as he did.

An hour later, he stared out the window of the waiting room off the emergency department of the Forest County General Hospital. A train, heading east, rattled along beyond the parking lot. As the boxcars carrying cattle and other goods from the west rushed by, he let the hypnotic motion sooth his desire to flee to the freedom outside. He hated hospitals, and all he could think about was the last time he'd waited for a doctor to come and tell him if the woman he loved had lived or died. Only to discover she'd kept secrets and had risked their unborn baby's life.

He shook his head and turned away from the brightness of the day to the constraining dimness of the waiting room with its uncomfortable gray plastic chairs and fake wood tables scattered with last month's tired magazines.

His twin sister sat with their mother while their father paced the length of the waiting room, drawing curious stares from the three sets of parents waiting to have sick kids examined, and a cowboy with a dirty, blood-soaked towel wrapped around his hand.

"Mr. and Mrs. McPherson?" The masculine voice had Wyatt turning in its direction. A tall, lean man in blue scrubs and a white coat stood at the door of the waiting area.

Dad stopped his incessant pacing, and Mom sat straight in her chair as she held onto Audrey's hands.

"What's going on, Doc?" his father asked in a gruff voice.

The doctor rubbed the dark stubble of a five o'clock shadow on his chin. "Come with me."

They followed him into a claustrophobic room with more gray plastic chairs and another fake wood table in the center. The doctor gestured toward the chairs. "Please, sit down."

Once they settled around the table--Wyatt and Audrey sitting on either side of their mother with their father stoically standing behind them--the doctor closed the door and sat across the table from them.

Dad cleared his throat, but his voice still came out rough. "How is she, Doc?"

"I'm Doctor Dan Forsyth. Rachel is in critical condition and has been moved to the intensive care unit, but I feel confident she will pull through." The doctor shook his head and glanced at his hands as he cleared his throat. "I knew Major McPherson from Afghanistan. She and I worked at the same hospital when she and Colonel Webster were shot. I know what PTSD can do to a person. But she's a fighter, and she'll get through this."

"You worked with our daughter?" Mom's voice broke on the last word.

"Yes, I was a government contractor." Forsyth smiled. "I moved to Colton when my contract was up partly because of what Rachel said about the place. I couldn't believe such a perfect little town could exist."

Wyatt wasn't so sure he'd call Colton perfect, but it did have its own kind of charm. What surprised him was that Rachel spoke so highly of a place she'd avoided for years.

Audrey glanced at him as if she was thinking the same thing. "When can we see her?"

"She's sleeping, but I think her parents can visit for a few moments tonight. Then it would be best if you all go home and wait until tomorrow. I suspect she'll be awake by morning."

Wyatt had to get out of there. He stood and Audrey looked at him. "I need some air." Before anyone could question him, he kissed his mother's cheek and patted his father on the shoulder, then left the room as the first tears stung his eyes. *Dear God, Ladybug, what made you think suicide was the answer?*

He had no idea where he was going when he opened up the throttle of his Harley, letting the cool wind whip through his hair and dry the tears on his cheeks, until he turned into the gravel drive of the C Bar M Ranch.

* * * *

Dawn pulled into her driveway and stared at the Harley sitting by the barn. But she didn't see its owner until she caught movement by the door. Wyatt leaned against the wall and watched her park her truck. Her heart sped up as she got out of the rig.

From the way his forehead pulled down over his eyes, and the deep frown tugged on his lips, something bad had happened. She stopped halfway to him and folded her arms across her chest.

He stepped away from the barn, and before she knew what was happening, his arms were wrapped around her like his life depended on it. She snaked her arms around him and held on tight. His body pressed against hers, but there was nothing sexual in the embrace, despite her heart's rapid beating and the tightness in her lower belly. Her nose filled with his wonderful scent of leather, fresh air, and his unique musk. His breathing was ragged, and from the way he trembled, she wondered if he was crying. But a man like Wyatt would never cry unless his world had imploded.

Several moments passed before he lifted his head from her neck and met her gaze. The pain in his blue eyes broke her heart.

He took a deep breath and looked toward the pasture next to the barn. "I'm sorry."

God, his voice was so deep.

"I… uh…" As he shook his head, the chilly breeze lifted his hair, and the setting sun turned the auburn strands scarlet. Her hands tingled at the memory of the softness of his hair.

"Wy, what's going on?" She'd never seen him so rattled.

As he closed his eyes, he stepped out of her arms, but took her hand. "Rachel tried to commit suicide."

She sucked in a breath. "Dear God. Is she okay?"

"She will be. She's in the ICU and had her stomach pumped." He wiped his free hand over his face. "She overdosed on her antidepressants and washed them down with a bottle of Ma's Christmas brandy."

"Oh, God." She squeezed his hand and those electric eyes met hers. "C'mon. Let's go inside."

He nodded and let her lead him across the driveway and up the porch steps. Taco waddled and wiggled over when Dawn opened the door. Dawn ruffled the dog's long ears and let her out. Taco recognized Wyatt and barked, but the need to do her business overrode any obligation she must have possessed to protect her mistress.

Wyatt followed Dawn into the living room. He'd let go of her when she'd opened the door and jammed his hands into the pockets of his bomber jacket. He never looked more lost.

She headed for the gun safe next to the kitchen, removed her service belt, and locked her Glock in the safe. Sensing him watching her, she took a deep breath and turned around. "Would you like some coffee?"

He shook his head. "How about something stronger?"

"Beer?"

"Yeah."

She went into the kitchen and returned with two Coors Lights. Why had he come to her? He could have gone to Zack and Tracy's or his cousin Dylan Quinn or his latest fling...The list went on. But instead, he was here, and she refused to ponder the reasons.

As he took the bottle from her, he sat on the couch. She perched on the edge of the wing chair next to the safe with the cold bottle between her hands. He tipped his bottle back and gulped about half.

"Do you want to talk?" Why else would he be here?

He lowered the bottle and stared at it as he leaned over his long legs. "She wasn't breathing, and her pulse stopped when Ma and I found her. I started CPR, and when Dad got there with the ambulance, he shocked her to restart her heart. We almost lost her." His voice dipped so low it broke.

"Damn."

He nodded and drank more of his beer. "I thought we lost her. What the fuck was she thinking?"

Wyatt often cursed, but his use of the f-bomb scared her as much as his being here. She set her bottle on the end table and moved to sit beside him. Although she had no idea why he'd come to her, he obviously needed comfort. Was she willing to provide it?

The pain in his startling baby blues had her heart seizing. She'd do anything to relieve his hurt.

Anything?

She slipped her arm around his waist. "She feels helpless."

Sweet Jesus, what would she do if she were in Rachel's shoes? She may have lost her baby, but Rachel would never know what it is like to have a baby grow inside of her. She would never have a child of her own.

What would Dawn have done if she hadn't stopped the bullet and it had hit Wyatt all those years ago? Would she have been as helpless and lost as Rachel losing the man she loved? But Dawn lost him anyway, and the child they'd created.

"I know she's hurting, but she has to stop holding in the pain. I know the timing of Audrey's announcement the other day was terrible, and I know she's grieving, but there has to be something that can be done to make things better." He closed his eyes and shook his head. "I was just settling in at the ranch, now I think it's best if I stay at Mom and Dad's to help with Rachel a little longer."

One of the many things she'd always loved and admired about Wyatt was the way he loved his sisters. But sometimes love wasn't enough. "I don't think that's the answer."

He met her gaze again. "What?"

For several moments, they stared at each other. Her sinuses burned from both fear and sorrow for her friend.

She averted her gaze to the fisted hand on her thigh. What had helped her get through her loss? "She needs to get out and around people. Your parents and you mean well, but I can only imagine she feels like a burden on you all. If you delay your move, you'll only manage to make her feel more stifled."

He shifted beside her and rested his hand over hers. She snapped her eyes to him.

"I suppose I see your point." Swallowing so hard his Adam's apple bobbed, he set his empty bottle on the table beside him. When he turned back to her, he wrapped his arm around her. "What do you think we should do?"

He was asking *her*? She shrugged, feeling strangely comforted by his touch and agitated by it at the same time. "She's a nurse. Why not see if she can volunteer either at the hospital or at one of the nursing homes? Maybe if she's working again, she will be able to heal."

"In other words, if she's busy, she doesn't have time to dwell on the rotten things going on with her?"

She shrugged. "Not really, but she has to feel like she's needed. Like she's in control of her life again."

After she'd lost their baby, she'd come back to Colton, and as soon as her doctor released her to go back to work, she'd begged her dad to give her a job with the sheriff's department. Keeping busy helped her deal with not only the loss of her baby, but her broken heart.

He searched her face and eyes as if he demanded to know all of her secrets. Dawn couldn't breathe as she watched him close in, then she gasped when his lips landed on hers. The kiss was nothing like the one from the other night. This one was tender, but passion sizzled under the surface.

She turned into him. He pulled her into his lap, and gripped her waist, holding her close. Licking her upper lip, he demanded entrance. Taking his face between her hands, she straddled his legs, pushed him into the back of the couch, and took his onslaught with welcome fervor.

* * * *

"Wyatt," Dawn whispered against his lips, but unlike the other night, she didn't stop him. She opened the snaps of his shirt and shoved it aside. He hissed between his teeth when she kissed down his neck to his pulse point.

His heart thumped in his chest with a hungry need he didn't realize was possible. He'd never wanted her more than he did right now. He wanted the fiery sensations of her hands caressing over his chest to help him forget the pain he carried for his sister and anger at his not being able to protect her.

How could he ever forgive Dawn for her betrayal? And yet, here he was, seeking comfort from her. Was he willing to make love to her?

Was he going to use her like this?

She moaned in his mouth and ground against his hardening cock, and his desire took over any conscious thought.

He groped for the buttons of her uniform blouse. When he couldn't get them open with his trembling fingers, he gripped the edges and pulled. Buttons flew to the left and right, but he didn't care. And apparently, neither did Dawn. She shrugged out of the shirt.

The small pucker above her left breast had his breath freezing in his lungs. He touched the scar, and she trembled as their eyes met.

Had she taken a bullet for him?

Why on God's Earth would she have done that? He'd had things under control that night.

He couldn't bare thinking about the pain and shock he'd been consumed with when the doctor had come out of the OR of the Dallas hospital to tell him Dawn would be okay, though the bullet grazed her heart. However, the child she carried couldn't be saved.

If he'd been a few minutes later, Rachel would have been beyond saving. He'd have failed his sister as he'd failed saving his baby.

"Stop thinking," Dawn whispered, as she leaned in and kissed him, plunging her tongue deep into his mouth setting him on fire all over again.

As he stripped her of her bra, she worked open his belt and fly. When she wrapped her hot hand around his erection, he broke the kiss with a curse. He opened his eyes when she slipped off his lap. Her dark brown eyes burned, scorching him as she kissed down his chest, stopping to lick over his erect, sensitive nipples. All the while, she pumped his cock. She stroked her thumb over the sensitive head of his penis, and the electric shock zapped through him and landed in his balls.

"Dawn." He lolled his head back, but couldn't tear his gaze from hers.

She shifted to her feet, took off her boots, and pushed her tan slacks and panties to the floor. As he watched her, he toed off his boots, then removed his jeans and underwear.

She slid her gaze over his body, and her breathing came in quick spurts as she reached up and pulled the band from her hair. The long black waterfall landed around her shoulders and reached the curve of her ass.

Dear God in heaven, she was beautiful.

Blood rushed so fast out of his head, his vision fuzzed, causing him to blink. He filled his lungs with air scented by Dawn's distinct fragrance of honeysuckle and spice.

She crawled back into his lap. He gripped her waist and held her in place. "I don't have any condoms."

He wheezed as if he'd run a twenty-mile race. At this point, if they couldn't follow through, it would about kill him. He was beyond a cold shower.

Touching his face as she had earlier, with both hands caressing his cheeks and jaw, she smiled. "It's okay. I'm on the pill. And I trust you." She swallowed and her smile wavered a little. "I haven't been with anyone since we were together."

Then why was she on the pill?

She must have sensed his question. "After..." Again she swallowed and the smile disappeared completely. "After I lost the baby, I went on the pill to regulate... things."

He nodded and pulled her to his mouth. At the moment, speech was as beyond his capabilities as were regret and anger at her reminder of the child he'd never know. As their lips melded, she took him deep into her body and moaned into his mouth.

Tight, wet heat engulfed him. The shock hit his balls and light flashed through his head. He was going to come before things even had a chance to get started. He broke the kiss, and air rushed out him, hissing between his gritted teeth as he got a grip on his control.

She arched her back into a beautiful bow. Her breasts rose high as she lifted up and slid back down, starting a relentless rhythm that had him panting. She opened her eyes and met his gaze as the first ripple tightened around him, cutting through his fragile control like a knife.

She closed her eyes again and a long gasp escaped as her orgasm shattered her.

He couldn't hold back. The fireball barreling down his spine and through his groin was too much. Squeezing his eyes closed and gritting his teeth, he gripped her hips, taking over, and thrust into her deep and hard. She quaked around him as he exploded into her.

She fell onto him and buried her face into his neck. He brought his hands slowly up her back and threaded his fingers into her honeysuckle-scented hair. He had no idea how long they stayed like that, the only sounds being their rapid heartbeats, ragged breathing, and the refrigerator kicking on and running.

Then reality smacked him between the eyes.

What the hell had he done?

Chapter 8

Oh, hell.

Dawn shivered from the cool air hitting her naked back as much as from the realization she'd had sex with Wyatt.

Had she used her body to comfort a man who could never love her?

Shifting off his lap, she reached for the afghan folded over the arm of the couch. She turned her back to the man she'd just played cowgirl with and wrapped the soft wool around herself.

She closed her eyes and tried to forget the intense pleasure she'd experienced with him and the hollow emptiness that now replaced it.

She suspected the rustling sounds behind her were from Wyatt getting dressed. During the intervening eternity of dead silence, she remembered she still had to feed her horses, and poor Taco scratched at the screen door.

Thinking about the mundane was easier than concentrating on the sensations of his essence on her inner thighs and the chill settling in where only moments before there had been burning heat.

He cleared his throat, and she forced her eyes open, then looked over her shoulder. Wyatt stood completely dressed, but his cheeks were still flushed from the strain of what they'd done.

Handsome as the devil her people had long considered the White Man of being.

"Some white men still think all we are good for is lying on our backs with our legs open."

But what if he was the one on his back? She could almost hear her mother's response. *Semantics.*

"I... eh..." He stabbed all ten fingers into his tussled hair.

God, if he said he was sorry, she'd break right here and now.

The phone rang, but she ignored it, letting the machine pick up.

She turned, gripping the ends of the blanket that covered her from shoulders to feet, but she was still naked to him in a way going beyond nudeness. Her soul was on display.

She closed her eyes and waited for him to leave.

"Sheriff, this is Tilly. I convinced Tyler Demello to talk to us. He'll be here in an hour. I notified the DA and the Rangers. Call the station."

"Hey." She swallowed, hoping her tongue would form the words she needed it to. "I'll see you around. I have to feed the horses and call Tilly to find out what's going on."

Her legs threatened to crumble, but somehow she managed to sound normal as if they'd spent the afternoon sipping beer and talking motorcycles.

His gaze slid from hers, and he nodded. "Dawn… Thank you for being here."

Oh, sweet God, that was worse than *I'm sorry.*

Slipping in past Wyatt when he left, Taco barked, then pressed against Dawn's leg. As Wyatt's Harley roared to life outside, Dawn sniffed and shook herself into action. Looking down at the dog, she realized how lonely she was and how much she wished things could be different between her and Wyatt.

That was the reason she so easily gave herself to him. He'd come to her during what was a painful time, and she'd let the feeling of connecting emotionally with him carry her away.

Dawn… Thank you for being here.

Her mother was right. All he would ever want from her was sex.

And like the damned fool she was, she easily gave it to him.

"C'mon, girl, let me get you some dinner. Then it's back to work for me."

Thank God. If she was lucky, tomorrow, she'd be there all night and day too. When she finally came home, she'd be so tired she wouldn't have the energy to think about how stupid she was, or how good Wyatt McPherson felt buried within her.

Taco wiggled her tail and let out a happy bark.

Too bad her life couldn't be as easy as her faithful old puppy's.

* * * *

An hour and half later, Dawn walked into her office, with Tilly trailing behind. She picked up Demello's file from her desk and turned to face her second in command. "Is he in the conference room?"

Tilly nodded. "The DA will be here in a few minutes."

"What about the Ranger?" She fished in her desk drawer for a pen. As she scribbled on a scrap of paper to make sure it worked, she looked up, and her stomach folded in on itself.

"I'm here." Wyatt entered and removed his hat. He must have gone home and showered, because his hair was still a little damp and curled at the ends. He'd also changed into dark jeans, a white western shirt, and leather vest. His silver peso star pinned to the left side of the vest winked brightly when it caught the overhead light.

Tilly pursed his lips. "What are you doing here? I thought you were on vacation. I heard about Rachel. She's in mine and Barb's prayers," he said, referring to his wife as he patted Wyatt's shoulder.

He cleared his throat and looked everywhere but at her as he spoke. "As for the vacation, Captain Rider called me and told me he yanked my request this afternoon. Said, since the sheriff and I have worked together before and drugs are involved, I'm too perfect for the case to let loose." He rubbed his neck. "As for Rachel, thanks. She needs all the prayers she can get."

Tilly nodded and clearly wondered by the narrowing of his eyes what Wyatt was doing here and not at the hospital, but he didn't ask.

She wasn't that polite. "Why are you here… and not with your family?"

He shrugged and fiddled with his hat by turning it around in his hands by the brim. "Only Mom and Dad could see her tonight. Audrey and Lance are with them, and I hate hospitals too much to hang out there. I figured I would be of better use here."

Dawn's legs threatened to give out. She sat in the chair behind her desk and opened the file, although her vision was too blurred to see the paper of the report, let alone the writing on it.

How was she going to work with him after her performance earlier?

Would he expect a repeat?

Was she strong enough to resist if he did?

She was vaguely aware of Tilly speaking, but she couldn't comprehend his words.

Fisting her hand around the pen she'd fished out of her drawer until her fingers hurt, she forced herself to get a grip. She couldn't let Wyatt know he rattled her so much. When she could speak, she stood and rounded the desk.

"Get Wyatt up to speed on Demello. I'll go meet Pete," she said, referring to the DA, then escaped as fast as she dared.

She found Peter Grant talking to his cousin, Deputy Doug Grant, outside of the conference room. As she approached, Doug cuffed Pete on the arm and headed back to his desk.

Pete nodded at her. "So, what do you think will come out of this little meet and greet?"

"Hopefully, a confession and the identity of the thug killing these kids." Dawn sensed Wyatt before he stopped beside her. She glanced at him and Tilly. "Ready?"

"Yep. Let's go." Wyatt was close enough to touch as he reached for the door handle. "After you, Sheriff."

He met her gaze, and her belly clenched at the memory of his lips on her as their bodies melded. She hurried through the door into the conference room, the men following her.

Tyler Demello sat next to a man who stood as they entered. He wore an expensive suit, his short brown hair gleaming of high dollar Dallas salons. His calculating dark eyes easily took her in with a glint of disdain. "Sheriff Madison. I'm Greg Meyer, Tyler's attorney."

Dawn hit *Record* on the recorder on the table and shook the Dallas lawyer's hand. His gold Rolex gleamed in the fluorescent lights overhead. "Yes, I remember you, Mr. Meyer. We've eh... worked together before."

He gave her a tight-lipped smile and settled his jacket sleeve back into place. He got her meaning. High priced defense lawyers and the police never *worked together*. The cops wanted to tar and feather the rich scum the attorneys were getting paid mega bucks to save from the vat.

She indicated the men standing beside her. "This is Lieutenant Wyatt McPherson of the Texas Rangers, Lieutenant Tillman Kennedy, and Forest County district attorney Peter Grant."

Wyatt nodded toward the tall, well-dressed woman standing behind the teenager. "Ma'am."

"Elizabeth Raines. Tyler's mother." She crossed her arms over her silk blouse and pursed her carefully painted full lips. She didn't look old enough to have a seventeen-year-old son. Then again, according to the grapevine, she was married to a man five years older than her son, and half her own age. "Are you charging my son with this preposterous charge, Sheriff?"

Laying the folder on the table, Dawn pulled out a chair and sat directly in front of Tyler. He'd sat with his arms crossed before him throughout the entire greeting. He might have agreed to this meeting, but he hadn't left his attitude at home. "I have no choice, Mrs. Raines. Tyler was caught with six ounces of coke. We think he's a dealer, if he's a user with that much product... Well, either way, we have a problem."

The woman's surgery-perfected face paled, and she slid into a chair beside her son. "Tyler?"

He glanced at his mother before looking back at Dawn, and swallowing so hard his protruding Adam's apple moved up and down in his scrawny neck.

"I have to warn you, Tyler. Whatever you say here, can and will be used against you." His lawyer interjected before Tyler had a chance to confess to possession. Despite the sheriff's department having already established the fact by finding the drugs on the boy. "I have to advise you to allow me to answer your questions."

"Yes, Mom." Tyler totally ignored the lawyer. Some of that attitude was a good thing after all.

Dawn let out a breath. He wanted to talk, and she wasn't wasting a minute of it before Meyer reeled him in. She opened the folder and removed a photo.

Before she had a chance to show the picture to Tyler, Wyatt pulled out the chair beside her and slid into it. His scent filled her nose, and she flashed back to the salty sweetness of his skin as they had sex only a few hours ago.

"What do you know about Christopher Larson and Justin Vaughn?" Wyatt asked, his tone low and hard.

Tyler glanced at his tattooed hands. "I know they were also dealers."

"Are you, or were they part of a gang?" Dawn studied the dark marks over his knuckles. She didn't recognize them as any gang symbols she was aware of, but she'd also been out of the loop on what went on in the inner cities for several years now.

He shook his head and looked up at her, his dark eyes guarded, but not completely hidden behind his mask of defiance. His black hair fell over his forehead, making him look younger than his seventeen years. How did a rich kid like him end up so messed up?

"Don't you dare say anything else, Tyler. I won't have any son of mine going to prison. I won't be the laughing stock of the Junior League again." His mother glanced over at the lawyer. "This meeting is over."

Tyler's dark eyes hardened as he glared at his mother.

Ah... And there was Dawn's answer.

Before Raines could get out of her seat, Pete stepped forward from the quiet place he'd taken up against the map of Texas to watch the questioning. "Mrs. Raines, just for the charges your son's already incurred, he's facing at least five years in prison. And I'm not talking some cushy juvie boarding school. I'm talking the state pen. This is at least his second offence. I'm prepared to go after him as an adult."

Tyler's face paled. "Those other charges were tossed out."

Pete nodded and leaned over his hands beside Dawn. "My mistake. However, you are a dealer. Chris Larson was a dealer. Justin Vaughn was a dealer. I don't know about you, but that's a lot of drugs for a county that has ten times more cows than people."

"Mr. Grant, what are you getting at?" Meyer leaned forward.

Dawn all but smiled. She knew exactly where Pete was going. "Would you mind telling us where you were Monday morning around four AM? Because I have a witness who says you weren't home."

Tyler's eyes got big, and his mother gasped. "Are you suggesting my son killed those two thugs?"

Wyatt stood and leaned over the table. "That's exactly what we're suggesting, Mrs. Raines."

"No!" Tyler shook his head so fast he sent his punk hairdo flying around his face. "No. I didn't kill Chris or Justin. We were all dealing for the same man."

Meyer rested his hand on his shoulder to stop the flow of words. He gave Pete a hard stare. "Okay, Grant. I see where this is going. What can you offer my client if he cooperates and tells you what you want to know?"

Pete straightened and seemed to be calculating his options in the way he rubbed his jaw. "A plea bargain. Tyler tells us whatever he knows, and I'll reduce the charge to possession."

"No, not good enough." Meyer leaned back in his seat. "We want all the charges dropped."

"I'll reduce the charges, but I can't drop them." With a brow raised, Pete sat in the chair next to Dawn. "Take it or leave it."

The other lawyer started gathering his notes and glanced at Raines. "I believe we are finished here. We'll see you at the arraignment."

"Then we go after your client as our prime suspect in the murders of Larson and Vaughn," Wyatt said from behind Dawn.

She glanced at him. His jaw twitched and the hardness in his features surprised her. In all the years she'd worked with him, she'd never seen him this cold.

Was it directed at her? Or at the drug dealer?

* * * *

Wyatt didn't believe for a second Demello killed anyone, but the accusation got the desired effect. The bigwig lawyer sat back and agreed to Pete's plea bargain. He hated it. Punks like this one had cost him so much, but he'd learned a long time ago that to catch a big fish the little ones sometimes had to be let go.

He didn't have to like it or make it easy on the shithead.

After a few moments of whispered conversation between Demello and Meyer, the lawyer said, "My client does have a concern about his and his family's safety."

"My department will keep you and your family safe." Dawn picked up the photograph she'd removed from the folder and placed it upside down in front of her. She glanced at it and swallowed. "I promise no harm will come to you, Tyler."

"So, now you wanna share what you know?" Wyatt came around to the side of the table and leaned over it. Getting close to Dawn wasn't a good thing and sitting beside her again wasn't doing anything for his mood.

He'd been a weak fool earlier that evening, but he wanted to talk about the sex. Had it meant nothing to her?

Was it nothing more than a mercy fuck?

Dear God.

His skin was too tight over his bones. He physically ached from the stress and heartache of the day. But he had to get his head back on straight and concentrate on what the kid was saying.

The sooner he solved this case the quicker he could get the hell away from Dawn.

As far as the fence they shared between his ranch and hers allowed.

Great.

"I only know that we all worked different parts of the county. I hit up the Heights," he said, referring to the sub-division built on the Circle M land. "Chris handled the ranch hands and cowboys that came into his father's bar, and Justin took care of the high school crowd."

Wyatt folded his arms over his chest. "Nice little arrangement you had there. What happened?"

The kid shrugged and looked down at his folded arms.

Dawn leaned in and slid a photo toward him. "Have you ever seen this man?"

Jesus, it was a photo of her brother.

Demello glanced at it and shook his head.

"Are you sure? A source told me that a man known as Outlaw is your supplier."

She'd been busy the past few days.

"Yeah, but none of us ever saw him. He only talked with us on the phones he'd sent to us."

"How did he first make contact?" Wyatt couldn't believe Dawn was considering Talon. Although a lot of circumstantial evidence pointed to Talon, he knew he wasn't their dealer.

Tyler shifted in his seat and glanced at his mother. "Through Justin Vaughn. I'm not sure exactly how or when Outlaw contacted Justin. Chris believed it had been when Justin was arrested back in the spring. Anyway, Justin told me a new supplier was looking for some dealers. I'd just moved to this effing hick town and figured what the hell. I needed some cash and had plenty of people willing to pay.

"How'd you get the product?" Dawn slipped the photo back into the folder.

Tyler shrugged as if the answer was obvious. "We'd get a text to pick it up."

"Where?" Wyatt held his breath. If they knew where and when, they could catch this bastard.

"It varied. Sometimes, it would be the dumpster behind the Longhorn. Sometimes at the mall. We'd get a call and be told to drop off the cash we owed and pick up new product."

Dawn leaned back in her chair. "That's showing a considerable amount of trust. Could you contact Outlaw if you had a problem?"

"Yeah, through texting." Tyler shifted in his seat.

"Where's this phone now?" Tilly glanced at Wyatt before turning back to the kid. "We'll need to see it."

Wyatt step forward when Tyler reached into his back pocket and pulled out a small, thin smart phone. Tyler laid it on the table with a hand that trembled. Good, the kid was terrified, but Wyatt got the impression his fear didn't come from the police.

Tyler looked from Tilly to Dawn. "This is the phone, but I can't give it to you. If Outlaw calls and I don't answer, he'll know something is up."

Dawn picked up the phone and handed it to Tilly. "Call the FBI and get someone here who can download the information from the phone and bring it back." Tilly nodded and left. She folded her arms over the table and leaned in. "Thank you, Tyler. We'll get the phone back to you, but you have to promise if Outlaw makes contact, you'll call the police immediately."

Meyer squared his shoulders. "My client will agree to the terms only if we can discuss ways to lessen the charges brought against him."

Wyatt shook his head, but it was Peter Grant who answered with a snort. "Your client just admitted to drug dealing, and you expect me to bargain him out of it?"

"Stop!" Tyler banged his fist against the table. He scowled at the lawyer. "Shut the hell up, will you? I'm willing to help them. As long as they keep me and my family safe."

Dawn's shoulders lifted up, then went down on an exhale. "We'll do everything we can." She glanced at her notes, rubbing the side of her neck as if the muscle ached under the smooth tan skin, she asked, "Did you ever think of cheating him?"

Wyatt watched the motion and wished he could massage away her tension as he'd done so many times in the past. He turned away and took a deep breath. She didn't wear perfume, but he was close enough to smell the honeysuckle-scented soap she'd always used.

"Sure. But he assured us if we tried, we'd be dead."

"Is this what happened to Chris and Justin?" Dawn asked.

Tyler shrugged. "Maybe. I don't know. I know they wanted more money."

"How long has this been going on?" Wyatt paced. He couldn't stand still. Not when all he wanted to do was take Dawn out of the room and away from all this crap.

"About three months."

Dawn glanced at notes she'd taken in a small notebook. "My source related that this new supplier wanted a lot of your profits."

Who had Dawn talked to?

Tyler narrowed his eyes as if he wondered the same thing, then nodded. "Yeah, I guess. He wanted ninety-five percent of what we made."

Wyatt let out a low whistle and stopped pacing. "Not much for you, considering the risks."

The kid shrugged and uncrossed his arms. "Nope, not really. I was cooler with it than Justin and Chris. But they needed the money more than me." He glanced at his mother, who sat staring at her son with wide eyes and a mask of complete horror on her pale, painted doll face. "I also knew how to cut the coke so that I had more of it to sell on the side." Tyler looked down at his hands. "We thought getting involved would keep us safe. Outlaw promised the cops wouldn't bother us as long as we played by his rules. Chris and Justin didn't like it. And now they're dead."

Chapter 9

The sun was coming up by the time they were finished questioning Tyler Demello. Dawn had Doug Grant escort him and his mother home, and stay there until she could send a day shift deputy. The DA and Tilly had left to head home.

Wyatt stood from the chair before Dawn's desk and paced the length of Dawn's office, sipping strong coffee. He was too tired to stand and too wound up to sit.

Dawn set her cup on the edge of her desk. "Wyatt, get out of here. Go to your family. We can go over Tyler's interview later."

He turned to her and shook his head. "No. We need to figure this out. When I left the hospital after… before I came here last night, the doc assured us Rachel would be okay."

Had she forgotten the raw emotions that they'd shared last night? What had it meant? He wasn't sure if he was asking the silent question to her or to himself.

She looked down at her desk. "Then at least call someone to make sure that's still the case."

"Audrey said she'd call me if anything changed." He set his mug on the edge of her desk.

Dawn pursed her kissable lips. "Call your sister. I'd like to know how my friend is, even if you think she's fine."

He smiled and nodded. "Okay." He unclipped his phone from his belt and hit the button to call his twin sister.

Audrey answered on the first ring, but her "Hello?" came out sounding tired.

Wyatt glanced at Dawn as she sipped coffee from the bright green mug he'd given her all those years ago. She met his gaze, and the concern in her deep brown eyes pulled at his heart. Running his free hand through his hair, he turned away. "Hey, sis, it's me. Sorry if I woke you. How's Rachel?"

"Wy, hi. No, I'm up. She's still sleeping, but the doctor said she's improving and doesn't suspect there will be any problems when she wakes up."

He closed his eyes as relief washed over him, weakening his knees. "Thank God. Are you home?"

There was a rustling sound in the background and a murmured conversation he couldn't make out. "No. Lance and I stayed over at Mom and Dad's, but we're all at the hospital now. I didn't want to leave them alone last night. Especially if…" She cleared her throat. "Well, I thought it best to be here since you had to work."

"Thanks, Audrey. I'm not sure Ma understood that I had to go when the captain called." After he'd left Dawn's place, he'd run home to shower and change. Getting Dawn's scent off his skin had been a priority. On his arrival at the hospital, he'd learned about Demello when his commander at the Rangers had ordered him to the sheriff's station. He could have told the captain about his sister's attempted suicide, but since his vacation had been rejected, he'd figured it was best to get back to work and find the killer. The sooner they found the creep, the sooner he'd get away from Dawn. That reason was what kept him here now.

"Mom'll be okay, Wy. She's scared, that's all. Lord knows we all are. I wish I knew how to help Rachel, but sometimes, I wonder if my being around only makes things worse. Especially now with the pregnancy." She sighed over the phone. "But I do know, whatever happened to cause Rachel to do this, we won't let it happen again."

He smiled. Audrey had always been a glass half-full kind of person. "Hey, I gotta go, but call me if you hear anything."

"I will. Love you."

"Love you too, sis." He disconnected the call and faced Dawn. Clipping his phone on his belt, he sat in the chair in front of her desk and met her expectant gaze. "Audrey said she'll be okay. The worst is over."

Dawn breathed out a relieved sigh. "That is the best thing I've heard in a long time. Now, she just needs to find her way out of this depression."

"Yeah, but that'll be the hard part."

She smiled and flipped open the folder. "But she also has you. You'll help her through it. If there's one thing I've always lo--eh--liked about you, it is your dedication to your sisters." Dawn's near slip not only set her cheeks flaming, but his heart to pounding.

Had she almost said *love*?

She cleared her throat and shuffled the papers in the file. Pausing, she smiled and looked up at him. "Remember George Fink?"

Wyatt narrowed his eyes and leaned back in his chair. "The bully who tormented you and Rachel during second grade?"

She nodded and picked up her cup, hugging it in her hands. "He picked on Rachel more than me. He was scared to death of Talon. But he never expected you to come to her rescue."

He laughed. "All the little turd needed was a talking to. After that, he left my baby sister alone, and you too, if I remember correctly, and then he moved away. The only bully who never seemed to get the memo not to mess with my friends was Chet."

She set her cup down with a scowl. "Yeah, Chet. He's not a bully anymore, but he is one big pain in my ass."

"I'm surprised you didn't send Hendricks to babysit Demello." He sipped his cooling coffee.

She shook her head and pinched her fingers together. "I'm this close to suspending him."

He grinned around his mug. "I wonder how long he'll last before he hangs himself."

She shook her head. Fatigue showed in the redness of her eyes and the frown lines of her forehead. "Hopefully, it's soon. And preferably before the election."

They were both avoiding the big red elephant doing cartwheels in the room. He chuckled and retrieved the coffee pot to refill their cups. As he poured the dark brew into hers, she met his gaze and held it. Her breath caught, and the pulse at her neck fluttered. He affected her as much as her nearness did him, but they had no future together.

He swallowed and backed away to return the pot to the burner. "I've been thinking about where the drugs are coming from and think I'll call a friend I know in Border Patrol."

"I was thinking the same thing." She pulled a printout of a map of southern Texas from a folder. "If we could get a handle on where the drugs are coming from, we might be able to follow the trail into town."

"What do you think?"

She turned the map upside down so that he could see it from his seat. Using a pen, she pointed to Highway Six at the dot that indicated Colton. She traced down the map to Interstate Thirty-five where the roads intersected on the south side of Waco. "I think the drugs are coming from the south." She continued down the blue line, indicating the major connector between Austin, San Antonio, and Nuevo Laredo, Mexico.

Tapping the pen on the border town, she looked at him. "Remember the Blood Dragons?"

"How could I possibly forget?" The Dallas gang was supported by one of the biggest drug cartels in northern Mexico. He and Dawn brought down five of the gang's members after a six-month investigation in drug trafficking. "You're thinking Outlaw is getting drugs from the Cotreras Cartel?"

"Yeah." She tossed the pen on top of the papers scattered over her desk.

"I'll talk to Dave Alton and see what he's been watching."

She smiled and leaned back in her chair. "I thought he retired from Border Patrol?"

"Nope. He was promoted. I don't think the old bird will ever retire." Wyatt picked up his hat from the chair near the wall and set it on his head. "I'll call Dave, and then I'm headed over to the hospital."

I wish you'd come with me.

The lack of sleep was causing him to go crazy.

He was almost to the door when she said, "Wy?" She waited until he looked over his shoulder. "Drive safe."

He nodded. "You too."

* * * *

Dawn sighed as Wyatt closed the door behind him. She had to get some sleep, but going home and facing the couch were twelve hours ago she and Wyatt had done the dirty was not something she was ready to do.

But she had to go home eventually. She'd asked her dad to let Taco out and feed her horses, but she couldn't expect her parents to take over her responsibilities forever.

Now that she was alone, and her brain was too mushy to think of much else, the scene from where she'd found Wyatt at her barn to him walking out the door was on a constant rerun loop. But that wasn't the only thing that replayed.

She closed her eyes and went back to the day her life shattered around her.

Her skin itched, and a chill prickled her bear arms. Something was going to happen, but good or bad, she had no idea.

"Got the money?" The dealer stepped out of the shadow of the pillar holding up the interstate. At this time of night, about the only thing on the highway was truck traffic. The street, running under the bridge and to the left of the deal, was abandoned.

Eduardo Guerrero was the leader of a small gang, setting up shop in this area. And he was a killer. He had three warrants out for his arrest--two for murder and one for armed robbery. It irritated her that she couldn't haul his ass in for those, but she'd learned a long time ago these thugs knew how to get out of things like that. To get them off the street, the gang had to be toppled.

Armed to the teeth under their leather and denim coats, Guerrero glanced at his lieutenant, who stood back. They didn't trust her yet. She was losing the edge she had a few months ago when she and Wyatt took down the drug ring within the Blood Dragons.

Turning thirty had been such a pain in the ass.

Especially when she was pretending to be someone who'd just turned twenty-one.

Hell, she could barely remember being that young.

The lieutenant nodded at the dealer and headed toward the street, a switchblade and a gun stuck into his belt. His name was Dominic Sanchez, and he had at least two warrants for drug dealing, and one for armed robbery.

"Si." She slipped into the Hispanic accent she'd perfected last year and gave Eduardo a come-hither smile. He'd been eyeing her up since she'd met him last month. "A grand."

He glanced around and held out his hand. His long coat opened to show what looked like a military issue Beretta tucked into his belt. "Give me the cash, and you'll get your product."

She reached into the large bag slung over her shoulder and pulled out the money, making sure to give the kid a nice look of the goods her low-cut tank showed off, but just a quick peek. The last thing she wanted was to seem too eager.

For one thing, she was wired to the hilt with a microphone sown into the top's seam and a small camera fixed in the center flower decoration between her boobs. Second, the greasy creep made her skin crawl, and finally, Wyatt watched and listened in the van out on the street.

She would have preferred not to be so skimpily dressed, and not because she minded the thugs' lustful stares or the bite of the September night's air, but she missed her Kevlar vest.

This was the last time she would do this. Her fear of Wyatt's reaction to the news wasn't worth the possible danger she put herself and their baby in.

Eduardo handed her a white package wrapped in cellophane. Cocaine. She smiled again and tucked it into the bag. The denim hobo purse hit her bare thigh below her cutoff shorts. She suddenly wished the weight were her Glock and not a small fortune of nose candy.

A car door closing and yelling in the street cut through her like a cold wind as she looked in the direction of the van.

Oh, God, no!

Sanchez held Wyatt with a switchblade knife at his throat as he marched the man she loved across the street. Wyatt glanced at her with a stoic set to his jaw and a gleam in his eyes.

Dear God, he had a plan. She'd seen that expression more than once.

Things happened so fast from there. Wyatt somehow pulled the gun from the kid's belt and shot Sanchez before he had a chance to realize what was happening. At the same time, Eduardo aimed his gun at Wyatt's head. She rushed Eduardo and grabbed for the gun. The thug pushed her off, and before Wyatt reached her, the gun discharged.

The pain above her left breast bloomed into a scream of...

"Dawn?"

She jerked her eyes open. Her head rested in her arms on her desk. Sitting up, she swallowed back the sob in her throat. God, how she hated reliving that night over and over again.

Rubbing the sleep and the remnants of the dream from her face, she said, "Chet, what's going on?"

He shrugged and sat in the seat Wyatt had vacated earlier. "Nothing much." Nodding toward the sheet of paper on her desk, he folded his hands over his chest. "I figured you'd want the report on the Cartwright twins versus Joe Farley."

She stretched her neck to the left, then the right, trying to get the kink out of it. How long had she been asleep? She glanced at her watch. Crap, she'd slept at least two hours. "Since you're smiling, I can assume everything worked out."

He chuckled and shifted in his seat. "Yep. Hey, I heard some scuttlebutt about that Demello kid being here all night. What's that all about?"

Dawn glanced at the old stained Mr. Coffee in the corner, but the thing was dry as the Badlands and looked as unappealing too. Damn. She needed a cup of joe.

"You aren't on the case anymore, Hendricks." She got up to make a pot of coffee.

A finger of apprehension tickled down her spine from him watching her as she filled the pot from the water cooler next to the file cabinet.

"So you've said, but I still care what happens. When you lose the election in a few weeks, this will become my nightmare."

She narrowed her eyes at him over her shoulder. "Let's keep politics and your wishful thinking out of it."

As she poured the water into the reservoir, he asked, "Did he talk?"

She dumped coffee grounds into the basket and turned around. "Not much. Only gave us some details of how the supplier does business."

"What do you know?"

She put her cup under the flowing stream of dark, pungent coffee, wishing she could hook up an IV of the stuff. "This guy's bound to screw up." Stirring in some of the powdered creamer, she looked over her shoulder at him again. "Trust me. They always do."

* * * *

Dawn downed two pots of coffee and signed off on some of the reports piling on her desk before heading home at around three in the afternoon. She had the air conditioner blasting icy air into her face and the radio turned up to ear splitting, so she could stay awake as she drove.

She knew better than to let herself get this exhausted. But after her dream, she didn't want to be alone.

Being alone gave her time to think.

What if Wyatt did have everything under control?

What if she hadn't rushed Guerrero?

Could Wyatt have shot the kid before being shot himself?

She shook her head to dispel the questions as much as to prevent her eyes from closing.

As she crossed the bridge over Oak Springs Creek, she tapped the brake to enter the turn. The pedal went to the floor with no resistance, and instead of going slower, she sped up.

Oh crap!

The brakes were out. She couldn't panic, not now. Hoping to slow down, she put the truck in low gear. But it was still too fast for the curves in this stretch of Blackwell Road.

A horn blared as she rounded the curve near the entrance of the Estrada ranch. She was over in the other lane, and a truck rushed toward her. Jerking the wheel, she got out of the oncoming pickup's path and lost control.

The last thing she saw before impact was a mailbox containing the name *McPherson*.

* * * *

Wyatt put away the cans of spray paint and the stencil of his name he'd used to repaint the old mailbox. He hadn't decided on a name for his place, but figured calling it the McPherson Ranch was okay for the time being. As he wiped his hands on a rag, he looked around at the old junk Luis Estrada had left in the tool shed beside the barn. Rusty garden implements and hand tools hung on a pegboard made from sixteen-penny nails hammered part way into a piece of plywood. The lawn mower parked in the corner was missing its left front wheel.

Thank God, the house had been emptied out. The Estradas moved out over the weekend and headed for Phoenix. On Columbus Day, he'd moved the bulk of his stuff in with help from his family.

Fortunately for him, he didn't have much. An old leather couch and recliner, flat screen TV he'd mounted to the wall, a kitchen table and chairs, some gym equipment, and his bedroom furniture.

A car horn blast sounded from the road, and he looked out around the doorframe of the shed. A pickup truck with the logo of the CW Ranch swerved to miss a dark blue truck taking the curve in that stretch of the road way too fast.

"What the hell…" He rushed out of the shed to the driveway as the Ford F-150, which he recognized as Dawn's, crashed into his newly painted mailbox and took out part of the picket fence before coming to rest against the hundred-year-old oak tree standing in the middle of his front yard.

"Dawn!" His heart slammed against his ribs, and he took off at a dead run, jumping over the low fence surrounding the yard. Steam and smoke rose from the ruined engine, and the sour odor of gasoline filled his nose. "Dawn, are you all right?"

He reached the driver's door and was vaguely aware of the CW pickup pulling into his drive.

A door slammed and the driver of the truck asked, "Wyatt, is she okay?"

"Oh God, Dawn. Are you okay?" Wyatt reached for the handle of her door. His heart raced as images of when she was shot came rushing through his brain. He hadn't been able to protect her then, and now she'd crashed against his tree. The airbags had deployed, and their deflating mess cushioned her. She moaned but wasn't awake. Blood trickled from a nasty cut on her forehead.

"How bad is she hurt? She was on my side of the road coming at me like a bat out of hell." Wyatt recognized the voice of Jeremy Greenberg, the Cartwright's horse trainer, as he ran up beside him.

He didn't look at Greenberg. He was too scared for the woman in the broken truck. "Call for an ambulance."

The ambulance and a fire truck took twenty minutes to get to the ranch. Wyatt stayed with her the whole time.

His dad climbed out of the passenger's seat of the fire truck as soon as the thing stopped, which surprised him. He must have needed to get way from the mess at home as much as Wyatt. Dad and the two EMTs from the ambulance rushed over to the crashed truck. He glanced inside at Dawn. "Is she okay?"

Wyatt met his dad and nodded. "I think so, but she hasn't come to yet. She must have hit her head pretty hard."

His dad motioned for him to step back as his crew and the EMTs got her out the truck and strapped on a gurney. "We'll take good care of her, son."

He nodded and ran his hand through his hair. He must have lost his hat when he jumped over the fence. Funny, he hadn't even missed it until now. He looked around, and sure enough, the old Stetson lay on the grass near the fence. "I know."

Wyatt jerked his chin toward Greenberg, who leaned against his truck, talking on his cellphone and smoking a cigarette. "He said she was driving erratically and swerved to miss him."

"Want me to call for a deputy to come out here?" Dad narrowed his eyes on him.

"Yeah, but call Tilly direct. He'll be in charge until Dawn's back on her feet."

"Chief, we're ready to go," one of the EMTs called from the back of the ambulance to his father.

Wyatt swallowed and met his Dad's searching gaze.

Dad jerked his head toward the ambulance. "Go with her. I'll stay here and wait for Tilly. I've had my share of hospitals for a while."

"Thanks." With his heart racing, Wyatt nodded and ran for the open gate. On the way, he scooped up his hat. "Hey, wait. I'll ride along."

Chapter 10

Dawn woke up, her body blazing in pain from her head to her feet. With more energy than the action should have required, she lifted her hand to her pounding head and moaned when she met a large bandage on the right side of her face.

"Welcome back, Sheriff Madison. I'm Dr. Forsyth."

She turned toward the sound of the voice to find a man wearing a white coat at the foot of her bed, looking at a medical chart. She must be in the county hospital. "What happened?"

"You were in an accident." The doctor closed the chart and put it back in a slot on the footboard. "You have a concussion, and I put ten stitches in a cut on your forehead." He moved to the side of the bed and pulled a small flashlight from his pocket.

"Uh…" She blinked when the bright light stabbed through her skull as he checked the pupil of her right eye.

"Sorry." He moved the light to the other eyeball. "Good." He finished and moved away with his torture light.

"How long will she be in here?"

Wyatt? He stood near the window with his hands in his pockets. Her heart did a funny little flip-flop in her chest. What was he doing here?

She quickly answered her own question. He'd probably been here with Rachel when she was brought in and felt obligated to see her.

The doctor turned toward him. "At least overnight for observation." He folded his arms and smiled at her. "Do you remember anything?"

The last thing she remembered with any sort of clarity was leaving her office. "Not of the accident."

There was a rap on the door, and the sound hammered through her head.

"Is it okay to come in?" Tilly filled the doorway, holding his tan Stetson in his hand. "I have some news about what happened."

The doctor headed toward the door. "Sure. Just don't stay too long."

"Thanks Doc. You're the new guy on staff." Tilly entered the room and faced the doctor.

"Yes. I just moved here about two weeks ago."

Tilly smiled and held out his hand. "Tillman Kennedy. My wife, Barb, is one of the nurses here. She said you were over in the war. What branch of the service?"

"Ah, Mrs. Kennedy. She keeps me in line." The doctor shook Tilly's hand with a broad smile. "I was a contractor over in Afghanistan. But I did six years in the Navy. That's who paid for my training."

Tilly laughed. "Well, Barb is good at keeping folks in line. I think you'll like it here."

"He knew Rachel from over there too," Wyatt said from his spot at the window.

Tilly tossed his hat onto a chair in the corner. "Barb said you're her doctor. Take care of that girl, Doc. And this one too." He pointed at Dawn.

"I will." Forsyth smiled and nodded toward them all. "It was nice to meet you."

Tilly opened the door and held it. "You gotta come to the American Legion sometime. We vets get together about every Friday night."

"Thanks for the invite. I will sometime." He looked back at Dawn. "I'll order something for the headache."

"Thanks," Dawn said as the doctor left the room.

"Wow, imagine him knowing your sister." Tilly closed the door after him.

"I'm told it's a small Army." Wyatt moved back to stand next to her bed. "What did you find out?"

Tilly cleared his throat and shifted his feet. "The brakes were cut."

Dawn couldn't believe what she was hearing. "What?"

Tilly scratched at the gray scruff growing in at his cheek and nodded. "I saw the cut in the line myself. Whoever did this was hoping you'd wreck."

"And no doubt not walk away from the crash. Blackwell Road is full of turns, not to mention the creek." Wyatt shoved his hands into the pockets of his jeans and paced the length of the small room. "If my mailbox hadn't slowed you down before you hit that old oak tree in my front yard, Lord only knows if you would've survived."

"I crashed in front of your house?" She got a flash of memory--a mailbox with a name painted in black.

He ambled to her side and sat in the chair next to the bed. "I'd just finished repainting that darned mailbox before you crashed into it."

Tilly chuckled and leaned against the wall. "She didn't like your paint job, eh?"

She couldn't help but smile. "I'm sorry."

"Mailboxes can be replaced. You can't be." Wyatt's grin and the intensity of his eyes made her breath catch and her heart beat a little faster. He laid his hand on her shoulder and gave a gentle squeeze. The sensation tingled through her.

No way could she respond to him.

Another knock on the door echoed through her head like a gunshot, and much to her disappointment, Wyatt let go of her. Tilly opened it, and her mother and father rushed into the room. Tilly waved and exited after they entered.

Her mother came to the bed and hugged her. "Oh, my baby, are you okay?"

She glanced at Wyatt, who stiffened as if he was ready to leave, but something in his gaze had her believing he didn't want to go.

"I'm fine, Momma." She hugged her father.

He kissed her forehead next to the bandage. "What happened?"

"I'll tell you later."

"Hey?" Her brother's voice came from the doorway.

She let go of her father and stared as Talon edged through the door. In his arms, he carried a beautiful little girl with hair the color of wheat and big hazel eyes. "Talon?"

"I have someone I'd like you to meet." He took a few steps toward her bed. "Jessie Mae, this is your aunt Dawn."

The little girl snuggled close to Talon's shoulder. In her other arm, she held a raggedy stuffed animal that might have been a bear, and sucked on her thumb.

"Hi, Jessie Mae." She swallowed and met her brother's gaze. "That's why you disappeared?"

He nodded and looked at Jessie Mae. Dawn wasn't sure she'd ever seen so much love shining from her brother's normally cold eyes as she did in that moment.

"She's gonna be living with me from now on."

* * * *

He and his brother-in-law stood in the parking lot of the county impound. Staring at the sheriff's truck, he shook his head and shoved his hands on his hips. "You know we have to get rid of the kid. We can't have him running off his mouth again."

"Did you figure out who else has been talking?" His brother-in-law moved around the front of the Ford, looking over the damage.

"I have a few ideas. I think it was Ella Larson's girl, Annie. But according to what I heard, she left with Charli Quinn this morning for Nashville."

The peacock stopped looking over the truck. "I'll take care of the Demello kid."

He scowled at his brother-in-law and pointed at the truck. The idiot had one thing he had to do and fucked it up. "Like you took care of the bitch?"

The idiot stopped in front of him. He thought he was a big deal because he carried a few muscles and was a few inches taller than him. "It's not my fault she hit the damned mailbox and slowed her momentum. If she'd hit just the tree or landed in the creek, she'd be dead." The peacock married to his sister puffed up his chest. "It was you who didn't want me to just put a fuckin' bullet in her head. Now what?"

Turning away, he took his hat off and wiped sweat from his brow. He needed another hit soon. His need for coke was coming sooner and sooner. He couldn't function without it anymore. "We have to scare her enough so she can't focus on catching us."

"And how the hell do we do that?"

He looked over his shoulder at his partner and smiled as a plan formed. "You'll see."

* * * *

Wyatt paced the hall outside of Dawn's room. Seeing her in that hospital bed brought back every bad memory he had of the shooting.

"So, who do you think has it out for my girl?"

Wyatt turned at the sound of Tom Madison's voice. He cleared his throat and shrugged. "Whoever killed those kids."

Tom wiped his hand across his mouth and nodded as he sat in a chair along the wall. "Of course, question is what triggered them into hitting Dawn?"

"I think talking to Demello last night was the trigger." Wyatt sat beside the former sheriff and his father's best friend. "The murderer shouldn't have known he talked, but it seems like he does." He leaned over his legs and looked down at his hat in his hands. "Thing is how did they find out?"

Tom steepled his fingers on his lap and peered at them as if deep in thought. "Hard to say. Maybe someone tipped off the killer."

"Maybe. But who?" He squinted down the corridor. The only people in the know, as far as he knew, were the police and the DA. "Sure, the kid could've said something to someone on the outside, but I doubt it. He's scared shitless."

He looked over his shoulder as Tom stretched his long legs out in front of him, crossing his scuffed cowboy boots at the ankles. "Do you think someone inside the department might be involved?"

Wyatt sat up. "I doubt it. I've known every one of those guys all my life, and I'd trust my life with any one of them."

Tom pursed his lips. "Sometimes, the guy least suspected of a crime is the most guilty."

The door to Dawn's room opened and Talon entered the hallway. He glanced at Wyatt and Tom. As he approached them, he shoved his hands into the pockets of his leather jacket. Talk about freaking shockers. Seeing Talon Blackwell with a kid topped the list.

Talon leaned a shoulder against the wall and tilted his head to look at his boots. "So, am I still on the short list of suspects?"

Tom looked at Wyatt, waiting for his response too.

Twirling his hat in his hands, he took a deep breath. Wyatt didn't have any evidence exonerating Talon, except what his gut told him. "Are you willing to tell me what you were doing in front of the Longhorn on the morning Chris Larson was killed?"

Talon shifted his feet and turned around to lean his back on the wall. With a smirk, he shook his head. "I can't. But I will tell you the reason I was in town had to do with my daughter."

"Were you meeting someone?"

Talon met his gaze with eyes that could freeze carbon dioxide into dry ice. "Yeah, but I'm not telling you who, so stop asking. Like I said, I was in town to meet someone who had information about that little girl in there." He pointed toward Dawn's room. "Her mother doesn't want to be named, and I respect that request even if I hate the reason for it."

Tom sighed and stood. "She doesn't want anyone to know she had your child?"

Talon looked at the man who had raised him as his own with hard eyes. "Can you blame her? I'm one of the infamous Blackwell bastards. Besides, I'm an ex-con."

With a frown, Tom shook his head and tilted it toward the floor. "I'm going back in."

After Tom went through Dawn's door, Wyatt faced Talon. He would never understand what Talon's beef with his stepfather was, but now wasn't the time to ask. "So, her mother's from Colton?"

Talon only shrugged.

"I know you went to Las Vegas."

That registered a response. Talon scowled and straightened. "Who told you?"

Wyatt glanced at his hat and sat it on his head. "I'm a Texas Ranger. I have my contacts. But even if I didn't, your sister has hers. I know you flew out of Dallas last Wednesday night and stayed at a hotel called the Lazy Cactus. Let me see if I can figure out what you were doing while you were there." Leaning back in his plastic chair, he counted each point he made on his fingers. "The girl's mother is from Colton. You showed up at Black Diamond Casino where Maggie Pratt is a showgirl on Thursday nights. Thanks to the Colton grapevine, I also know Aida Mae Pratt is excited Maggie's got a job on some cruise ship. Although she makes it sound like she's a cruise director, we all know Maggie's an exotic dancer."

He smiled and looked at his extended three fingers. "Doesn't take too much math to add this up. Maggie Pratt is that little girl's mother. She called you and told you to come get the girl."

He tapped the three fingers against his temple. "Or rather, she contacted her sister. You were at Beth's the night Larson was killed. She didn't want you parked outside of her place, so you parked your truck down the street and around the block. That's why you were in front of the Longhorn. Though, I have no idea why you'd be there at four in the morning. Unless she didn't want to risk anyone seeing you at her daycare center."

Talon fisted a hand and chuckled, but it was as humorless as his amber eyes. "Guess that's why you're a hot shot Texas Ranger, huh? But I'm not admitting to anything."

Wyatt stood and rubbed the scruff on his cheek. He needed a shave. "Don't worry. Your secret's safe with me."

As he headed down the hall, Talon's low voice stopped him. "McPherson, if you fuck my sister over again, you won't like the consequences."

He turned and glared at his childhood best friend. "What's that supposed to mean?"

Talon flashed an arctic smile as he passed him. "You're a smart guy, figure it out."

Chapter 11

Talon nodded to the nurse seated behind the station in the intensive care unit. "I'm here to see Rachel McPherson."

The nurse, whom he vaguely recognized as someone he'd gone to school with, frowned and closed the chart on the counter in front of her. "Only family and close friends are allowed to see her."

"Believe it or not Rachel and I are close friends."

Before he turned away, she pursed her lips and leveled her gaze on him. "You have five minutes.

With a single nod of his head, he turned away from the desk and headed toward the room his mother had told him was Rachel's.

The nurse didn't try to stop him as he opened the door. The air in the dim room was heavy with the scent of antiseptic and the incessant beeping of a heart monitor. He swallowed as he took in the machines and IV attached to the woman lying in the bed.

She looked small and frail, something Rachel had never been. The sight of her broke his heart. As he stopped next to her bed and sat on the chair, she turned to meet his gaze. He had no idea what to say to her, but he couldn't leave the hospital without seeing her.

"Talon?" Her voice was weak and hoarse.

He nodded and averted his eyes to his hat, which he held with a death grip. "You know there was a time I wanted to die. I had a plan, and even thought about doing it. But in the end, I couldn't go through with it."

She turned away.

Swallowing the dredged up pain of the memories, he went on. "When I was sent to prison for something I didn't do, I was done. Done with being the bastard son of Jock Blackwell. Done with constantly fighting for everything I've ever had. Done with life."

"I'm so tired of the pain, but I hate the pity in everyone's faces more. Why didn't God just take me too?" The sorrow cracking through her weak voice shot through his heart.

He reached over and brushed strands of red hair from her cheek and forehead. "I know it seems like the only way out, but death isn't the answer."

"My mother bathes me." She stared up at him with beautiful blue eyes so full of pain and self-disgust it soured his stomach. "Did you know that? She doesn't trust that I can do it myself. Wyatt moved in with our parents because of me. He hasn't lived at home since his sophomore year of college. What the hell do I have to live for?"

He wiped the tear from her cheek. "They love you. They do these things to take care of you, to help you heal. You have a lot to live for, Rachel."

Huffing, she looked at the ceiling. "I have nothing. My fiance is dead, and I will never be able to have a child. Did you know that was all I ever wanted?" She closed her eyes and took a deep breath.

"You still have your family. And you still have your friends. Let us know what you need us to do for you and what you don't. Rachel, we are all here for you. You just have to let us in."

But Rachel McPherson never let anyone too close, including the people who loved her. He'd bet that was the real reason she never brought her fiance home, no matter how much she loved him.

She turned away and he stood. He'd left Jessie Mae with his mother long enough. "The next time you get that low, call me."

Meeting his gaze again, she reached for his hand. "You've always been there for me, Talon. Thank you for being such a great friend."

He smiled and squeezed her cool fingers. They reminded him of twigs of straw that would break with the gentlest of pressure. "I'll always be here."

The door opened and a nurse came in. His five minutes were up. He let go of her hand. "I'll see you later."

As he passed the nurse, he nodded and then headed out the door. Damn it, was he going to let himself get caught in Rachel McPherson's web again?

* * * *

Tilly unlocked the door to Dawn's office.

Wyatt entered and turned on the lights. "Thanks. I won't be long."

Dawn's lieutenant shrugged. "She told me to let you, and only you in."

He nodded and glanced around the familiar office. Before she'd taken over the job of sheriff, Zack Cartwright had sat in here. Wyatt and Zack had spent a lot of time here mulling over clues while looking for the cattle and horse thieves a few months ago. Now, he and Dawn were looking for a murderer and drug dealer.

Tilly left him alone. Wyatt sat in Dawn's chair and looked over her desk with a smile. She'd always been a neat freak, and her desk reflected it. He pulled out the center drawer to reveal her pens, pencils, and all the other stuff, like a stapler and roll of tape. He closed it and looked to the stacked bins on the left side of her desk containing all of her active files. The only things sitting on top of the desk were a calendar, laptop, phone, and her coffee cup.

He picked up the bright green oversized mug and turned it upside down. A smudged *Happy Birthday, Babe* was written in black Sharpie on the bottom. He'd been surprised when he'd seen her still using the mug. With a smile, he remembered the day he'd given it to her two months after they'd moved in together.

"Happy birthday." He carried a tray of breakfast food into their bedroom.

She moaned and turned over. "Yeah, right."

He laughed and sat down beside her on the bed. "Oh, c'mon. You're only thirty, not ninety."

Dawn glared at him, but when she looked at the tray of pancakes covered with whipped cream and a big birthday candle stuck in the middle, her face softened. She picked up the green mug of coffee and took a sip. "This is new."

"Yep. It's one of your birthday gifts."

She glanced at him. "One?"

He settled the tray over her lap and leaned back against the pillows. "I also weaseled us a long weekend off together. I thought we'd ride the Harleys up to Chickasaw National Park in Oklahoma. I rented a cabin."

"Oh, I like that idea." She covered her finger with whipped cream and smeared it over his lips. "A lot." Then she kissed him.

He couldn't remember if she ever ate the pancakes he'd slaved over cooking. But he vividly remembered her licking whipped cream off more interesting body parts than his lips, and the amazing weekend they'd shared in the intimate little cabin.

Swallowing hard, he shook the memory away and set the cup in its place. He was here to see her files on the case, not go through her personal items.

He found the files for the case and glanced at his watch. Dawn would be leaving the hospital in a few minutes.

"You look good there. Maybe you should consider running for sheriff." Wyatt looked up to Chet, standing in the open doorway. He stood and picked up the files. "Nope. I know who I'm voting for." He had to bite his tongue to keep from adding, *and it's not you.*

Chet sat in the chair in front of Dawn's desk. "Can't believe someone would cut the brakes on Dawn's truck. Any idea who it could've been?"

"You know we don't."

With a nod, Chet looked at his hand. "I heard through the grapevine Talon Blackwell was back in town. Maybe he doesn't want his sister snooping around. Is he being brought in for questioning?"

"Talon's not our killer." He had to leave soon if he planned to meet Dawn at her house. He didn't understand his need to make sure she was okay, but something drove him to take care of her.

"How do you know that for sure?"

Wyatt rounded the desk. "He'd left town to pick up his daughter from her mother."

The way Chet's eyes bugged out of his narrow face would have been funny if Wyatt cared what the deputy thought. "Blackwell has a kid?"

"Yeah. Cute as a button too." Wyatt motioned toward the door. "I'm headed out. I know Tilly wants to lock up."

Chet stood and followed him out the door. He gestured toward the files. "What you got there?"

"Case files." Wyatt waited for Tilly to lock up, then headed for the back door to the parking lot. He glanced at Tilly and set his hat on his head. "I'll be back."

Tilly waved with a smile. "Tell Dawn I'll talk to her later."

He caught the puzzled twist on Chet's lips as he opened the door. "Will do."

* * * *

"Hold up, and I'll help you out." Dawn's father turned off the engine of his Explorer as he looked over his shoulder at her. He knew her too well.

Sighing, Dawn let go of the back door handle and waited for him to get out from the driver's seat and open her door. She'd won one battle already. Her parents had relented to bringing her home after leaving the hospital and not their house.

Her mother exited the passenger side and came around from behind the rig as Dawn climbed out of the back seat. She hoped her parents missed her wince as she stepped out on her left foot. She'd sprained her knee when it hit the dashboard, and it hurt like a son-of-a-gun.

The last thing she wanted was to stay with them. Talon and his daughter were camping there since his shack wasn't any place for a kid. What a shock she'd had when he dropped the oh-this-is-my-daughter bomb. She didn't want to subject the little girl to all of the tension surrounding her and Talon. Jessie was trying to adjust to her new family. Besides, Hunter and Chief still called the place home. But she hadn't presented the real reason in her argument to Dad and Mom: She'd been on her own too long to move back in with her parents, even if it was temporary.

"Are you sure you don't want to come over to the house for tonight?" Mom grabbed the plastic bag holding the clothes Dawn had worn to the hospital and closed the door. A worried frown furrowed Mom's forehead and played on her lips.

"No, Momma. I'm fine. I just want a hot bath and to watch some TV." Which was a complete lie. She'd call the station and asked Tilly to bring the case files to her. Dawn glanced toward the front porch. A flowerpot containing a chrysanthemum had been shattered. Damn, with Taco at her parents' for the past two nights, the raccoon visiting the barn must have gotten a little braver and come onto her porch. "Just keep Taco for one more night."

"I'll send Hunter over to feed your horses tomorrow." Dad closed his door.

Before she could tell him she could take care of her animals, the rumble of an engine drew her attention down the driveway. Her heart jumped at the sight of the black Silverado's driver.

"Doesn't he know you have to rest?" Mom twisted her lips into a frown.

Her father chuckled and pocketed his keys. "I don't think he's here for work, Frannie."

Wyatt parked behind the Explorer. As he stepped out of the truck, he put his black Resistol on his head. From the looks of his leather vest and star pinned to it, he'd been working. He glanced around and seemed as much at a loss as to what he was doing there as she was. "Hey."

"Hi. What's going on?"

He glanced around again and walked toward her. "I wanted to make sure you didn't rush off to work. Tilly and I have things covered, so you take as many days off as you need."

She folded her arms and shifted her weight onto her right leg. "We have a murderer to catch."

"You have to rest," her mother chimed in. "You heard Dr. Forsyth. No work for at least three days."

Dawn glared at her and headed toward her front door. "Okay. So, let's go in. Then y'all can get out of my hair and I'll rest."

Wyatt grinned, causing her tummy to tumble over itself. "I'm here to make sure you do."

Her mother took her arm as if she needed help walking. "How did you know she was out of the hospital?"

Wyatt shrugged and looked as sheepish as a little boy caught red-handed with his fingers in the cookie jar before supper. "Tilly told me when she was going to be discharged. So, I left the station in time to meet y'all here."

He'd go through all that trouble? "You know that could be considered stalking?"

"Are you going to arrest me, Sheriff?" Wyatt grinned, moving in beside her, and put his hand on the small of her back.

She shivered, but covered the action by scowling at him. "I should."

Her dad smirked and took her mom's hand. "C'mon, Fran. I think Wyatt can take it from here."

Mom glared at Dad. "I'm not leaving until I know she's settled."

Dawn shook her head as she climbed the steps of the porch and immediately stopped when she noticed the door ajar. "Dad, was Hunter or Talon over here this morning?"

"Hunter fed your horses, but he wouldn't have gone inside." Dad came up beside her. "And when your mom and I stopped by last evening to pick up a change of clothes for you, we made sure to lock up."

Wyatt let go of her as he reached under his vest and pulled his Colt out of his shoulder holster. Her mother gasped at the sight of the gun and took Dawn's hand to keep her from going inside.

Wyatt nodded toward her dad, who positioned himself in front of her and Frannie, then pulled the Glock he'd carried since his days as sheriff. As Wyatt slowly pushed the door open with his Colt at the ready, he stepped inside. "Oh, damn…"

Dad moved inside with Wyatt. "What the hell happened here?"

"What?" Dawn shook off her mother's hand and entered her door. Everywhere she looked broken pieces of her life lay on the floor. The couch where she and Wyatt had sex was ripped and smashed into unrecognizable tatters. Her beautiful Cherokee and Comanche paintings, broken and cut, lay like confetti on the white fluff of the couch like in a bed of snow. Her handmade afghan her grandmother had woven for her was torn and frayed. The end tables and TV shattered as if beaten with a sledgehammer.

With a whimper, she entered the kitchen. The bright pottery dishes she'd collected over the years littered the floor in colorful shards. Even the cabinet doors weren't spared in the small kitchen. Most of them were torn from their hinges and broken in half or splintered on the tile floor she'd laid herself when she pulled out the linoleum after she'd bought the trailer.

"Oh, sweet Jesus." Her mother sobbed. Dawn wrapped her arm around her waist, glad she could lean on her mom. "Look at the refrigerator."

Dawn turned and gasped. Big, black blocky letters filled the white door. They said, *The next time you won't be so lucky, bitch.*

"The bedroom looks as bad as it does out here." Putting away his gun, Wyatt waded through the debris in the living room from the direction of her room. He stopped in the doorway between the kitchen and the living room.

She pulled her gaze away from the warning and met his narrowed eyes. "What do we do now?"

Mom wiped away tears. "That settles it. You're coming home with us."

"No." Dawn leaned against the wall. She needed to sit down, but her dining chairs resembled kindling. "I can't stay with you."

"Nonsense." Her mother sniffed and put her hands on her hips. "Someone wants to hurt you. We can make room for you."

"We can't risk putting Talon's little girl in danger." Dawn blinked at the stinging in her eyes. She wouldn't cry in front of her parents and Wyatt.

"She's right." Her dad wiped over his mouth with the back of his shaky hand. She'd never seen him so rattled. He pointed to the fridge door. "Whoever this is, isn't messing around. This place is turned upside down and inside out. You hit a nerve, and you have to keep hitting it, but you need to be safe."

Mom gestured around the room. "Exactly! And we can keep her safe."

She fought the panic threatening to overtake her by replacing it with frustration at being talked about in the third person while standing right there.

"Dawn will stay with me."

She snapped her gaze to Wyatt. Surely, he didn't mean...

"I think it would be the best for everyone, don't you?" His eyes burned with an intensity she didn't recognize.

Would it be possible to live with him and not end up in his bed?

* * * *

Wyatt called the sheriff's station to alert them about the break in. He marveled at Dawn's strength as she picked through her ripped and shattered belongings to determine if anything had been stolen. But then, he'd have been more surprised if she'd broken down and cried.

Her parents stood by and watched with concern and sorrow etched on their faces.

Unable to stand by and do nothing but wait for Tilly to show up, he made his way back down the short hallway to the bedroom and stopped in the doorway. Dawn sat on the floor amidst the broken furniture and the debris of her clothing. The damned thugs hadn't been satisfied with just ripping her stuff. They made sure she'd never reuse any of her clothes by dumping motor oil over them. The pungent odor burned his throat when he took a deep breath and entered the room.

She must not have heard him as she rummaged through what looked like torn bits of photos. The sob that broke loose as she picked up a dark black and white scrap of a picture had him stopping behind her.

"No." She shook her head and shifted through the bits of old pictures faster. "Damn them!"

He laid his hand on her shoulder. "Dawn?"

She let out another sob and tears streaked her face as she fitted the jagged pieces together on her lap. The distinct fuzzy image of a sonogram took shape as she found another scrap. "Why couldn't they leave it alone?"

The shock of her words had him letting go of her shoulder and stepping back. He stared down at the grainy, ripped photo and a plethora of emotions hit him in the gut like a roundhouse kick--anger, pain, and betrayal were the first, but then surprise and sorrow slipped through. Had she cared enough for their baby to keep the sonogram photo? Of all the things Dawn possessed, was the only thing she cried over a fuzzy picture of a child never born?

He looked away and took a deep breath. "Dawn… I'm…" What could he say?

With a sniff, she shook herself as if trying to get her emotions under their usually tight control. She stood, then wiped her eyes as she faced away from him. "Sorry. I think all of this has gotten to me."

"Tilly and Deputy Grant are out here," Tom called from the living room.

She cleared her throat and limped out of the room, all traces of the emotion she'd displayed completely gone. "Thanks, Dad. C'mon, let's go figure out who would do this to me."

Wyatt closed his eyes and took a deep breath. Maybe she didn't care that much about the baby after all. He couldn't bear looking at the torn photo on the floor. Turning away from the room, he followed her out into the living room.

What the hell had he been thinking by insisting she stay with him?

* * * *

The sun was setting by the time she left her shambled home. The investigation was still going on, but when Wyatt saw her take a bunch of ibuprofen for her various pains, he insisted they leave. Her mother wasn't happy with the arrangement, but Dawn couldn't put her family in danger. Someone was out to get her, which meant she was getting close to figuring out the identity of the murderer. Her dad and brothers had taken her six horses back to his barn. Mom packed up some of her own clothes for Dawn to borrow until she was able to buy a new wardrobe.

God, her head hurt. She rubbed her temples as Wyatt pulled into his driveway.

He parked the truck beside the white clapboard two-story. "You shouldn't have stayed there so long."

She looked out the window at the big, old farmhouse. One day she wanted a place like this built on her share of the ranch. A home where she could raise a family.

Right. She had to find a man first. An impossible feat since she didn't even date.

The opening passenger door startled her. Wyatt held out his hand. "C'mon. Let's get you inside."

She shifted out of the seat but ignored his hand. "So, you're all moved in?"

He shut the door and took the bag her mother had packed from the back of the truck. "Mostly. I don't have much, so it didn't take long to move in."

She followed him up the steps to the wide wraparound porch. "You know you don't have to do this. I can find a place in town. Or stay at the station until I can get my place cleaned up."

He unlocked the door and opened it, but waited for her to enter. "Nonsense. I have the room and you need--"

"Don't you dare say protection. I'm the damned sheriff, and I know how to take care of myself."

A muscle in his jaw ticked as if he gritted his teeth. "I know you can, but you don't have to do it all by yourself."

She signed and looked into the darkened entry. "I know." Meeting his gaze again, she realized how close they stood. "I'm sorry. I guess I'm being cranky."

He tilted his head toward the inside, and his lips twitched in a kissable one-sided smile. "You're tired, hungry, and I know you're in pain. C'mon. Let's get something to eat."

Before she could even think about carrying through with the crazy thought of kissing him, she entered the warm interior of the entry and was hit with the subtle scents of oil soap, ink from the box of crumpled newspapers Wyatt had used for packing, and leather. As with most Victorian homes, the oak stairway greeted her on the left of the entry. There was a dark living room on the right and a parlor on the left.

Wyatt turned on the lights, and she followed him down the hallway to the huge country kitchen. A formal dining room sat behind the parlor, an office and a pantry were next to it. She'd been in the Estrada's home many times as a child. The place always had a warmth and character that made her feel safe and comfortable. But it was different this time. Instead of the scent of Stella's chocolate chip cookies, she breathed in the overwhelming fragrance of cleaners used after the Estradas moved out.

"Please, make yourself comfortable." Wyatt's voice broke into her thoughts as she stood in the middle of the kitchen, looking around. Despite the differences in the place, the same feeling of belonging prickled through her, even though Wyatt's small round dining set replaced Stella's huge country trestle table that she, the Estrada kids, and Talon played fort under when they were kids. She smiled at the memories.

"Oh. Sorry. I was just remembering all the times Mary Estrada and I hid under the table from our brothers when Stella babysat us." She sighed and pulled out a chair from the dinning set, which was much too small for the size of the kitchen.

He headed to the refrigerator and poked his head in. "Audrey never liked this house." After he retrieved a plastic storage bowl, he removed the lid and closed the door. He put the bowl in the microwave before turning with a wicked smile playing on his lips. "She calls me crazy for buying the old place."

"She still thinks it's haunted?"

He shrugged and pulled two plates from the cupboard. "Who knows? The rumor is Stella's great-grandmother Rebecca Cartwright still roams these big old rooms."

She took the plates from him and laughed. "Well, if a member of the Ferguson clan buying her land doesn't anger the old gal, nothing will."

Looking over his shoulder, his eyes twinkled with mischief as he pulled another storage bowl from the fridge. "I guess time will tell. So, if you hear any chains rattling in the attic tonight, you've been forewarned."

"I'll remember that." She took the bowl of potato salad and set it on the table.

He retrieved the steaming bowl of something spicy-smelling and a bag of sandwich rolls. After he set them on the table, he came back with a pitcher of sweet tea. She grabbed two glasses and some silverware, and then they sat down to eat.

"This smells great. Your mom's barbequed pork?" She poured some tea into the glasses.

"You know Ma. She loves to cook." He opened the rolls, took one out, and passed them to her. "She brought it and the salad over on Tuesday. I swear she thinks I'm starving to death."

She laughed and took some of the potato salad. "She always thought you were too skinny."

He glared at her, and she grinned as she bit into her sandwich. As the thought of Wyatt's perfectly muscular body under her hands burned into her mind, she moaned and was glad her mouth was full of his mother's delicious barbeque.

They ate in silence for a few moments. The easy way she'd relaxed with him surprised her, considering everything that had happened. She remembered the reason she was sitting here eating with Wyatt and set her half-eaten sandwich on her plate.

He frowned and sipped his tea. "I know that look."

She shook her head. "We have to find this jerk. Something we did hit a nerve, and I want to know who is trying to scare me off the case."

Leaning back in his chair, he wiped his mouth on a paper napkin. "I talked to Dave Alton this morning."

"Does he know anything?"

Wyatt stood and retrieved a tablet from the edge of the counter. He handed it to her as he sat again. "Border Patrol and the DEA have been watching a trucking company called North-South Transport."

She read Wyatt's barely legible scrawls and looked up. "The company ships textiles from Mexico to Dallas and is owned by a Lester Gilman? Why does that name sound so freakin' familiar?"

He finished off his salad. "Because we put that two-bit con artist in prison on fraud and drug charges three and half years ago. He was released six months ago and went to work for his father, who was the original owner of North-South. Lester's dear old dad kicked the bucket five months ago when he fell from a ten-story balcony. Guess who the sole inheritor was?"

"Lester. How convenient."

He grinned and shrugged. "Oh, it gets better."

"Please do tell. The suspense is killing me."

Chuckling, he poured them more tea. "North-South Transport's main supplier of those textiles is none other than Alvarez *Textil*."

"As in Hector Alvarez, cousin of Ignacio Cotreras, boss of the Cotreras Cartel?" She massaged the tightening muscles of her neck.

"Bingo." He stood and stepped behind her. She glanced over her shoulder as he placed his hands on her back with the thumbs massaging the sore spots in her neck. "Can you guess the route North-South Transport takes to get from Monterrey, Mexico to Dallas?"

She almost moaned with relief and pleasure. How could she forget the magic of his massages? Heat bloomed in her core, and she had to force her mind to concentrate on his voice. "Highway Six. They pass right through town."

"Two for two." He hit a particularly tight spot, and she let out a moan of satisfaction.

"Feel good?" He chuckled and worked down her back.

She glanced over her shoulder at him and shivered at the heat in his deep blue eyes. This had to stop or she'd end up in bed with him again. Standing, she broke the connection. "We need to find that driver who showed up at the Quick Fill at the same time Chris Larson was killed. Has the FBI found anything yet?"

"I'll contact them and find out." He put his hands on his hips. "But first, you need to get some rest. I'll show you to my room. I don't have a bed in the guest room yet, so I'll bunk in the living room."

Chapter 12

Standing in the doorway of Wyatt's bedroom, Dawn stared at the king-sized bed and swallowed hard. It was the same bed they'd shared all those years ago. Wyatt set the suitcase Dawn's mother had packed for her on the dark blue and white bedspread.

"The bathroom is right here." Wyatt pointed to the door on the right of the hall. "I'll use the one downstairs. Just let me grab some clothes and my razor."

Dawn sucked her bottom lip between her teeth while Wyatt opened drawers and pulled out clothes. He passed her in the door and went into the large bathroom, which had been carved out of one of the bedrooms years ago when plumbing had been introduced into the old house, then came back with a shaving kit.

What did she do next? Letting herself drown in the blue sea of his gaze wasn't an option. Clearing her throat, Dawn looked at her hands. "Thank you. You really didn't have to do this."

"I know and I told you it's the least I can do." The huskiness of his voice had her meeting his eyes again. He jutted his chin toward the opening of the bedroom. "Go on. Get some rest. Tomorrow, we'll figure out what to do next. Goodnight, Dawn."

"Goodnight," she said as he turned away and headed down the hall. Was she the only one who saw the double meaning in his words? What would happen next, not only with the case, but with them? As he disappeared down the stairs, she whispered to herself, "Why are you doing this, Wyatt?"

Shaking her head as the light in the hall went off from below, she entered his bedroom and sucked in a deep breath. Beside the bed, a heavy oak dresser sat against the wall. The moon shimmered through the bowed window, and a box of books sat on the window seat.

She went to the suitcase on the bed and rifled through her mother's borrowed clothes for something she could wear to bed. A new pack of underwear, socks, two white blouses, a pair of dressy black jeans. "Damn, Mom, how could you forget night clothes?"

She sat on the edge of the bed and pulled out a pair of the underwear. Thank goodness, her mother had a new pack lying around. She'd have to make do with the bra she wore until she could get to the store to buy new clothes. Bra size was the only size she and her mother didn't share.

She had to find something to wear to bed. Without thinking about it, she went to the closet door and opened it. A narrow shelving unit divided the space in half with Wyatt's clothes hanging on the right. She could easily imagine the closet shared by a husband and wife. Swallowing at the sudden lump, she remembered when she and Wyatt shared his closet in Dallas.

She reached for one of his shirts and held it up to her nose. His musky scent mingled with the clean fragrance of fabric softener. How many times had she worn his shirts to bed?

With a sniff, she took the shirt off the hanger and closed the door. She'd feel better after a hot shower and a good night's sleep.

She put the shirt on the bed and reached into her jeans pocket, pulling out the scraps of the sonogram photo. Refusing to let grief wreck her again, she pieced the bits together on the dresser top. She'd tape them when she got the chance. Of all the photos she'd collected, this was the only one she had to save.

She gently touched the blurry white image of her son's tiny face. "Oh, angel baby, I love you."

Sniffing again, she picked up her borrowed clothes and headed for the bathroom before the tears could start flowing.

* * * *

"Where's Wyatt?" Dawn's throat hurt as she opened her eyes and tried to focus on the hospital room. The beeping of a machine thundered in her ears.

Her mother feathered her fingertips over Dawn's forehead. "He's not here, sweetheart."

Her chest hurt. Why was she in the hospital? "What happened? Where's Wyatt?"

Mom glanced away. "He's not hurt if that's what you're asking. He's working." She took Dawn's hand and met her gaze again. Tears filled

Sara Walter Ellwood

Mom's eyes, and Dawn had a sinking feeling. "Do you remember what happened?"

She shook her head. "Not really."

"Sweetheart, you were shot in the chest and had surgery to remove the bullet."

As the memory of being shot came back to her, Dawn groaned and looked around the room again.

Her father stood by the end of her bed with his hat in his hands. "Wyatt was the father of your baby?"

Mom looked over her shoulder at Dad. "Tom, not now."

He came around to the other side of the bed. "She's got to know." Dad pulled a stool over and sat next to her bed. Clearing his throat, he took her other hand.

If they knew about the baby, did Wyatt know too? "Know what?"

"Sweetpea, you lost the baby," Dad huskily said, and Mom cried as she squeezed Dawn's hand.

Pain shot through her as sharp as when the bullet had hit her. "No." She sobbed and pulled her hands from her parents' grips. Grabbing at her lower belly, she shook her head. "No, not my baby boy."

"Wyatt didn't know, did he?" Mom's voice trembled with her tears.

Dawn shook her head. "I didn't know how to tell him. We never talked about kids or even the future. I got pregnant the first week we were together."

"How long were you together?" Dad wiped away her tears with a rough thumb.

"Five months. Oh, God, that's why he's not here. He found out about the baby and..." She couldn't say the words.

"He's left, sweetheart. He told me he couldn't believe you would've done this." Her mother's pain-filled voice pounded what was left of her heart to dust.

Dawn jerked awake and sat up in bed. For a moment, she didn't know where she was. Sucking in a breath, she lay back and glanced at the clock. Six-thirty. Thank God, morning had finally arrived. The night had been filled with bad dreams.

She tossed off the covers and sat on the edge of the bed. Her bare feet hitting the cold wood floor caused a shiver to slither down her spine, and she had to go to the bathroom.

After using the toilet, she washed her hands and splashed cool water on her face. As she dried herself on a hand towel, she met her reflection in the mirror. Her eyes were red and slightly sunken from lack of sleep, but she'd be okay once she got some coffee in her system. The bandage on her forehead was loose on one side, so she removed it and gently washed the neat line of small dark stitches. She could go without covering it for now.

She left the bathroom and heard a grunt in the room across the hall. Curious, she peeked around the doorframe. Her breath caught in her throat at the sight greeting her. Wyatt, dressed in only a pair of shorts, faced the window and lifted free weights. He grunted as his right arm and shoulder flexed as he lifted the large barbell. After lowering the right arm, he curled his left. Sweat glistened over his back, and the damp tips of his chestnut hair curled. How long had he been working out?

Heat simmered in her belly and tingled through her. She had to turn away, but she couldn't. All she wanted was him.

He must have either heard her gasp or sensed her. Turning, he set the weights on the floor and grabbed a towel off the treadmill. After he wiped his face, he picked up a water bottle and chugged.

"I'm sorry." She turned to go back to the bedroom before she did something irrevocably stupid.

"That's my shirt."

His husky voice stopped her. Damn, how could she have forgotten she was dressed in only his shirt? She looked down at the row of pearl snaps. The bottom hem hit mid-thigh. "Ah… I'm sorry."

"You said that already."

She swallowed and shook her head. "I mean about the shirt. Mom didn't pack anything for me to wear to bed."

* * * *

Sweet Jesus, she was a vision standing there in his shirt with her black hair, tangled from sleep, hanging around her shoulders and down her back. Her deep tan skin against the stark white cotton enticed him. He ate her up with his eyes as his groin ached with the need he'd tried to work out of his system.

Sleep had been almost impossible last night as he lay on the cramped couch, thinking about her lying in his bed. When the cold shower hadn't worked sometime around four o'clock, he'd gotten up to take care of the horses, made sure the cattle had hay and water, then came in and headed to the bedroom he'd turned into a gym.

He'd finally worked her out of his system, when he'd turned to catch her watching him with a naked fire in her dark brown eyes. She wanted him every bit as much as he did her.

His touch on her face startled her. She met his gaze, and the lust shining in her eyes snared him. He had to have her. He tangled his fingers into her hair, pulling her to him as he backed her into the wall. She gasped as he brought his mouth down on her lips hard.

As he plunged into her mouth, drinking her in, she curled her fingers into his bare chest and wrapped her leg around his. He had to stop. Having sex with her again wasn't an option, but his body--his heart--wasn't listening to the reason of his mind.

He picked her up, and she straddled him as he carried her into his room. Kissing her, he laid her on the bed, and stripped the shorts off his body. She sucked in her bottom lip as she devoured him with her gaze. As he leaned over her, he yanked open the snaps of her shirt to reveal full breasts tipped with hard, dark nipples.

She moaned as he sucked one of the tips into his mouth, relishing the salty-sweetness of her skin. The thumping of her heart and hissing of her breath were sweet music in the buzz of his ears. He released the hard bud after giving it a good workout and latched on to the other one. She clawed at his shoulders and back as she arched and writhed under him.

Moving down her belly, he nibbled on her smooth skin until he reached the edge of her panties. He shifted onto his knees and pealed the white cotton from her, revealing the dark tangle of curls between her legs. His breath hitched as he thought of burying himself in her, but he didn't want to rush. He couldn't let this happen again, so he intended to make every second count.

"Wyatt. I need you."

Loving the breathlessness of her voice, he grinned as he suckled on the tender skin of her ankle, causing her to wiggle and moan. "All in due time, babe."

She curled her fingers into the sheets and groaned. He nibbled up her long, toned leg and tingled with the anticipation of sampling her. Parting her curls, he groaned as he took her swollen clit into his mouth.

* * * *

"Oh, God!" Dawn arched off the bed as he sucked her. The tension coiling in her core tightened to the breaking point. "I'm gonna come."

She shattered into a million bright lights and rode a high of bliss. He stayed with her until the last shiver quaked through her; then he kissed up her tingling belly, over her supersensitive breasts to her neck. She wrapped her arms and legs around him, welcoming him into her.

He pulled back to meet her gaze and feathered damp hair from the side of her face. "You're so beautiful."

Was she imagining the raw emotion in his amazingly bright eyes? She threaded her fingers into his hair and pulled him to her lips. As she kissed him, he started to rock his hips. The slow, gentle motion was nothing like the raw sex they'd had days ago on her couch. This resembled the love they'd made years ago.

Her heart ached with the memory.

She tightened her legs around him and twisted her body, changing their positions. He chuckled as she sat up on him.

"You really don't like me on top, do you?"

She ignored the pain in her injured knee as she leaned over him, lifting off his erection and slamming back, causing him to groan. She kissed him, then said against his lips, "But you love when I'm on top. So, shut up and enjoy the ride, cowboy."

His laugh died on a long growl as she set a rhythm meant to drive them both to orgasm.

* * * *

"Wow." Dawn fell onto her back next to him and pulled the sheet over her.

Wyatt rolled over on his side, propped his head with his hand, and brushed his fingers over her flushed cheek. Did they have a chance? "You're amazing. You know that?"

She shook her head and sat up, then pulled on the shirt. As she faced the window, she ran her hands through her hair. "This can't keep happening."

He picked up his shorts from the floor and tugged them on. "You're right. It can't." He rounded the bed and headed for the dresser. "I'm going to take a shower and head to the station. You can…"

He stopped and stared at the torn photograph of the sonogram, lying on top of the dresser. She'd saved it. His fingers trembled as he touched the tattered pieces. He turned and faced her. "Why didn't you tell me you were pregnant?"

She hugged herself and glared at him. "Why did you leave me when I needed you most?"

He took a few steps toward her. "Don't turn this on me. Were you that driven by your damn career you were afraid I'd want you to quit if I found out you were pregnant?"

Shock and pain twisted her face into a hard mask. "Do you really believe that?"

"You tell me." He slashed his hand through the air as he closed the distance between them to stand toe-to-toe with her. "All you ever wanted was to be sheriff of this damn town. While we were in vice, getting promoted to detective was your ambition. I think getting pregnant threw a really big wrench into those plans." Her face paled with disbelief, but he ignored it and rushed on. "What were you planning to do, Dawn? Have an abortion?"

The loud smack on his cheek surprised him more than it hurt. "Fuck you, Wyatt. I loved that baby. I wanted to tell you, but I had no idea what you'd do. I'm Native American. You're white. I got pregnant the first or second time we had sex."

The tears swimming in her dark eyes ripped at his heart as her meaning sank in. Had he been so wrong about her reasons for not telling him?

Before he could respond, she headed for the door and turned at the opening. "You're the one who left me in the hospital after I took a bullet meant for you. You have no right to judge me."

The slamming of the bathroom door echoed around him as his cell phone started playing Toby Keith's *Beer for My Horses*.

Chapter 13

Wyatt glanced at the caller ID. Talon Blackwell? He connected the call. "McPherson here."

"I need to talk to you. I'm worried about Rachel."

He leaned against the windowsill and took a deep breath. "What do you know about my sister?"

"Enough to know she'll try killing herself again the moment she's let out of that hospital."

The sense of urgency in Talon's voice surprised Wyatt as much as Dawn's keeping the sonogram had. "Where are you?"

"I'm at the diner in town."

He glanced at the closed bedroom door as the water went off in the bathroom. He didn't need this right now, but he had to do what he could to save his sister. What the hell would Talon Blackwell know about Rachel? He closed his eyes. "You have a lot of explaining to do about how you know all this about my sister."

A harsh laugh met his ear. "I could say the same thing about my baby sister, McPherson."

The phone went dead. He stood and ran his hand through his hair. A niggling memory wormed its way into his mind. After Rachel had found out about Lance and Audrey's affair, she'd run off. No one could find her, but a week later, she'd showed up with Talon Blackwell and announced she was joining the Army. He set the phone on the windowsill.

How had his life gotten so damned complicated? Protecting his family and the woman he loved shouldn't be this hard.

* * * *

"Thanks for picking me up." Dawn climbed up into the big blue Dodge truck and closed the door.

Zack narrowed his eyes on her with open curiosity. He looked out at Wyatt's house as he shifted into gear. "No problem. How're you feeling?"

"Sore. But I'll live. Mom said you stopped by to see me in the hospital, but I was sleeping. Thank you anyway." Her knee started hurting again after her long shower, and now her head throbbed.

"I'm glad you're okay." He watched her buckle her seatbelt with concern shining in his dark blue eyes. "Wyatt said you were lucky you hit his mailbox first. You should've bunked down at the office if you were that tired."

She didn't want to talk about the accident. Or the lie Wyatt and Tilly came up with to tell everyone so that they could keep the real cause for the accident off the Colton grapevine. "How're Tracy and the kids?"

He pulled onto Blackwell Road heading toward the sheriff's station in town. "The kids are great. Tracy's mom and mine are driving us crazy about our wedding plans, but we're all good."

They were quiet for a long time. She'd called him after she heard Wyatt leave, knowing she couldn't stay in the house after what happened that morning. As she stared out the side window at the pastures, she sensed him glancing at her.

"Okay, color me nosy. What were you doing at Wyatt's?"

With a sigh, she looked over at her best friend. "I'd spent the night."

"Oh."

She shook her head and bit her bottom lip. "Someone broke into my house and destroyed the place. All the furniture, my clothes... everything. But we are keeping it quiet since the last thing I want on the grapevine is that I was attacked and threatened. The accident had also been an attempt on my life. My truck's brakes were cut. I didn't fall asleep while driving."

"Damn. Any idea who might be responsible?"

"Nope." God, she wanted everything to get back to normal. "But I know it's the murderer."

He sighed and shook his head. "I can't say I'm sorry I quit when I did, but I am sorry you fell into this."

"Me too. Kids are dying, and I can't catch the thug killing them."

"Are we done dancing around the bush?"

"Thought you enjoyed the two-step." She wanted to tell Zack everything, but how could she spill her guts to him? They were still friends, but now he was so happy with Tracy, and her life was such a pile of flaming crap. They didn't have as much in common as they used to.

"Not with you, I don't. What the hell's going on between you and Wyatt?"

Leave it to Zack to jump on the big pile of crap making up most of her personal problems. She briefly met his gaze. "Wyatt and I lived together when we were on the Dallas PD."

He swallowed and stared out the windshield. "I know. He told me when I questioned him about what was going on between you two after you started acting like a snapping turtle on the rustling case."

"What did he say?"

Shrugging, Zack rubbed the back of his neck. "Not much. Just that you ended it."

She glared at him. "That bastard. Figures he'd blame it on me. I didn't end anything. He left me when I lost our baby after I was shot."

He stopped at an intersection and looked at her. "You were pregnant?"

Averting her eyes, she sighed at not only the disbelief in his voice but the hurt too. She and Zack once shared everything. "I was almost five months pregnant. Because I barely showed, Wyatt never figured it out, and I never told him about the baby."

"Why not?"

Closing her eyes, she sniffed as the pain from the memories hit her. "I was afraid he'd do to me what Jock Blackwell did to Mom. And he proved me right." She shook her head and looked out the window as the truck moved through the intersection. "When I got shot, I lost the baby, and he found out about the pregnancy. I woke up and he was gone."

"You never talked to him about it?"

She shook her head and bit her lip. God, how could this still hurt so much? "When I was discharged, my parents took me back to his apartment. It was obvious he hadn't been there for days. I packed my stuff, came home to Colton, and put my notice in at the PD. Never going back. Later I found out Wyatt went after the gang leader who'd shot me, then quit himself and joined the Texas Rangers. The next time I saw him was when he showed up on the Parker case two months ago."

"Jesus." He blew out a breath between his teeth. "So, what's going on now?"

"I have no idea. We had a fight this morning. I think he believes it's my fault we lost our baby," she said with a shrug. What had he meant about her wanting an abortion and her career being more important? At the time, she'd been so angry she hadn't thought about the meaning behind the words. "But he hadn't wanted the baby anyway." *Had he?*

"How can you be so sure about that? You both need to sit down and talk about this." He looked over at her again and shook his head. "Dear

Sara Walter Ellwood

God, Dawn. Has it ever occurred to you Wyatt may have been pissed that you never told him about the baby and upset that he lost his child?"

It had, and she'd long ago dismissed the possibility. "If he wanted the baby, he wouldn't have left me. If he'd loved me, he wouldn't have left. There's nothing to talk about."

He was quiet for a long time. "I think there is. Wyatt's nothing like Jock Blackwell, Dawn. You of all people should know that. Are you sleeping together?"

She laughed, but it sounded choked even to her own ears. "Not sure if you can count two bouts of wild sex as sleeping together."

She sensed him staring at her for as long as he could take his eyes off the road. "Dawn, you're in love with him, aren't you?"

Nodding, she wiped at her nose with the back of her hand. She would not start bawling like a baby in front of Zack. She wouldn't! But the truth hurt too much, and a tear leaked out. "I've loved him since I was a little girl."

* * * *

The bell over the glass door jingled as Wyatt stepped into Ella's Diner. The din of conversation and the aromas of buttermilk pancakes, bacon, and copious amounts of strong coffee greeted him. He moved into the dining room and searched the crowd for Talon.

His old friend sat in the back corner in a booth and stared out the window next to his table. As Wyatt weaved his way through the dining room, tipping his hat to those who wished him good morning, Talon turned to watch and sipped his coffee.

Wyatt slipped into the booth across from Talon and removed his hat. Zelda Marion, one of the regular waitresses during breakfast and lunch, rushed over and smiled. She pulled a pen from behind her ear and readied her pad for order taking. "What can I get ya, Wyatt?"

He forced a smile. "Just coffee this morning."

She tucked the pad away in her apron and stuck the pen back behind her ear. "Comin' right up."

Once she rushed off to get his coffee, Talon set his mug on the fake red marble table. "I want to help Rachel."

Before Wyatt could answer, Zelda returned with a steaming mug of black coffee and the pot to refill Talon's cup. "I heard about Rachel's troubles and the sheriff's accident. Hope both those gals are okay. Let your mammas know I've put them on my prayer list."

Wyatt stared into his mug of coffee. "Thank you, Miz Marion. Ma will be happy to have your prayers for Rachel. She really could use them right now."

Talon shifted in his seat. "Dawn will be okay. Thanks for your concern."

She nodded and looked from Talon back to Wyatt and smiled. "If you gents need anything, just give me a holler."

When they were alone again, Wyatt leaned over his arms and narrowed his eyes at Talon. "How the hell are you going to help Rachel?"

Talon's hard eyes softened a little. "I know where she is emotionally. At least, I understand what feeling trapped is like. She needs someone who can understand her but won't feed her self-pity and depression." When Wyatt bristled at the implication of that last insinuation, Talon added, "Not that you, your parents, and Audrey don't mean well, but how would you feel in her shoes?"

"Like shit."

"Exactly. She's dependent on y'all, but she doesn't have to be, nor does she want to be. She needs to feel like she has something to live for, and that she's not a burden on the people she loves. Rachel hates that more than she does anything else."

Wyatt leaned back and huffed. "How would you know?"

Talon's gaze never wavered. "I know your sister better than you can possibly guess."

What did he mean by that? Sure, Talon and Rachel had known each other since they were kids, and he and Talon had been best friends growing up. Something in Talon's conviction spurred all kinds of questions. The same kinds of questions that nagged him when Talon showed up the day they'd brought Rachel home from the VA hospital and they'd talked for an hour.

"I don't like this."

"Who does? Rachel is the sweetest, kindest person I know, but life sure as hell hasn't treated her well, has it?" Talon shook his head and glanced out the window. "She deserves better than this, Wyatt. She needs to find her way again, and I think I know how to help her."

"How?"

Talon met his gaze again. "I talked to Dr. Forsyth about what he thought would help her. She needs something that will fulfill her desire to help people. He said that she loved nursing."

Wyatt narrowed his eyes and fisted his hands on either side of his coffee mug. He understood Forsyth knowing that about Rachel; he'd worked with her. But what the hell business did Talon have involving himself in her healing? "You talked to Rachel's doctor? What gives you the right to think you know more about her than her family does?"

A muscle in Talon's jaw ticked as he stared Wyatt down. "I may not be family, but Rachel has always been my friend. I care about what's happening to her." He shook his head and gazed out the window. "I'm involved because I want to help her get past this pain."

With a deep breath, Wyatt picked up his cup and let the warmth calm his anger. Maybe Talon figured something out that the rest of them hadn't. Wyatt didn't have to like it, but he hated not being able to help his sister even more. "What do you suggest? I doubt the hospital would hire her as a nurse."

Talon shifted in his seat and picked up his own mug. "Maybe not. But there has to be something that would make her feel important again. You should talk to someone at the hospital and see what they suggest."

Wyatt couldn't help the self-deprecating grin. "You know your sister suggested the same thing."

Talon finished his coffee and picked up his hat. "Sometimes, she has a good idea. I gotta go. I'm meeting a contractor in less than an hour."

"As in a building contractor?"

Talon stood and opened his wallet. As he tossed a five on the table, he nodded. "Yeah. I need a house and soon. Living with my mother and Tom is not gonna work. Jessie Mae and I need our own space."

Talon turned and almost ran into his sister and Zack Cartwright. Wyatt's heart sped up at the sight of Dawn standing slightly behind Zack as if she hoped he would shield her in some way. Wyatt recognized the way she tried to avoid looking at him as vulnerability, and he wanted to take her into his arms.

"Talon?" Dawn looked up at her brother.

"Mornin'." Talon put his hat on his head.

Zack smiled and patted Talon on the shoulder. "I guess congratulations are in order. Welcome to the trials and tribulations of fatherhood."

Talon returned his smile. "Thanks."

"If you need anything, call." Zack removed his hat and ran a hand through his hair. "Being a single father of a little girl can be a challenge. Maybe the girls can meet up sometime. I know your girl is still little, but Mandy would love playing with her. She loves babies."

"Thanks. I might take you up on your offer." Talon nodded at his sister and headed toward the door.

Wyatt stared at Dawn, who finally met his gaze. "You're supposed to be at the house."

"I have work to do." She glanced at Zack. "Let's get out of here."

She turned to leave, but Zack touched her elbow, stopping her. "Not so fast." He gently eased her toward her brother's vacated seat. After Dawn sat, Zack leaned over the table and lowered his voice. "I don't know everything that's gone down between you two. But I do know what not talking and getting the important things out in the open can do to a relationship. You two need to talk."

Zack straightened, settled his hat onto his head, and ambled through the diner, stopping occasionally to say howdy to those who greeted him.

When Dawn shifted to get up, Wyatt reached over and took her hand. She snapped her gaze to him, and he took a deep breath. "He's right. We do need to talk."

Zelda stopped by to refill his cup and asked Dawn what she would like. "Just coffee with cream."

"And please bring us each an order of the number two breakfast special. I'd like my eggs over easy with bacon. The sheriff would like hers scrambled with a side of sausage, and we both want white toast." Wyatt smiled at Zelda, who perked up at the prospect of them ordering more than coffee.

"Comin' right up." After slipping her pad and pen into her apron, she collected Talon's empty mug and the cash he'd left on the table before heading back to the counter to put the order into the kitchen and grab Dawn's coffee.

"You shouldn't have wasted the food. I'm not hungry."

Wyatt sipped his coffee. "Well, I am, and you need to eat."

She looked out the window. He could see her anger in the set of her jaw. He sighed and glanced around the crowded room. Zack was right. They needed to talk, and although this wasn't the best place for the conversation, he intended to have it.

Zelda returned with Dawn's mug of coffee and set a creamer pitcher on the table. Dawn mumbled a "thank you" and poured milk into her coffee. "What did you and Talon have to talk about?"

"Apparently, he and Rachel are old friends, and he thinks he can help her."

She looked up at him and furrowed her brow.

"I should have realized they were close by the times he came to her rescue when we were all kids, but I didn't realize the friendship lasted into adulthood." His and Talon's hadn't.

Dawn hugged the mug of steaming coffee and stared into the depths.

He leaned over his arms. "I would never have done to you what Jock Blackwell did to your mother, Dawn. It hurts that you think I would have."

* * * *

Dawn looked up. The sorrow, pulling at the fine creases at the corners of his eyes, and the downward tilt of his lips shot a tinge of pain through her heart. "But you left me."

He shook his head and averted his eyes to the table. "No. I didn't. You left me. I came home, and you were gone."

"I came home with Mom and Dad. I wasn't sure you wanted me anymore. They told me they hadn't seen you since the night I'd lost the baby. Where did you go?" Had she misjudged him? Her heart raced and ice filled her gut.

He took a deep breath. "After I found out about the baby, I had to do something. God, I was angry. At you. At the kid who shot you. At the world. I went after the thug, then took a ride to McAllister. I have a buddy from the police academy who lives there and is in the Amarillo office of the Texas Rangers. He talked me into joining."

Zelda took that moment to deliver their breakfasts and refilled their coffees. Neither of them made any move to eat. Zelda looked from her to Wyatt, who gave her a half-smile and said, "Thank you."

"Enjoy your breakfast." As she turned away, she shook her dyed bright red head; the sky-high beehive hairdo she'd worn since high school in the sixties never moved.

"And instead of coming home to see me, you joined the Texas Rangers." Anger bubbled up in her sour stomach. She pushed the plate filled with fluffy eggs, sausage links, and home fried potatoes away. "You're mad at me? You accused me of wanting an abortion?" She lowered her voice when an older woman glanced at her. She sure as hell didn't want any of this mess to end up on the Colton grapevine. "Let's take a good long look at your relationship history. Maybe you can see things as I did."

She held up her fingers to count her reasons for not knowing his intentions when she'd discovered the pregnancy. "You took me to my senior prom, and I nearly gave you my virginity, but I stopped before things went too far. Then you went back to college and never gave me the time of day for almost ten years. I figured you were mad that I didn't give in."

She clicked off another digit. "Then you and that TV reporter, Vanessa Burk, dated and lived together for years after college. But you didn't show any indication you wanted to marry her. In fact, when she proposed, you moved out."

With another finger, she counted off another doubt. "I got pregnant too early in our relationship to even know if what we had was real. You never once mentioned wanting a future with me, Wyatt." She lowered her hands. "How the hell was I supposed to know anything?"

He picked up his fork and poked at the fried potatoes on his plate. "I figured you didn't want a future." Giving up the pretense of gathering potatoes on his fork, he laid it on the plate and stared her down. "All you ever wanted was to be a police detective. If you had known me at all, you would have figured out I never wanted to stay in Dallas."

She leaned back in her seat. "I never wanted to stay in Dallas, either. You knew that."

"True. You wanted to be sheriff. I figured you never told me about the baby because you didn't want it."

She shook her head. Pain hit her so hard she gasped. "I would never have done anything to intentionally hurt my baby." Her voice cracked on the last word.

"I've danced around this question long enough. Why the hell didn't you take yourself off the case?"

She hugged her coffee cup, the anger replaced with an empty, cold nothingness. The warmth did nothing to take the chill from her gut or the numbness from her fingers. "I planned to tell you about the baby after the deal and call the captain to be removed from the case. I was so scared that night, Wyatt. Not just for me and you, but for our baby. The sonogram picture I have had been taken earlier that day. I loved the idea of having a baby--your baby. But until then, the pregnancy didn't seem real. I'd learned the sex that day, and for the first time, the glob of cells growing inside of me looked like a baby."

She averted her gaze to the table. "Our baby. I was afraid you wouldn't want it. God, I prayed Mom was wrong about all white men being like Jock Blackwell. I prayed that you wouldn't leave me like you had before--like you did Vanessa when she wanted to get married and you didn't. I hoped you did love me and would accept our baby." She forced her eyes to him and was taken aback by the sorrow etching his handsome face.

"I never really loved Vanessa. I loved you." His low, gruff voice blasted her like a bugle. "How many times did I have to tell you that?"

She sniffed back the sting in her sinuses. She wasn't going to start crying! She glanced out the window and took a deep breath, fighting the tears threatening to fall. "And I loved you. How could you ever think I'd kill our baby?"

Before he could answer, Tilly rushed to their table, causing her to jump at the abruptness of his out-of-breath appearance. "I saw your truck outside," he said to Wyatt, then turned to Dawn. "Elizabeth Raines just called. Tyler Demello is missing. But that's not all." He swallowed hard and rubbed his hand over his lower face as if what he was about to say burned his mouth. "Deputy Grant's been shot."

Chapter 14

Dawn stepped out of Tilly's SUV and rubbed her hands on her borrowed black slacks. The only parts of her sheriff's uniform she had were her tan Stetson, jacket, badge, and gun.

Two other sheriff vehicles pulled up and parked on the street. The body lying next to a brown Tahoe with the Texas Star painted on the door brought her up short. "Do you have any idea of what happened?"

Tilly cleared his throat. "The call came in as I was headed to the station this morning. When I saw Wyatt's truck at the diner, I stopped, knowing he'd want to know."

Wyatt parked his truck next to the curb behind a sports car. The driver stopped Wyatt and spoke, but Dawn couldn't hear the exchange. Wyatt pointed down the street and the driver pulled away and headed toward town.

Dawn frowned as she noticed other cars stopped along the wide street and the drivers gawking at the scene.

As Wyatt approached Dawn, she looked at the two deputies stopping to stare at the body. "Hendricks and Simms, take your vehicles and block either end of this street. If we don't close it, we'll have half the town here."

Chet nodded and tapped the other deputy on the shoulder.

Wyatt headed toward the body, and she forced her feet to follow him.

Doug, who had been on the force ever since her father hired him the day he'd graduated high school, lay on his back and stared at the clear blue sky with sightless eyes. He'd been shot in the chest, and a pool of dark blood pooled under him on the blacktopped driveway. The coppery scent mingled indecently with the fragrances of fresh cut grass and autumn leaves, making her already sour stomach churn.

By the size of the hole in his bloodstained uniform shirt, he'd been shot at nearly point blank range. How could anyone get that close to him? His orders had been explicit to keep everyone away from the house. Had he known his killer?

Doug had been one of her best deputies despite his goofy personality. She'd known him since grade school, but he was a few years younger than her. His father was a history professor at Colton College, and his mother taught Sunday school.

His wife would be heartbroken, and his two-month-old daughter would never know her father. Fighting the tears that stung her sinuses and clogged her throat, she glanced at Tilly. "Has anyone contacted his wife?"

"No, not yet." He shook his head and shuffled his feet.

She patted him on the shoulder and glanced at Elizabeth Raines huddled against a man on the front stoop of their Spanish inspired two-story. A potted gardenia lay on its side, and dark soil spilled out from the broken glazed pot. Had Doug's killer knocked it over? Or had Tyler tried to escape? "I better talk to the Raines." She glanced at Doug's body. "I'm leaving you in charge of this part of the investigation."

He nodded and she turned to look at Wyatt standing behind her on the brick walkway. The Glock holstered at her hip weighed heavily as she approached Tyler's mother. She didn't want to think about what they would find when they found Tyler Demello, considering how brutally Chis Larson and Justin Vaughn had been murdered.

Wyatt's black Resistol shaded his face, but she could tell by the hard tilt of his mouth his thoughts were running with hers. When they reached the couple on the small porch, he removed his hat and held out his ID to the tall dark-haired man. "I'm Lieutenant Wyatt McPherson of the Texas Rangers."

The man glanced at the ID and worry furrowed his brow. "Cory Raines. I'm Tyler's stepfather."

"Mrs. Raines." Wyatt shoved his badge back into his pocket.

Dawn introduced herself to Mr. Raines, then looked at his wife. "We need to ask you some questions about Tyler."

Tyler's mother pushed away from her husband and stiffened.

Cory Raines nodded and looked from Wyatt to her. "Please come in."

He moved to the side, opening the door to allow them entry. As they filed into the spacious entry, she caught sight of expensive art and posh furnishings. Elizabeth led them into the room on the left, and stopped between a creamy leather couch and a black overstuffed chair.

Other than the worry tugging on the fine lines around her eyes, the woman looked as impeccable and as mad at the world as she had the other evening when Tyler came to the station. As she folded her arms before her, Dawn noticed the tremor in her perfectly manicured hands. "You assured us we would be safe."

Her husband moved in and wrapped his arm around her shoulders. "We want Tyler found."

"We want the same thing." Dawn swallowed the sudden cotton in her mouth. How could this have happened?

Wyatt glanced at her and pulled a notepad from his back pocket. "What do you know about Tyler's disappearance?"

"He didn't disappear. He was abducted." Elizabeth rubbed her arms with her hands and moved away from her husband. "When we woke up this morning, we found the glass in Tyler's window cut and he was gone. His room is a mess. Then we found Deputy Grant dead in our driveway." She shuddered and shook her head.

Why didn't the murderers kill Tyler like they had the other two boys? Dawn glanced at Wyatt and knew he was thinking the same thing. "Can we have a look in Tyler's room?"

Elizabeth nodded and sniffed. "Please find my son."

* * * *

As Wyatt entered the first floor bedroom, he pulled a couple pairs of rubber gloves out of his jacket pocket and looked around. The window facing the backyard was open, and a large hole was cut into the glass below the lock. He could easily imagine the abductor cutting the hole, opening the lock, then lifting the pane.

On the wall above a desk holding a laptop, a poster of some rapper hung next to the window. A backpack sat beside the desk. Scattered on the floor were a few articles of clothing. Punk jewelry and soda cans littered the dresser. Spread out over the floor was the bedding with a large lump under it as if the pillows hid from prying eyes. The room held a chill from the breeze blowing in the wide-open window and held the scent of cut grass from the neighbor's yard.

Dawn took the pair of gloves he held out to her. He didn't miss that she avoided touching him. "Looks like he was yanked out of bed."

He turned to the Raines, standing in the doorway. "Have either of you touched anything in here since finding the room like this?"

Elizabeth shook her head. "No. We called the police right away."

As Dawn pulled on her gloves, she knelt beside the broken glass on the floor. "Wyatt, take a look at this."

Pressed into the carpeting were several pairs of muddy boot prints. From the haphazard placement of them, there may have been a struggle.

A line of blood drops went from the open window to the edge of the comforter, concealing the pillows on the floor.

She lifted the comforter from the floor, and Elizabeth let out a scream. Her husband gasped and pulled her close to him. A puddle of blood stained the tan carpeting, and lying in the middle of it was Tyler Demello. He was stabbed in the belly and had several slashes over his arms.

How the hell had his parents slept through the racket this must have made?

When Dawn met his gaze, the taut lines around her eyes showed the fear and pain she held inside, which pulled at his heart. The deaths of these kids were taking a toll on her. "We have to call the FBI forensic team in here ASAP. If there's mud and blood here, there's more outside."

He nodded and knelt beside her. Although he figured it was a futile move, he laid his fingers on the boy's neck to check for a pulse. When the first beat fluttered under his fingers, he blinked and pressed harder into the artery. He focused on the kid's chest to look for breathing.

"Wyatt?" Dawn's soft voice shook. "I think he's breathing."

He met her wide-eyed gaze as the flutters under his gloved fingers became recognizable as a weak pulse. "Call an ambulance. He's alive."

Elizabeth, who had gotten herself under her Junior League polished control, took a step into the room. "He's alive?"

Wyatt yanked on the sheet, balled it up, and held it to the oozing wound on Tyler's belly. He glanced at the boy's mother. "He's alive but barely. Please stay back."

She narrowed her eyes at him, but her husband pulled her back and said, "C'mon, Liz. Let them do their job. You don't want to disturb any evidence that could catch the guy who did this."

Dawn clipped her cell onto her belt. "The ambulance is on its way. I'm calling dispatch to get a hold of the FBI." She pointed to the drops of blood leading to the window. "We need to get these boot prints casted and that blood analyzed. I have a feeling it's not Tyler's."

"That not all we need the FBI for." At the pucker of her forehead, he swallowed and remembered what her father had said the other day in the hospital. "We need them to protect Tyler and his family." He flicked a glance at the Raines and lowered his voice to a whisper. "It may be time to reconsider who the killer might be. I have a feeling he may be closer then we think. In fact, he might be working with us."

The furrow in her forehead deepened until his meaning blossomed in her mind and unfurled the creases of puzzlement like a flower opening to the sun. "You're thinking we have a possum in the henhouse?"

He nodded and smiled despite the gravity of the implication. "Exactly."

* * * *

Chet punched the office door, putting a dent in the cheap wood. His worthless sack-of-shit bother-in-law sat behind his desk, he looked up and frowned as he wrapped the cut on his arm in gauze from a first aid kit. "What the fuck?"

He kicked the offending door wishing it was Gene's ugly mug. "The kid isn't dead."

That got the asshole's attention. He sat up and narrowed his eyes. "What are you talking about?"

Chet leaned over the desk into Gene's face. "Demello. The bitch and McPherson found him, and he is still alive. He's been taken to Dallas and is in the hospital there."

Gene leaned back into his cushy leather chair. "You'll have to off him."

Chet shook his head and spun around. He hated feeling caged in. Running his hands through his hair, he sucked in a breath. Damn, he needed another hit. "How the hell am I supposed to do that? He's surrounded by FBI agents and Rangers."

The idiot his sister married leaned over his arms on the desk. "You're running for fucking sheriff! You should be able to get close enough to make sure he can't talk."

Chet had about enough of the know-it-all. He grabbed Gene by his shirt collar and pulled him over the desk. "I think Madison and McPherson are on to me. If you would've killed the bitch like you were supposed to…"

Gene scowled and gripped Chet's wrist hard enough to cause him to wince and let go. "She would be dead if you would've let me put a bullet in her head."

Chet hated to admit even to himself the peacock was right. He stepped away from Gene's desk and took a deep breath; it did nothing to relieve the gnawing need burning him from the inside out. "We have to figure out what our options are."

Gene shook his head and sat back in his chair. "You need to win that election in a few weeks so you can find a scapegoat to take the rap for those murders."

Nodding, he shoved his hands into the pockets of his jacket. As the memories of what he'd seen at Madison's trailer flipped through the fuzz of his mind, he turned toward Gene. "I think I know how I can get rid of Dawn Madison and possibly Wyatt McPherson too."

Gene furrowed his brows. "You going to let me in on the plan?"

He grinned. "Destroying a person's place gives you a very personal look at what they're hiding."

Chapter 15

Wyatt finished the text message informing his captain of Tyler Demello's status. The boy had been rushed to surgery soon after they'd arrived at the hospital. A few moments ago, he'd been moved to intensive care. By the way the hospital staff tossed glares at the FBI agents when they reminded them where they could and couldn't go, Wyatt suspected they hated their presence.

Sighing, he clipped his phone on his belt and leaned back in his chair. The last time he'd sat in this hallway had been three years ago when Dawn got shot. He'd been expecting the memories to come and clobber him, but they hadn't. Instead of the pain of betrayal flooding his heart, the ache of what he may have missed with Dawn filled him.

What would have happened if he'd stuck around and they'd actually talked things out? Why had he run?

Dawn talked with Tyler's father near the door of the boy's room. The well-known fertility doctor was dressed in an expensive suit and bore the air of someone rich, but by the way he fisted and opened his hand, and by the deep creases in his face, Wyatt could tell that he was genuinely worried about his son.

Wyatt focused on Dawn and frowned. She leaned against the wall as if she needed it to hold her up. Pain and fatigue showed in her drawn and pale face. The knee of the leg she favored appeared twice its normal size beneath the black fabric of her borrowed slacks.

When Dr. Demello turned away, Wyatt stood and headed straight for her. "I think it's time to get you home."

She turned toward him, and her eyes narrowed for a beat before they widened. "I can't leave."

Shrugging, he looked around. "We both know no one but immediate family, hospital staff, and the FBI can get within a hundred yards of the kid. He's safe, Dawn." Not for the first time, Wyatt admired her for her commitment, but if she didn't get out of here soon, she would drop. "Let me get you back to the ranch where you can get some rest. You weren't even supposed to be working yet." He smiled before she had a chance to voice the protest he imagined coming. "Besides, your momma will already have my hide for not keeping you at home. Do you want me to be on the receiving end of her wrath?"

She let out a small laugh, then tilted her head to the side. Humor he'd not seen for a long time shined in her deep brown eyes. "Like the time you and Talon stole all her tomatoes from the garden to throw at Jock Blackwell's house?"

He rubbed his jaw and chuckled. "Yeah, like that." He set his hat on his head and nodded toward the exit. "So, let's go."

With a wince she couldn't stop, she pushed away from the wall and lost her balance. She would have fallen if Wyatt hadn't caught her. "Damn. My knee hurts."

He guided her to a chair. "Sit down. I'm going to find a nurse with a wheelchair."

With narrowed eyes, she shook her head. "Just give me a minute. I'll be fine."

"No. For once in your life let someone take care of you." Before she could make a fuss, he turned toward a passing nurse. "Miss, do you have a wheelchair handy? Sheriff Madison was in an auto accident yesterday and has been on her feet all day."

"Wyatt. I'm fine." He heard the words through gritted teeth.

Dawn stood, but she fell back into the chair. The nurse stepped forward and frowned. "I think he's right. In fact, I'd recommend you having it looked at."

"No." Dawn glared at him. "Just get me a chair. I'll call the doctor when we get back to Colton."

The nurse pursed her lips as if she wasn't sure she believed her, but soon turned to fetch the wheelchair.

Dawn leaned her head back and closed her eyes. She gave up too easily, which had to mean she knew he was right, or she was glad for the intervention but too proud to admit it.

When the chair arrived, the nurse helped her onto the seat and glanced at Wyatt as she took the handles. "Which exit are you parked closest to?"

"The E.R. I'll pull my truck up to the door."

"Good. I'll meet you there." She started pushing the chair through the staring FBI agents and medical staff, while he took off for the elevator.

When would she stop pushing herself to the brink?

* * * *

Dawn stared out the window as the dark highway between Dallas and Colton flew by. Soft country music played on the radio. She and Wyatt didn't speak. What was there to talk about? She'd said more than her piece that morning--*God, had it been that morning?*--at the diner.

The sex that happened before then seemed like a lifetime ago.

"I have nowhere to go," she said more to herself than to Wyatt as they entered the city limits of Colton.

"I'm taking you back to my place." The deepness of his voice had her turning her head toward him. He glanced her way, and their eyes met for a brief time before he had to look back at the road, but she recognized the shadowy seriousness shining in the depths. "I think it's time you and I have a talk."

"Thought we already did this morning at the diner."

Again, his piercing blue gaze touched hers as he stopped at the red light in the center of town. "You asked me a question before Tilly came in. I think I owe you an answer." He looked back at the road when the signal changed to green, but she got the feeling he did so more to avoid her than to make the turn. "I don't know what I thought, Dawn. About the baby. About whether you'd want it or not. I spent a lot of years trying to figure that out. I…" He shook his head and rubbed his jaw. "I was hurt you didn't tell me."

Sighing, she closed her eyes and leaned her head back against the seat. She was too tired to do this again. "I told you why I didn't."

"Yes. And that's what hurts. I thought you knew me better than that. I'm nothing like Jock Blackwell."

She turned her head and looked at his handsome profile. The set of his jaw showed her the pain in his heart, but the sight did nothing to alleviate the hurt she still held deep in her own. "Then why did you run? If I'd honestly hurt you so bad by not telling you about the baby. If you wanted our baby so much, why didn't you face me then?"

"Let me get you home, and we'll finish this."

She shook her head. He was still running. "Okay."

A few moments later, they pulled into his driveway. He helped her out of the truck and into the house. Once he helped her settle on the couch, with her bum leg propped on a pillow, he gently placed a bag of frozen peas over her swollen knee. When he handed her a couple of pain pills and a glass of milk to wash them down, she'd had enough.

She set the empty glass on the end table. "Now, are you going to tell me the real reason you bailed on me?"

He faced the fireplace and tossed his hat onto the leather chair that matched the couch. "I should have been able to protect you, Dawn. I failed. The same way I failed my sisters, especially Rachel."

What? "I don't get it? I can take care of myself, and I can't imagine a brother loving his sisters more than you do."

He faced her, the shadows in his eyes causing her heart to flutter. "That's just it. Did you know I set up Lance and Rachel?"

She shook her head.

He sat in the chair next to her and leaned over his long legs to study his hands. "I didn't think he was good for her, but I went against my gut. Lance was home from college and Rachel was still in high school. I knew she had a crush on him, and when he asked me if I'd get him a date for the Fergusons' roundup barbeque, I knew exactly who." He shook his head and fisted his hands. "So, if I'd gone with my gut and told him to go find his own damn date, my little sister might not be suffering like she is right now."

She couldn't believe the guilt radiating off him. "Wyatt, you had no way of knowing what would have happened. Besides, Lance made his own decisions when he cheated on her with Audrey, and so did Rachel. No one forced her to join the military."

He shrugged as he leaned back in the chair. "I know you're right, but I can't stop thinking about it. Just like I can't stop wondering where I went wrong with you. I should have been the one protecting you, not the other way around."

As if a dark veil lifted from her eyes, she realized the truth about Wyatt, and the fact that he honestly believed that horseshit made her angrier than she'd been in a long time. She shifted to face him. "You egoistical, chauvinistic idiot!"

He narrowed his eyes and sat up in his chair, but before he could respond, she said, "You left me, not because of my losing the baby, but out of some caveman notion that you should have saved *me*? Is that why you left me? You couldn't stand that a woman took a bullet meant for you?"

"No. It's not about you being a woman and me being a man. It's hard to explain. I feel the same way about my dad." Standing, he ran his hands through his hair, setting the chestnut strands standing on end and askew. He paced to the windows and turned with his shoulders drooping like a great weight sat upon them. The pain shining through his eyes had her gasping. "It's because I love you so damn much I'd rather die than see you hurt."

When his words seeped in and their meaning fractured her anger, something warm filled the cold places in her heart. Hadn't she fallen so desperately in love with him because of his compassion for others? Despite the pain in her knee, she tossed the melting bag of peas aside and stood. He stepped forward as if to stop her, but she shook her head and held out her hand to halt him.

Swallowing the sudden lump in her throat, she asked, "Don't you get it? I've always felt that way about you. That's why I had to stop that thug." She put her hands over her flat stomach and closed her eyes against the terrible truth. "I didn't think about our baby in that moment. All I could think about was you." Tears burned her sinuses, and she didn't stop them from flowing. She didn't have the strength in that moment. "I know it's awful, and I know you will probably never forgive me, and there isn't a day that goes by that I don't think about our beautiful baby boy." She opened her eyes and sucked in a breath at finding him standing only inches from her. He laid his hand on her cheek, and she leaned into the warm callused strength of his hardworking palm. "But I couldn't let you be taken from this world, Wyatt." She couldn't manage more than a whisper as she drowned in the fathomless blueness of his eyes. "You're too damned special. I know you're nothing like Jock Blackwell."

He wrapped her up in his arms and kissed her. His soft lips were firm on hers and his tongue demanded entrance. She leaned into him and opened, offering him her total surrender. Clinging to him in a way she never thought she would again, she gave him everything as their tongues danced and teeth nipped.

He broke away panting for air. Before she could catch her own breath, he swung her into his arms.

"Wyatt?"

He searched her eyes, and a small unsure smile touched his lusciously moist lips. "Just let me take care of you for one night. Okay?"

She shivered at the husky quality in his voice and nodded. A few moments later, he laid her down on his bed. Unable to do anything but watch him, he slowly removed her shoes and socks. As he began massaging her aching arches, she leaned back and moaned.

When he stopped, she opened her eyes to him unbuttoning her blouse. The fire in his eyes when they met hers was hot enough to burn her to a crisp, if she hadn't been already a flame with her own desire. She reached for the snaps of his shirt and yanked it open. He shrugged it off as she caressed over the scattering of dark curls covering his chest.

Leaning forward, he set her skin blazing as he kissed and nipped the skin below her ear. She gripped his hair and pulled him from her neck. His gaze swirled with fear of rejection and questions.

She licked lips that still tingled from his kiss earlier. "Make love to me, Wyatt."

A wicked grin lifted one side of his lips, and his eyes darkened to the color of a twilight sky. "It would be my profound pleasure to do so."

She couldn't stop the giggle as he nipped her shoulder and flicked open the front clasp of her bra. The laugh quickly died when he pulled back and touched the pucker above her left breast where the bullet had entered her chest. He leaned over, and above her lips, he whispered, "I forgive you. Now, you need to forgive yourself."

She gasped from the force of those words. "I forgive you. Don't you ever leave me again." Forgiving herself had never occurred to her, but she realized in order to fully heal the emptiness inside, she had to. She caressed his handsome face, the stubble of the dark beard on his cheek enticing her fingers.

The passion of his kiss took her breath away. When they separated, panting from a lack of air, wanting to feel skin on skin, the need to join as one drove them to frantic motions as they got rid of the rest of their clothes.

Once they were both naked, Wyatt took his sweet excruciating time to lavish her feverish skin with caresses, kisses, and nipping. From the healing cut on her forehead, to the scar above her breast, to her sore knee, and every place in between. He spent a long time on her breasts until she arched off the bed and fisted her hands in his hair. She was a trembling mess by the time he skimmed his lips over her tummy. Shifting between her legs, he leaned over her. She was more than ready for him and welcomed him into her as he thrust forward. Closing her eyes and moaning his name, she wrapped her uninjured leg around his hips and her arms around his neck as he filled her.

He buried his face into her neck as a groan escaped from deep inside of him; then he slowly pulled out and thrust in again. "Oh, God, Dawn, I don't know how I've lived without you."

She gasped at the meaning of his words and held him, breathing in his musky, outdoorsy scent. The heat of his body covering her comforted as he moved within her again, and the coil of her climax tightened. So many sensations she'd forgotten built within her as she let her heart soar and break free from the years of doubt and pain.

"Wyatt, I love you!" she screamed when her orgasm hit, taking her to a place she was sure she'd never been.

He moaned deep into her neck as he thrust into her one last time and trembled as she held him.

* * * *

Time stood still as Wyatt let her words and the bliss of his climax flood him. When he found the strength to pull away, he sought her gaze. Had she meant what she said, or were the words something tossed away in the heat of passion?

She gasped as she tried to catch her breath. In her eyes, he saw an opening to her soul he'd never noticed before. Shifting his weight, he leaned over her from the side and brushed his fingers through her long, black hair, spread over his pillow. "Did you really mean that?"

She licked her swollen moist lips and slowly nodded. "I never stopped loving you."

Joy he hadn't let into his heart for a long time filled it to bursting. He smiled and kissed her. As he pulled away, he cupped her face and caressed his thumb over her high blushed cheek. "I never stopped loving you. I tried. But I never quite got you out of my blood."

A beautiful smile curved her swollen lips and lit up her moist eyes. "Where do we go from here?"

He couldn't believe they were having this conversation. "First, we have to catch ourselves a murdering drug dealer, and you have an election to win." He shrugged as the future he'd always dreamed of spread out in front of him like a bright patchwork quilt. "I don't know, maybe then we find out what kind of rancher I am and what kind of rancher's wife you might become."

Her eyes widened as shock replaced her smile. He hoped like hell he hadn't spoken too soon. "Wyatt?" She gasped and laid her hand over her heart. "Are you…"

Clearing his throat, he covered her hand, and it fluttered in his grasp as he squeezed. "Not now, but I hope someday you'll be ready."

She sniffed and a tear escaped the corner of her eye. "Luck would have it I have almost seventeen hundred acres of prime pasture right next door waiting for a rancher to let loose some cattle."

"Do you have a rancher in mind?" Was that hoarse voice his?

Pulling him to her, she whispered before capturing his lips. "Yeah, I do."

Chapter 16

With her elbows planted on the table, Dawn rested her chin on her hands and watched Wyatt make breakfast. He had to be the sexiest man alive while he flipped pancakes and fried bacon. His jeans fit just right, and it wasn't a stretch to remember what that incredible tight ass looked like naked.

Glancing over his shoulder as if he sensed her staring at him, he cocked an eyebrow, and a lopsided grin tilted his lips. "I can almost see the X-rated thoughts in that head of yours."

She laughed and leaned back in her chair. "Guilty as charged. What will you do with me, Lieutenant McPherson?"

He turned away from the stove with two plates in hand, one stacked with steaming golden pancakes and the other heaping with fragrant crispy bacon. As he sat next her, he set the plates on the table. He leaned toward her and kissed her. "Oh, Sheriff Madison, be careful of what you're asking. You might find yourself in trouble."

Before she had a chance to respond, a loud bang sounded from the entry as if something had been thrown at the front door.

"What the hell?" He rushed into the entry, unlocked the door, and threw it open.

Dawn had followed him to the doorway of the kitchen and leaned on the frame. "What happened?"

He ran onto the porch, but no one was there. "I don't know." He picked up a brick with a piece of paper wrapped around it and held it up. "But I think this is what hit the door."

He headed toward her and removed the rubber band and a sheet of copy paper. "Damn."

As she watched his face turn from one of curiosity to anger, her gut tied into knots. "Wyatt?"

He handed her the paper. "You better read this."

The print was typed and in bold. She turned and leaned her backside onto the counter beside the door, taking the weight off her sore knee. "This is your warning, bitch. Drop out of the race for sheriff or the whole world will know you were pregnant and had an abortion while you were in Dallas, and that Wyatt McPherson was the father."

Only her family had known about the baby. Until yesterday, not even her best friend had known she'd once been pregnant. Did Wyatt's family even know? She looked up and swallowed. However, the reactions from his family and their friends didn't scare her, something else did.

Wyatt took her hand and helped her back to her chair. As she dropped into the seat, he kneeled before her. "We both know this isn't true."

"But I was pregnant. I did lose a baby." She stared at the paper in her shaking hand. "If the lawyers for the bastard who shot me find out our past relationship, they could have reason to request a mistrial. It was your testimony that put Eduardo Guerrero behind bars for the duration of his miserable life."

"You can't drop out of the race, Dawn." He took the note from her and tossed it aside, and then he held both of her hands. "First of all, you didn't have an abortion, and there's no proof I fathered the baby." He swallowed and shook his head. "We should come clean with our closest friends and family, but as for the rest, they can go straight to hell."

She nodded as a thought slithered into her mind. "If I drop out of the race, Chet will be uncontested."

He narrowed his eyes. "Why would the killer want Chet to be sheriff?"

"Because Chet is convinced my brother is the suspect and would spend all of his resources trying to prove it, buying the real killer a chance to get away." She closed her eyes as the gravity of everything swamped her. "We have to find the killer before he has a chance to make another move."

Her cell phone ringing startled her. Wyatt handed it to her, and she answered. "Sheriff Madison."

"It's Agent Green," said the male voice of the FBI agent-in-charge also working the case. "We found the truck that stopped at the Quick Fill the morning Larson was killed."

She looked at Wyatt. "Agent Green, I'm going to put you on speaker phone. Lieutenant McPherson is here with me."

As she set the phone on the table and put it on speaker, Wyatt sat in the chair beside her. "Agent, go ahead."

The agent cleared his throat on the other end. "As I was saying, the truck in the surveillance video from the Quick Fill the morning Larson was killed is owned by North-South Transport. When we finally found the truck and stopped it just north of the border, it was filled with textiles from Alvarez *Textil.*"

"Will the driver talk?" Dawn fisted her hand as she remembered her conversation with Wyatt the other night regarding the Mexican textile company owned by relatives of the Cotreras Cartel, one of the biggest drug organizations in Northern Mexico.

"Yeah." The agent chuckled. "He's talking, especially after we found bags of cocaine sown into the shoulder pads of the garments and threatened to charge him with the murder of Christopher Larson."

"What's he saying?" Wyatt leaned over the table as if he was afraid he'd miss what the agent said.

"He pulled up at the Quick Fill to deliver a shipment of coke, when a kid with a switchblade knife attacked him. According to the driver, the kid was demanding more money. The owner of the Quick Fill, Gene Murphy, pulled the kid off him and turned the knife onto the kid, stabbing him in the chest. Murphy and the driver then carried the body behind the Longhorn where y'all found him."

Dawn gasped and stared into Wyatt's wide eyes. Gene Murphy was the killer? When the silence grew too long for the FBI agent waiting on the other end, he said, "You still there?"

Wyatt swallowed and shook his head as if to clear it. "Yeah. It's just a shock that's all. We've known Gene for a long time."

"Keep us posted on the processing of the blood analysis from the Demello scene." She was numb. *Gene* was their killer?

"I've requested a rush on it. But if the kid can ID him, it would be quicker. I'll let you know as soon as I find out something."

"Thanks, Agent Green." She disconnected the call and leaned back in the chair. The air rushed out of her as she closed her eyes. "Well, it all makes sense now. The killer wants Chet to be sheriff because he would never suspect his own brother-in-law."

When she opened her eyes again, Wyatt had his cell phone out. "I think it's time to find out if Tyler Demello is awake yet."

* * * *

"I won't allow it. My son just woke up." Elizabeth Raines crossed her arms before her. "Up until now I've been able to keep his name out of the paper, but it's only a matter of time before someone figures out he wasn't in an accident."

"All you ever think about is yourself." Dr. Tony Demello scowled at his ex-wife. "He's my son as well. Tyler wants to talk to them, and I think it's the right thing to do. The sooner he identifies who did this to him the sooner the authorities can catch the creep."

Dawn bit her tongue to keep from saying the comments running through her mind. The woman was back to her egocentric self. By the eye roll she caught Wyatt trying to hide when he lowered his head, she knew he thought the same thing.

Wyatt shifted his hat in his hands. "Mrs. Raines, we won't be long."

Elizabeth looked from Wyatt to Dawn. "All right, but you only have five minutes."

The nurse let them into the room after Dr. Demello instructed her to do so. The FBI guard nodded in silent salute as they passed by and entered the door.

The dim room smelled of antiseptic, and the beat of a heart monitor provided a constant reminder of how close this boy came to losing his life. Dawn limped over to sit on the stool next to the bed.

Tyler watched her. "What happened to you?"

She smiled and shrugged. "You and I have something in common, I guess. The bad guy wants us dead."

He glanced at Wyatt as he stood behind her and licked his dry lips. "I guess I'm lucky to be alive."

"You could say that." Wyatt's deep voice trembled through her. "Tyler, do you know who did this to you?"

He closed his eyes and slowly nodded. "I don't know his name, but I recognized him before he stabbed me."

She looked over her shoulder at Wyatt. Excitement bubbled up at the prospect of finally having enough evidence to arrest the killer. She pulled out a photo of Gene Murphy. "Is this the man who stabbed you?"

He squinted at the photo and nodded his head. "That's the guy who runs the gas station in town. Yeah, he's the one."

Dawn's heart stopped as the implication settled on her. "Are you sure?"

Tyler shifted a shoulder under his green hospital gown. "Yeah, I'm sure."

She stood with help from Wyatt's hand on her elbow. "Thank you, Tyler."

Before they could rush out of the room, his weak voice stopped them. "But there was another guy there too. A sheriff's deputy."

Dawn was happy Wyatt was still holding onto her. The betrayal that someone in her department was a dirty cop shook her to the core. Killing kids was one horrible thing, but they had also murdered one of her best deputies. How someone could get that close to Doug and put a bullet in his chest now made sense. Doug had known his killer just as they had suspected. "Do you know who the deputy is?"

He nodded again and swallowed. "Deputy Hendricks."

They rushed out of the hospital as Wyatt called the Texas Rangers and she called Tilly. "Tilly, Demello woke up and told us who stabbed him. Keep everyone there and sitting tight. I'll be in as soon as I can."

"Who?" His voice shook with the question. He wanted these bastards off the street as much as she did, especially after they killed Doug, who Tilly had taken under his wing when the kid first started on the force. She couldn't trust Tilly not to do something stupid, like going after Chet or Gene alone. That could end up getting him killed.

"I'll tell you when I get there." She glanced at Wyatt as they rounded his truck to get in. "It's probably best if we keep this on the down low. I don't want anyone else to know Demello woke up. Got it?"

She heard him swallowing and could imagine the older man nodding, despite her not being able to see him. "Tilly?"

"Yeah, got it."

Dawn opened her door and climbed in. "Dawn, you and Wyatt be careful."

"You bet."

Wyatt jumped in behind the wheel and turned the key in the ignition. "My captain will notify the FBI and send backup."

He backed out of the space in the parking garage. She gripped her phone in her sweaty palm as they stopped at the intersection onto the busy Dallas street. "I can't believe this, can you?" She met his gaze as they waited for the green. "Chet has always been a bully, but God... A killer? Gene wasn't born in Colton, but he's been a pillar of the community since marrying Chet's sister and buying the Quick Fill."

Wyatt rubbed his jaw and shook his head. "Who would have pegged Leon Ferguson as a fraud and a killer, or Jake and Brent Parker as cattle and horse thieves?" The light turned, and he rushed out onto the street. "Just shows you really never can know."

She rested her head on the back of the seat, sudden exhaustion threatening to drag her under. "It means you can't trust anyone."

"That too."

* * * *

Chet sat down in the old worn leather chair at his desk and tossed his traffic book on top of the clutter of reports and campaign posters he'd hoped to post around town. He had to get rid of Demello before the kid woke up and talked. Hell, maybe Dawn and McPherson were already speaking to him. Wyatt had passed by Chet hiding out in his favorite spot for catching speeders on Highway Six not long after he'd thrown the brick at his house. At the time, Chet had wondered if he'd been spotted when he'd run into the stretch of woods between Wyatt's ranch and the Quinn's place.

He'd done some research on the date stamped on the sonogram photo he'd seen at Madison's house. It had been taken the day Dawn was shot in a drug bust gone bad. He'd also learned McPherson had killed the shooter's lieutenant, and his testimony put the other thug in prison for life.

It didn't take too much to figure out those two had probably been fuck-buddies. He didn't care. He had every intention of using that piece of information to his advantage.

When he heard Tilly at his desk, muttering something to himself, he narrowed his eyes on the old geezer. What was he mumbling about? "Hey, have you heard from the sheriff?

Tilly glanced at him. "Yeah. I hung up with her a moment ago. I just can't believe what she said."

He had to know what rattled Tilly so badly. "You okay, old man?"

Tilly shook his head and leaned over his desk. "Demello woke up and told Dawn and Wyatt who stabbed him."

Fuck! He cleared his throat and hoped like hell his voice came out normal. "Good. Do we know who?"

Tilly shook his head as if to clear it. "Dawn wouldn't tell me. Said she and Wyatt were coming here."

Chet had to get out of here and warn Gene. The idiot. If he'd listened to Chet from the get-go, they'd be kingpins in drug trafficking between the Cotreras Cartel in Mexico and Dallas. His plan was for Gene to buy a small trucking company and run the drugs. That hadn't been good enough for Gene. He wanted to go bigger, or so he thought. Gene had contacted an old college buddy, Lester Gilman, and bought into his trucking company, North-South Transport.

They still had to figure out a way to keep the law off their asses, and the solution seemed to offer itself up on a platter when Zack Cartwright resigned as sheriff. Gene had assured him there'd be no way in hell the town council and mayor would appoint Dawn Madison as sheriff, despite her being Cartwright's lieutenant. After all, Chet was the most logical choice, and if they went with seniority, Tilly Kennedy was an old fool with only two more years until retirement. Chet wasn't as sure as Gene. Everyone knew the damned Cartwrights owned this town, and they'd always looked out for those fucking Indian bastards.

However, Dawn's appointment hadn't been the only problem. When the kids they'd enlisted to deal the drugs started wanting more money and making demands, Gene insisted they had to die. Chet should have offed the dickhead before he had the chance to kill Christopher Larson. Hell, he should have gotten rid of him long before Larson had a chance to figure out the North-South truck that always stopped at the Quick Fill every Monday morning at four AM was their drug supplier. Now Chet had to save the idiot's ass.

Tilly said something, and he tuned into his ramblings. What did Tilly know? "…we're to stay here. I think they're going after whoever it is."

"If she knows who, surely she and Wyatt don't think they can take them down by themselves." Chet cleared his throat.

Tilly took a deep breath. "I don't think they will. Remember how they called the FBI in to watch Demello? I'm sure that's who'll respond. But I don't get why she wouldn't want us there."

He didn't give a rat's ass about the why of it or about the genuine hurt in Kennedy's voice. Standing, he grabbed his campaign posters. "I'm sure she has her reasons. I'm taking off for lunch. See you later."

Tilly shook his head. "She told me to make sure everyone stays put."

I'm sure she did. "I'll be back before she gets here. I'm starving, and I didn't bring anything. Want me to bring you something back?"

Tilly shook his head again and leaned over his desk.

Chet had no intention of ever stepping foot in the station again. As he left by the back door, he took a deep breath to slow his pounding heart. He needed another hit of coke, but there wasn't time for one. All of his careful planning was flying out the window. Damn that Indian bitch. If it was the last thing he did, he hoped to put a bullet in her head.

Chapter 17

Talon glanced at the little girl sleeping in the car seat beside him and put the old Dodge into park next to the gas pumps at the Quick Fill. He opened the door and climbed out.

As he filled the tank with unleaded, he checked his messages. The contractor he'd met with the other day was supposed to get back to him with an estimate. When he came across an unfamiliar number, he hit the play button.

Maggie's voice grated over the line. The usual bitter anger he choked on when he thought of the mother of his daughter bubbled in his gut. She and the loser she was dating had gotten married before they left Vegas to meet up with the cruise ship they were going to be working on in Las Angeles. He was about to hit delete when she said, "Keep a look out for papers from a lawyer. I met with one and had custody papers drawn up. We've decided we want our own family someday, and well, Alonzo never took much liking to Jessie Mae. Tell her goodbye for me."

The click on the other end jolted him. As the meaning seeped into him, and the words she hadn't said echoed in his brain, the old rusty knife he'd always associated with his father twisted in his heart. He glanced at the sleeping angel inside the old beat-up truck. Jessie Mae was her father's daughter.

The pump snapped off drawing him out of his thoughts. As he put the nozzle back into the bracket, he snagged his wallet out of his back pocket. With one more look at Jessie, he started around the front of his truck to go in and pay for the gas.

A black pickup truck turned into the parking lot, and his sister and Wyatt jumped out. Wyatt jogged over to him with a fearsome scowl on his face. Talon spread his feet and balled his fists. What had he done now?

"Get the hell out of here."

Wyatt's words had him blinking. "I have to pay for my gas."

"Not today." His old friend shook his head, and Talon followed Wyatt's glace to Dawn who stayed by the truck with the door open. She was down in a defensive pose, and he'd bet his next meal she had her gun out.

Talon may not have been the smartest man in town, but it didn't take him long to figure out what was going down. "Holy shit. Gene?"

"Yep, now get the hell out of here."

A shot shattered the plate glass window at the front of the store. Wyatt and Talon both hit the pavement at the same time. Jessie woke up screaming when another shot rang out and hit the side of Talon's truck above his head. His heart raced when he thought of Jessie being in possible danger, but he wasn't able to move.

Two more shots rang out, and he realized Dawn and Wyatt had fired this time. Wyatt got up on his haunches and yelled at Talon, "Go! We'll cover you."

Two shots came from the Quick Fill, which Wyatt and Dawn answered with rounds into the building as several other cars screeched to a stop in the parking lot with blue lights flashing. Talon scurried onto his feet and bent low as he rushed around the front of the truck. He jerked the door open and jumped in. Staying low, he cranked the key and hit the gas. The old Dodge tore out of the parking lot between two FBI cars and headed down Main Street.

Jessie's cry rang out with fear and pain.

He glanced at her. She had a death grip on her stuffed bear and looked toward the downed window. "It's okay, Jessie. It's only loud noise. It's gonna be okay."

The booming and popping of gunfire from the Quick Fill sounded through the open window, and Talon hit the button to roll it up, hoping to shut some of the noise out, but the passenger side wouldn't budge.

An FBI car had the street blocked at the corner, and he hit the brakes. An agent pointed her gun at him as she approached the passenger side and open window of his rig. "Stay in the truck and keep your hands where I can see them."

Talon put his hands in the air. "I'm just trying to get away. I was at the station getting gas. My sister is the sheriff."

She came up to the open passenger side window and looked at Jessie Mae, who'd been crying since the first shot rang out. "The kid's been shot."

What? He glanced at his little girl. She hugged Bear-boo in a death grip with her left arm. His heart stopped when he shifted the raggedy stuffed bear she carried everywhere to get a good look. Blood covered her arm and entire right side. "Oh, God!"

He leaned over to find where the blood came from. She'd been hit in the upper right arm, not far from the greenish bruise left when her mother's high heel had kicked into her. A large hole in the side panel triggered a memory of the shot hissing above his head and hitting the truck. The bullet must have come from a powerful enough rifle to drill through the steel and glass of the downed window, hitting Jessie's arm right above her elbow.

The agent put her gun away and spoke into a radio she must have had attached to her jacket. "Control, this is Agent Carson. I need an ambulance stat. We have a civilian child shot in the right arm. Bleeding uncontrolled."

Jessie met his gaze, her eyes glassy with pain and blood loss.

"Hold on, Jessie Mae. Help's on the way." His voice cracked and his heart ached. How could he have been so stupid to think the noise was the only thing causing her to cry? Why hadn't he realized she was in pain? What kind of father did that make him?

"Daddy, it hurts." She held out her blood-covered Bear-Boo to him and closed her eyes.

"Jessie!" Oh, God, no! She couldn't die. Not now that he'd found her. His stomach flopped at the sight of her arm hanging lip. From the look of it, the bullet severed her tiny bone. He ripped at his T-shirt and pulled the bottom off to make a rag, then pressed it to the bloody wound on her right arm.

The officer touched Jessie's throat as if checking for a pulse. She closed her eyes for a moment and nodded. "She passed out. Probably from the pain and loss of blood."

He looked at the woman through clouded eyes. "She can't die."

She rested her hand over his where he held the strip of cloth over the wound on Jessie's arm and gave it a squeeze. "She won't."

An eternity passed before an ambulance with a siren blaring skidded to a stop behind the FBI car, and two EMTs hopped out.

He had to believe her.

* * * *

The FBI agents they had been speaking with since leaving Dallas pulled in off Main Street, and a moment later, Talon's truck sped away, throwing up dust as it headed down the street.

She peered through the crack between the door and the frame to aim, and caught a glimpse of a figure moving between the shelving units inside the store. As recognition smacked into her, she gasped. She shook herself, as if to rattle the shock from her head, and fired. Chet Hendricks ducked behind a shelf holding potato chips, and her bullet hit it instead, sending flying bits from the bags.

Wyatt moved around the back of the truck to crouch behind her. "We have to end this before someone hits one of those gas pumps and blows us all to kingdom come."

She released the empty magazine from her gun and quickly inserted a full one. "Chet's in there."

Wyatt scowled. "Fucking figures. Nothing worse than a bad cop."

"Especially an arrogant killer."

She looked at the building, then glanced around. An old weathered lattice fence ran the length of the boundary between the Quick Fill and the property beside it. In the spring and summer, violet, fuchsia, and periwinkle-blue morning glories climbed the fence with an explosion of color from sunrise to noon. But now, the fence stood empty and dreary as it waited for winter. "I think I know how to get us inside."

He narrowed his eyes and rested his hand on her shoulder. "You aren't going anywhere near that building. For one thing, you can barely walk, and for the second, I need you to distract them."

As much as she hated admitting he was right, she nodded. Her knee hurt too much from crouching, if she had to do something fast or fancy, she'd be screwed.

"Okay." She ignored his raised brows at her easy agreement and pointed toward the side of the building. "I know there's a window on the side where Gene's office is. If you go back to the street and sneak along that fence on the other side, you can break through it and get inside using the window."

He reached around inside the truck and pulled out a Glock from the glove box. After checking the magazine to make sure it was full, he gripped it in his left hand and his Colt in the right.

He was sexy as sin when he looked like an old-time cowboy lawman. "Be careful in there."

He smiled and kissed her quick and sure. "Always. You keep shooting and make sure they don't know the cavalry's coming."

She focused on firing into the windows as did the three FBI agents.

Agent Mike Green, the agent-in-charge that she and Wyatt had been working with, knelt behind her, and she glanced back. He smiled and nodded. "What can you tell me about this place? I have two agents at the back door, but they're taking shots and can't get close."

"One of the shooters is a deputy sheriff." The thought of Chet being a dirty cop didn't so much surprise her as it made her angry that she hadn't seen through him. "We can assume the other one is his brother-in-law, Gene Murphy." She pointed toward the side of the building where she glimpsed Wyatt kicking at the fence. "Lieutenant McPherson is going to break through on the side. There's an office window there. Our job is to keep the two shooters as busy as possible so they don't notice him."

The agent nodded and touched the radio clipped to his jacket collar. "Villalobes. Come in."

"Villalobes here." A Hispanic accented male voice sounded over Green's radio.

Green sent out orders to keep the backdoor under fire as an ambulance siren sounded down the block. She furrowed her brow and looked back at Green.

He must have read her unspoken question because he said, "Agent Carson called an ambulance for the child in the truck that tore out of here when we arrived."

"The child?" Her heart fell into her stomach.

"Yeah, the kid was hit." Before Dawn had a chance to say a word, the agent backed away and fired a shot at the blown out hole where the window had been.

She closed her eyes and sucked in an unsteady breath. *No, God, please not Jessie Mae. Not another child lost to drugs.*

* * * *

Wyatt tucked the Glock into his waistband at his back and stuffed the Colt back into his shoulder holster when he came to the place in the fence outside of the window. Rot made the old lattice weak, and a few well-placed kicks made a hole big enough for him to get through. A Dumpster set to the right blocked him from the view of the two FBI agents shooting it up back there. They took return fire regularly as Gene Murphy shouted out jeers regarding the agents' marksmanship.

He studied the window, which thankfully was low enough to the ground that he could climb through, but it wasn't much bigger than two feet by three feet. How the hell was he going to fit through that thing? Without thinking too much about it, he pulled out his pocketknife and cut open the wire screen. After tossing it aside and putting the knife away, he tugged on the bottom sash. It lifted easily enough.

Removing his hat and dropping it to the dirty pavement, he sighed and shook his head. He hoped he didn't get stuck in the thing. Wouldn't that look good on his official record? "Here goes nothing," he muttered to himself and lifted his leg over the sill.

With a silent curse, he slithered into the hole, and swore again when his vest hung up on the edge. He wiggled a bit and got the rest of his body through the hole. Crouching in the dim office behind the desk, he palmed his Glock in one hand and Colt in the other, while he concentrated on the sounds of gunfire. At the door of the office, he peeked out. Gene pointed a military grade, illegal, automatic rifle over the top of an overturned candy display and fired out the back door.

Wyatt had to find Chet for his plan to work. From behind the counter, Chet fired another assault rifle through the front window on the opposite side of the room from Wyatt. He ducked behind the door and took a deep breath. Gene was a clean shot, but Chet would prove trickier since he could take cover behind the counter.

Who should he take out first? If he shot Chet first, Gene could get a clear shot at him. If he shot Gene, Chet could duck under the counter.

Wyatt closed his eyes and breathed in, trying to slow his racing heart. The best answer was to shoot them both at the same time. He didn't want to kill either one of them, but he had to put a stop to this shootout.

He opened his eyes, looked down at his guns, and whispered, "This is for you, son. Two more drug dealers off the street."

With one more long, deep breath, he stood in the doorway and aimed his left handed Glock at Chet and his right handed Colt at Gene, then fired.

* * * *

From inside the store, Dawn heard the double shots ring out. She held her breath as the gunfire stopped coming at them. Had Wyatt succeeded?

She stood up letting out the breath she was holding when Wyatt waved a newspaper around the frame of the shattered glass door. She looked back at the FBI agents. "Cease fire!"

Agent Green got on his radio and called out to the agents in back.

As she moved around the door of Wyatt's truck, her sinuses burned with the horror that Talon's baby girl had been shot, as well as with the joy of seeing the man she loved still standing and appearing to be unharmed. Ignoring the pain in her knee, she took off toward him in a limping run. She didn't care that the FBI agents would see her or anyone else for that matter.

Wyatt tucked his guns away and held his arms open to accept her as she landed in them. She held onto him with her Glock still in her hand as he kissed her.

"I'm so glad you're okay," he whispered before letting her go.

Movement inside the store caught her attention. Chet stood at the window with blood streaming from a shoulder wound. Wyatt had shot the bastard, but not incapacitated him. Without a thought, she pushed Wyatt to the side and fired. The answering shot from Chet went wild, hitting the side of one of the FBI cars.

Chet laid half way through the window with a bullet hole in the head and another in his shoulder where Wyatt had hit him. The FBI agents stormed the store and soon announced Gene was alive, but shot in the back and barely breathing.

Wyatt regained his balance and stared at her. She couldn't stop the tears. "I will always have your back, Wyatt. So, you better get used to it."

He shook his head and took her into his arms again. "As long as you let me get yours from time to time."

Then he captured her lips and kissed her so hard her toes curled inside her boots.

* * * *

Holding hands tightly as if they both needed a lifeline, Dawn and Wyatt rushed into the waiting room of the Forest County General Hospital. Her heart ached when she spotted her brother staring out the window, and her parents huddled together against the back wall.

She let go of Wyatt's hand and limped as fast as she could to her brother's side. He flinched when she laid her hand on his arm. The muscle under his tanned skin bunched and released. She held on as he turned his pain-riddled hazel eyes on her.

"How is she?"

"She's in surgery. The doc isn't sure they can save her arm."

Dawn swallowed at the painful lump forming in her throat and the burn in her sinuses. "I'm so sorry, Talon."

He nodded and looked back out the window. "You know her mother probably wouldn't care if her baby died. She called me earlier to tell me she's signing over full custody." He glanced at her again and shoved his hands into the pockets of his jeans. "But you know what. I love that little angel enough for both of us." His voice broke, and he turned away again to swipe at his nose with the back of his hand.

Dawn wrapped her arm around his waist and held him. "She's strong like her daddy. She'll get through this. We all will."

He sniffed again, but his eyes were dry and burned with anger. "Did you get the bastards?"

She looked over her shoulder and met Wyatt's gaze as he rested a hand on Talon's shoulder. It wasn't just for Talon's little girl or the three teenagers victimized by Chet Hendricks and Gene Murphy. They'd exacted revenge for their own loss, and for the first time in years, Dawn knew their baby had peace. They'd found peace.

"We did." Wyatt touched her cheek. "They're both dead."

Epilogue

Two months later.

Dawn brushed her long black hair in the rhythmic motions that would make the stuff shine, and closed her eyes. She still had to get dressed, but had time. Despite the excitement bubbling through her, she didn't want to rush her last moments alone.

She didn't regret not telling her parents or friends why she and Wyatt came to Cabo San Lucas, Mexico, for Christmas. They'd told them they needed to get away for a little while after everything that had happened, and no one questioned them.

Following the shooting at the Quick Fill, and the routine internal affairs investigation that occurred when a cop killed someone, Wyatt resigned from the Texas Rangers to become the rancher he'd always wanted to be. She'd won the election for sheriff, and loved keeping Forest County safe.

Jessie Mae would be in rehab for months, learning how to function without most of her right arm. But if any good came from the shooting, it seems the little girl found a friend in Rachel McPherson. And from the way her brother looked at her soon-to-be sister-in-law, Dawn had a good feeling about how things might turn out.

At a soft knock on the door, she opened her eyes and set down the brush. "Yes?"

"Dawn, you have about thirty minutes before we have to go."

She smiled at the sound of Wyatt's deep voice. Would she ever tire of it? "I'll meet you on the beach."

"I can't wait."

Standing, she reached for the simple white sundress she'd chosen to wear today. After pulling it on, she tied a blue and white beaded wedding belt around her waist. The intricate belt had been in her mother's family for at least six generations, and had been worn last by her cousin Jessica in Oklahoma when she married five years ago. Tracking the darned thing down without her mother's knowledge hadn't been easy.

With a quick glance in the mirror, Dawn smiled at her appearance. She'd never been a girly girl, but she liked being a woman, and today of all days, she was thrilled to be one.

She left the cabin and walked barefoot to the beach. The resort and the place she and Wyatt had chosen for their exchange of vows were located on the southern most point of the Baja California Peninsula.

The descending sun set the ocean and cloudless sky aflame with oranges, reds, and deep purples. Salt and an abundance of fragrant flowers--jasmine, gardenia, and a dozen more--perfumed the warm humid air. Christmas lights twinkled in the palm trees planted along the path, reminding her today wasn't just the eve of her new life, but also Christmas Eve. She paused on the stone path to take it all in. Wyatt waited for her at the bottom of the slope, smiling up at her.

He was dressed in black jeans rolled up above his bare ankles and a white shirt open at the collar to show off the top of his chest. If the jeans weren't enough to peg him as a cowboy, the cream-colored Resistol sitting on his reddish brown hair would do the trick. She returned his grin and hurried down the path.

"Dear God in heaven, you are a vision," he whispered as he held out his hand to her.

Heat rushed to her cheeks. How could he still make her blush after all these years? "Well, cowboy, you aren't too bad yourself."

Wyatt chuckled and kissed her fingers. "C'mon. We don't want to miss the sunset."

He led her to the edge of the white sand where the warm tropical ocean licked their toes. The justice who would marry them, his wife, and daughter were the only other people on the private stretch of shore.

Despite missing her family, she was happy Wyatt talked her into eloping. They planned to throw a big party back at the ranch in the spring and have her mother's brother perform the traditional Cherokee blessing, but it had always been Wyatt's dream to get married on the beach in Mexico.

In broken English, the justice read from the vows they had chosen. "Do you, Wyatt, take Dawn to be your wife? Do you promise to love and protect her as long as you both live?"

Wyatt lifted his hand to brush the loose strands of hair from her face that a soft breeze had sent fluttering. "I do."

"Do you, Dawn, take Wyatt to be your husband? Do you promise to love and protect him as long as you both live?"

She sniffed and tears leaked from the corner of her eyes. He feathered his thumb over the moisture, wiping it away. "I do."

"By the authority granted to me, I now pronounce you husband and wife." The women clapped, and the justice laughed. "You kiss your bride, *amigo*."

Wyatt pulled her into his arms, but she touched his lips before they could land on hers. Surprise widened his eyes and tugged his lips into a playful smirk.

"There's something I want to tell you first." She backed out of his embrace and took his hands, laying them over her abdomen. His expression turned to one of awe as understanding dawned on him. "I'm pregnant."

He laughed and pulled her to him, lifting her off the sand, then swung her around. "I don't know how this day could become more perfect." When he stopped, he let her body slide down his until her feet were once again touching the water and sand. "You've made all my dreams come true."

She wrapped her arms around his neck and smiled. "I think we've made each other's dreams come true."

He leaned in and captured her lips in a kiss full of promise as the sun slipped over the horizon.

Meet the Author

Although Sara Walter Ellwood has long ago left the farm for the glamour of the big town, she draws on her experiences growing up on a small hobby farm in West Central Pennsylvania to write her contemporary westerns. She's been married to her college sweetheart for over 20 years, and they have two teenagers and one very spoiled rescue cat named Penny. She longs to visit the places she writes about and jokes she's a cowgirl at heart stuck in Pennsylvania suburbia. Sara Walter Ellwood is a multi-published author and publishes paranormal romantic suspense under the pen name Cera duBois.

Turn the page for a special excerpt of Sara Walter Ellwood's

Heartstrings

He's determined to set things right, no matter the cost.

The last person Abby Crawford wants to face down is country music superstar Seth Kendall. Last time she did, she flat-out lied so he'd go to Nashville without her. She's never understood why their mutual best friend proposed, but she went with it so her baby wouldn't be fatherless. Now she's a divorced mother of a teenager, and secretly Seth's biggest fan.

Seth is home in McAllister, Texas for his father's funeral…and a chance to meet the daughter he's never known. He's willing to face the music of his own making and admit he's known about his little girl all along. For fifteen years he's kept his distance because Abby told him to follow his dreams without her, insisting she didn't love him. But now he won't leave until he knows his daughter and she knows him, even if it means facing the woman who broke his heart for good.

Confessing she's lied about her daughter's paternity all these years won't be easy for Abby, especially with her ex blackmailing her to keep the secret. And Seth doesn't know the hardest truth of all: Every love song he plays on his guitar still plucks her heartstrings.

On sale now!

Chapter 1

Seth Kendall parked his Escalade and stared out at the people who had known him all his life. What the hell was he doing here?

With a sigh, he opened the door, and all eyes turned in his direction as he got out. Why hadn't he stayed in Nashville as everyone assumed he would? Why did coming back here seem so important now, after being away for fourteen years?

The answers to those questions had plagued him the entire drive to his hometown of McAllister in the Texas Panhandle. The motivation wasn't his father's death at all. He'd come home because it was time for him to make things right, even if that meant causing a whole mess of hell to get it done.

He shrugged into his jacket. If it had been made of solid iron, it wouldn't have felt any heavier. The mid-August day was hot, but the sweat gathering under his Hugo Boss suit didn't come from the afternoon sun. People watched him all the time. That came with the fame he'd garnered as a country music superstar, but today, he didn't want to be gawked at. He adjusted the knot of his necktie and closed the door of the SUV.

He tipped his hat and nodded toward his father's friends and business associates as he headed toward the old church. None of the mourners spoke to him, but he could imagine what they were thinking. Everyone knew he and his father had despised each other.

Decorum required he remove his Ray-Bans and black Stetson as he entered the church, but he forced his expression to remain impassive. He combed his fingers through his hair and looked around. People chose seats, gradually filling the oak pews, and the low murmur of conversation mingled with the bagpipes playing a mournful rendition of his father's favorite hymn, *Amazing Grace*. He recognized almost everyone as he made his way to the front.

"Aunt Johanna." He stopped where his father's twin sister and the minister were speaking in hushed tones next to the open casket.

Johanna Kendall looked up at him with blue eyes reminding him of his father's. Dressed in a severe black dress and with her graying red hair pulled into a bun, she stepped forward and wrapped him in a hug. "Seth, I'm glad you finally made it home."

He held on for a moment before letting go. He'd come home for her. "How are you holding up?"

She shrugged and her eyes filled with misty sadness. "I'll be okay." Johanna used a white lace handkerchief to dab at her red-rimmed eyes. "I'll miss him. I never realized his heart was so bad. He always seemed as strong as a bull."

"We may not have seen eye to eye, but he was still my father." Hugging his aunt again, he held her and looked anywhere but at the man lying on the white satin inside the casket. He glanced at the pew behind him. As he sucked in a deep breath, he stepped away from Johanna and dropped his hat onto the seat.

Johanna moved away to speak with Glenda Marshall, the mayor's wife.

Seth held out his hand to the minister. "Reverend Keller."

"It's a shame you were unable to get away from your engagements to come home sooner. How're you doin', Seth?"

"I'm as good as can be expected, I guess." He shook the preacher's hand, then shoved both of his hands into his pants pockets. "I'm glad he didn't suffer." He didn't know what else to say.

He'd been in the recording studio when Johanna had frantically called him three days ago after she'd found John dead on the floor of his study. Unsure if he'd come home for the funeral or not, he finished the last songs for his next album, set for release in the spring. Now he wished he hadn't rushed to get the damned record done. At least then, he'd have had an excuse to escape as soon as this day was over.

Which was complete bullshit. He wasn't leaving here until he settled a score.

A heavy hand touched his shoulder. He turned to look into the rich brown eyes of one of his father's closest friends, and a man for whom he held a great deal of respect. He stuck out his hand and greeted the older man with a warm smile. "Judge Ritter, it's great to see you again."

Retired county judge Franklin Michael Ritter II smiled and shook his hand. He'd always reminded Seth a little of Mark Twain--tall and lanky with white wavy hair and a handlebar mustache. "It's nice to see you, too.

Though, I'd have preferred different circumstances. It's been a long time, son."

He didn't miss the quiet censure in the judge's tone. Or the way the man seemed to shake all over. His Parkinson's must have gotten worse.

"Oh, Seth, I'm so glad you made it home," an extremely petite woman said in a soft Georgia accent, and Seth found himself being hugged tightly around the waist. He returned Carolann Ritter's embrace, holding on for a moment. In so many ways, she'd replaced the mother he'd lost to a drug overdose. "We sorely did miss you over the years."

He forced a smile as she stepped away. Guilt needled him when tears shimmered in her brown eyes. Carolann and Frank had never made it a secret they loved him when he was a kid. Lord knew he never heard those words from his old man.

"Aw, Miz Ritter, I've missed y'all, too."

When a woman slowly moved in next to Carolann and Frank Ritter, his heart constricted. He forced the name through his tightening jaw. "Abigail."

"Hello, Seth." Dressed in a simple navy blue dress, Abigail Crawford Ritter stopped before him. She stared up at him with widened almond-shaped eyes the color of brandy. The naturally tan complexion she'd inherited from her Native American mother went pale and taut over her high cheekbones. She fiddled with the purse strap over her shoulder and pulled her long dark brown hair over her other shoulder. "We didn't think you'd be here."

He easily discerned the real meaning: *We don't want you here.*

The past slammed into him with blazing force, transporting him back to the manmade beach of the McAllister Reservoir. Returning him to the night he and Abby let their attraction turn into uncontrolled lust, and under the stars on a deserted stretch of weedy sand, she'd given him her virginity.

"Uh...I wasn't sure...I would be," he stammered and tried to shake off the memory of a passion he hadn't been able to forget. He forced himself to look beyond her.

"Sorry about your father." Mike Ritter stepped forward. His brown eyes were as hard as the bricks making up the walls of the church. Not quite reaching six feet, Mike was four inches shorter, and lanky like Frank. Mike was dressed in a suit as expensive as Seth's, if not more so. Since when was the county paying its sheriff enough for him to afford an Armani suit and snakeskin boots? Not to mention the Resistol hat in his hand.

Then Seth noticed the obviously pregnant brunette holding Mike's hand. An heiress to a fortune made from the railroad, oil and banking. "Tammy Jo McAllister?"

She smiled and slipped her arm around Mike's waist, while she rested her other hand on her baby bump. The gray dress she wore had *designer* written all over it. She must still have more money than King Midas and spent it like there was no tomorrow. "Hello, Seth. I'm now Tammy Jo Ritter."

An icy weight settled in his gut as he looked at Abby. She averted her eyes to the floor. "Mike and I were divorced two years ago."

The weight grew larger and radiated into his arms and legs. He couldn't keep coldness from leaking into his words. "Well, isn't that interesting? How's Emily?"

Abby's face lost all color as she looked at Frank and Carolann. Damn, they'd never learned the truth.

Mike's voice held an unmistakable warning not to push the issue. "Thanks for asking. She's fine."

He met Mike's glare with one of his own.

"I think we should sit down," she said in shaky voice before he could respond.

He snapped his gaze to Abby. Her eyes blazed with anger. She clenched her hands so tightly her knuckles bleached white against the dark blue of her skirt.

"I didn't realize you knew our granddaughter," Frank said without the least bit of curiosity. He obviously didn't catch any of the byplay.

I should know her. He'd keep up Abby's charade. For now.

"He met her at a concert in Amarillo." Mike's tone left no room for discussion on the blatant lie. "I think we should catch up on old times. After the service."

Seth glanced away from the cold eyes of the man who'd been his best friend growing up. Abby's dark eyes held no welcome either, which was a sucker punch in the gut. He wanted to see fire in Abby's brown eyes, but not from hatred.

"Yeah." He mentally shook himself. What was he thinking? She'd betrayed him. He looked back at Mike. "I think it's time to talk about those old times."

* * * *

Abby had feared this encounter since the moment her mother-in-law had called her with the news of John Kendall's death. She took her seat behind the Ritters and fisted her hands in her lap.

Mike had promised this day would never come, but she knew it would. How could she have been so stupid? She opened her hands, and cooling air hit the fine sheen of moisture coating her palms. Cold perspiration beaded on her forehead, and she resisted the urge to wipe it away. She had to control her emotions. If she wasn't careful, someone would notice her anxiety.

Mike glanced over his shoulder at her. He'd always been the solid one, her rock. He grounded her while Seth had been her dream. Her flight of fantasy. The one thing she could never really hold. Even now, even after their sham of a marriage had long ago dissolved into nothing but friendship, she had faith Mike would make everything all right.

Mike had stood by her when Seth left town to chase his dreams in Nashville. Seth had promised her he'd come home, he'd always be here for her, but he hadn't stuck around. He'd left and never came back.

Tammy Jo leaned against Mike's shoulder, and he shifted his focus to his new wife, wrapping his arm around her shoulders.

As Revered Keller began speaking about the kind of man her neighbor had been in life, she sensed Seth's attention on her and couldn't concentrate on anything the pastor said regarding John Kendall. Halfway through the service, she dared to look across the aisle at Seth. His gaze seemed to bore into hers, and the bitterness in the green depths of his eyes seared deep into her soul.

There had been a time when she was his second-best friend. She knew his secrets, and he knew hers, even things Mike hadn't known about them. She'd believed in Seth's dreams, had encouraged them when his father degraded and beat him for having them. In return, Seth had always been there for her when she'd needed someone to take her away from the reality of her life of living down her parents' sins.

She'd fallen in love with Seth, but she knew they had no future. Maybe if he hadn't wanted fame and fortune, they could have found a way to a happily-ever-after. Keeping him here would have destroyed him. And if she'd gone with him, it would have ruined them both. When Seth won a place on the new talent show *America's Rising Star*, she'd had to let him go--even if it meant lying to him to make him leave. But the passion they'd shared had haunted her ever since.

At the service's end, she met Seth's gaze across the aisle again. He had no intention of letting her forget what happened after that night on the beach when everything changed.

* * * *

The service had been typical and, thankfully, neither Johanna nor anyone else seemed to expect Seth to stand and give a eulogy, or worse, sing. He followed the hearse outside town to the Kendall family plot in a small grove of live oaks on the Double K Ranch where five generations of Kendalls were buried.

He had to talk to Abby. He wasn't the same boy who'd left her standing on her front porch the night he'd left town. But one thing hadn't changed; he'd never forgiven her for what she'd done after that night.

He got out of his SUV, went around, and opened the passenger door for Johanna. She leaned on him to help her out of the high vehicle, then they moved to stand beside the grave.

The scene of the pallbearers unloading his father's casket from the back of the hearse overshadowed his need to confront Abby. The oppressive midday sun beat down on him and glistened off the gray granite of the tombstone marking the grave where his father would be laid to rest. His gaze fell on the name of the woman he barely remembered.

Suzann Harris Kendall, born May 14, 1960, died July 28, 1983. May her voice charm the angels of heaven.

His mother. Dead at age twenty-three. He recalled that day almost thirty years ago when he'd stood here with his father and family. That day he'd wondered if his mother would hate him from heaven for ruining her life by simply being born.

It was a question he still wondered about.

A heavy lump settled in the pit of his stomach.

Dad, will you hate me in death for doing what you denied of my mother? For having dreams that didn't include you and making them come true?

He and his father hadn't had a relationship since he was about ten years old, when John had beat him for sneaking into the barn to play his mother's old guitar. But before then, his dad had been everything to him.

The first wave of regret hit him hard as memories of his early childhood fluttered to the surface, such as the Christmas when he was five and his father had given him his first fishing rod.

"You'll be sure to catch some big ones with that, son."

"Can we go now?"

"Not yet." His father ruffled his hair and grinned. *"But as soon as spring comes, we'll go to the lake, and I'll teach you how to fly fish."*

"Can Mike come along?"

John chuckled. *"You bet. I think Santa Claus brought him the same thing. And if you'd like, we can bring Abby, too."* He winked and added, *"I'm sure we can find a fishin' rod she can use."*

"Yahoo!"

Like the photographs in an album, the snippets of his childhood passed over his mind's eye. So many things from happier times.

"It's my one chance, Dad. Why are you doing this? Ruining my mother's dreams wasn't enough, now you have to ruin mine, too? I'm going to Nashville. I'm going to sing in that competition and I'll win. I'll get that record deal."

"If you leave, don't bother comin' back. You won't be welcome."

The bitterness of hateful words yelled in a fit of rage settled upon him. His back hurt with a phantom sting from all the times the belt had hit him. The shotgun his father fired the time he returned after winning the talent competition blasted his ears. The memory album slammed shut, smothering the spark of grief.

He swallowed the anger and the urge to drive away and never look back.

He looked up to see Abby watching him. No, he wasn't going anywhere.

At least, not until he claimed what his fear of becoming like his mother--washed-up and dead by age twenty-three--had denied him. The one person he'd let Mike talk him out of ever getting to know, by playing on his fears.

His daughter.

* * * *

The old Victorian house on the Double K Ranch was packed with mourners from the funeral. The Ladies' Auxiliary served beef barbeque sandwiches, baked beans, potato salad, and chocolate cake.

Abby had no appetite, but she carried her loaded plate out of the dining room with its old over-sized furniture to the wide wraparound porch. Several people milled around in small clusters, holding their plates and doing more talking than eating.

She smiled and greeted those who talked to her--not that many people did, but she didn't stop--and continued searching for Seth. She had to find out what he intended to do now that he was back in McAllister.

"Do you think Seth will stay in town?"

She stopped and took a deep breath before facing the woman behind her. Tammy Jo had never liked her, but then she'd never quite understood what Mike had ever seen in the spoiled heiress.

"I doubt it. He's famous. Nothing in McAllister mattered to him before." She turned to move away from her ex-husband's wife.

"I overheard him talking with his aunt."

When Abby looked at her, Tammy Jo smiled and glanced around at the people on the porch. She could barely keep the disdain off her supermodel face. So, she still considered herself better than the rest of them.

Tammy Jo met her gaze again and her smile widened. "Seth asked her what his father planned for the ranch. Seems to me he's thinking of moving here. How wonderful that would be. He's so famous."

"Yeah, wonderful," she muttered. Of course, Tammy Jo would think so, now that Seth Kendall was famous and rich. But there had been a time she wouldn't have given Seth a second glance.

Abby looked around again. She hadn't seen Seth since arriving at the house after leaving the gravesite.

She'd see about him staying. He had no business here. He'd promised to come back. Oh, he'd come back all right, only to leave again. He hadn't even wanted to see his baby. Chasing his dreams had been more important. Now, he could just keep on chasing them.

The numbed part of her heart belonging to Seth Kendall started to beat. The hurt was unbearable at the thought he'd leave her again.

Which was totally ridiculous. He had to go. His showing up now in Emily's life would serve no purpose but to devastate her.

Mike walked up beside her and Tammy Jo. He smiled at his wife and kissed her on the cheek. She rested her hand on her seven-month baby bump and looked up at him with softness in her hazel eyes.

Mike glanced at Abby and then back to Tammy Jo. Abby's heart skipped a beat at the answering love he held for his wife in his eyes. He'd never looked upon her like that, but then, neither she nor Mike had ever been in love.

"Sweetheart, I need to talk to Abby about Emily. Can you go find Miz Kendall and make sure she's doing okay? She's taking John's death hard."

Tammy Jo's smile turned cold. "Of course." High heels clicked across the porch as she strode into the kitchen.

The screen door closed with a bang, making Abby cringe. "You know she hates me."

Mike swallowed and looked down at his hands. "She thinks you have some hold over me." He met her gaze before turning away and heading off the porch. "C'mon."

She set her plate of untouched food on the wide banister and followed Mike out onto the lawn. They passed Martha Gordon and two of Tammy Jo's elderly aunts she took care of, as they sat under the trees in the garden eating and chatting. Mike nodded and tipped his hat at the older women.

"Sheriff Ritter, how you doin'? Getting ready for that baby?" Martha's smile showed extra bright against her dark brown complexion.

"I'm doing fine, Miz Gordon. And I can't wait until Tammy Jo has the baby." He smiled as they continued walking. "Aunts Edna and Bea. Good to see you ladies out and about."

The spinster sisters harrumphed and glared at Abby.

Martha glanced at the sisters and then back to her. "Good to see you, dear. The nursing home keepin' you busy these days?"

She didn't miss the curiosity in the woman's words, or the McAllister sisters' lips compressed into stern lines. "You too, Mrs. Gordon. Yes, I'm picking up some of Darlene Martinez's hours."

"Glad to hear you ain't causin' trouble."

Mike raised a brow at her and then looked over his shoulder at the women. "We leave all the trouble to our daughter."

Martha chuckled. "Now, I just bet that sweet little girl can cause a heap of trouble. But she sure was blessed with an angel's voice. Will she be singing at the Founder's Day picnic next month?"

Abby glanced at Mike before answering. Neither of them wanted Emily to sing publicly, but they also had long realized she had too much of her father in her to keep her quiet. "You know she will."

Edna leaned closer to her sister and said just loud enough for Abby to hear, "I remember John having the same trouble with Seth. That boy would sing to the cows just to spite his daddy. God rest his soul."

Abby's breath caught at the comparison.

Mike held her gaze a beat before tipping his hat and smiling at the women again. "Have a good afternoon, ladies."

Once they rounded the corner of the house and were out of earshot of the elderly women, Abby said, "Do you think people wonder where Emily's talent comes from?"

"No." He set his hand on her back and guided her to the white rail fence bordering the yard. "Talent may run in families, but that doesn't automatically mean it has to. Besides, I have a cousin from Georgia who is a rock singer. So, talent does run in my family if anyone ever asks."

He'd eased her mind a little. "You're probably right." She smiled and glanced at Mike as he looked out over the pastures. "You know most people think I'm hanging around you and your family because I want you back."

Mike met her gaze and shoved his hands into his pockets. "We were pretty convincing when we were married. Our divorce surprised the whole town."

"Yeah, we deserve an Academy Award for that performance."

"What's that supposed to mean?"

She laughed and waved the comment off. "Nothing. It's just amazing how easily we fooled everyone." She leaned over the fence rail and stared at the cattle grazing on the buffalo grass. "Thank you. I don't know what I would've done without you." She met his deep brown eyes and smiled. "And I'm also sorry."

"For what?"

She straightened and faced him as she pushed her hair from her face. A warm breeze blew across the flat grassland of the pastures. "You know what for. You and Tammy Jo. You were so head over heels crazy for her in high school. I wish I'd have known about your affair sooner. I'd have let you go then. It's the least I could have done."

She'd be lying to herself if she said his secret two-year affair with Tammy Jo hadn't hurt, but she couldn't be what Mike needed. She loved him, but not as a woman should love her husband. He'd always been more like a big brother to her. Her best friend.

Seth had been the one she'd burned for during those long nights while Mike slept on the far side of their bed. He never felt passion for her either. Soon after their marriage, they stopped trying to find it. Their nearly non-existent sex life had always been damned awkward.

He looked away and leaned his backside against a fence post. "I've always loved her. But I couldn't turn my back on you--or Emily."

He squinted against the glare of the sun. She'd always known what Mike sacrificed to be with her, to be a father to her baby, giving them a stable home.

The one thing she never understood was why he'd made the sacrifice. But now wasn't the time to ask. Of course, he wouldn't have told her anyway. He never had any of the other times she'd asked.

"Tammy Jo seems to be taking pregnancy well."

Mike chuckled and seemed to peer down at his expensive rattlesnake boots. He'd left his suit jacket in his Mercedes, and the tie must be there, too. Tammy Jo might be able to dress Mike up to look the part as a member the upper crust of society, but deep down Mike Ritter was still a cowboy who'd never wanted to do anything but ride rodeo.

"She is," he said. "The decorator just finished the baby's room. You ought to see it. The suite is fit for a prince."

She could imagine the expense of remodeling the old mansion in the center of town would probably feed a small country for a year too.

"So, she's having a boy?"

When he turned to her, the purest joy shone in his dark, warm eyes. "Yeah. But you have to swear to secrecy. Tammy Jo wants it to be a surprise for everyone."

She pushed loose hair from her face again, twisted the long mane and pulled it over her shoulder. "You got it. I'm happy for you. You always wanted a son."

The warm breeze ruffled the blond hair on his forehead under his hat brim. "That doesn't change what I feel for Emily. You know that, right?" He focused on her again. "I love her, Abby. That will never change. I've loved her since that first time I felt her kick when you were about four months pregnant. You remember that?"

"Yeah. You thought she was surely part bronco."

The large yard stretched in front of her. She, Mike and Seth had played a lot of tag and hide-and-seek on this patch of grass. A storm must be brewing somewhere. She folded her arms against the sudden chill in the air and hoped it didn't come to destroy their lives.

"You are her father in every way that matters. I know you love her." Facing him, she leaned her shoulder against a fencepost. "Mike, what are we going to do? Tammy Jo said she overheard Seth voicing an interest in the ranch. If he inherits the Double K and stays, what will we tell your parents? They adore Emily. But I'm not sure I can keep Emily in the dark if he's here. She idolizes him."

He took her by the hand and squeezed. His eyes flashed with anger. "We don't tell them a damned thing," he said, his voice pitched low. "Especially Emily. Besides, what claim does he have on her? My name's on her birth certificate. You said so yourself--I'm her father. He left you. He abandoned Emily. Hell, he came to the house and practically gloated, since I was married to you, he was relieved he didn't have to be saddled with a baby." He brushed his fingers over her cheek. "Abby, we can't tell anyone. Do you understand what the truth would do to them? To Emily?"

She nodded and clutched the folds of her skirt. The falsehood suddenly rubbed wrong on the painful spot in her heart belonging to Seth. "I suppose."

He smiled and stepped away from the railing. "I better get back before someone sees us and thinks the unthinkable." He squeezed her hand again before letting it go. "Abby, I've always been your friend. Nothing's changed. I'm here if you need me. Don't let your feelings for Seth sway you. Keeping Emily away from him is best for her. Think about how finding out about this will affect Mom. None of us want to bury her next."

She nodded and smiled, but it felt forced. He was right. Carolann's sick heart couldn't take the pain or the stress if she discovered the truth about her only grandchild. "I know. Now, get back in there to that jealous wife of yours."

He ambled across the yard and went around the corner of the house. She hugged herself and made her way to the old gazebo in the corner of the green expanse of grass. A grove of pecan trees provided shade for the structure. She plunged into the cool darkness when she stepped under the deeply pitched roof. Her eyes took a moment to adjust to the dimness.

She ran her hand over the chipped white paint of the banister.

"Remember when you, Mike and I painted this old thing?"

At the sound of the deep voice, she spun, her hand going over her heart. Seth stood up from the swing hanging from the rafters on the other side. "Seth..."

She sucked in a breath and it caught in her throat. Time had changed him, but it had also made him even more devastatingly handsome. The dark tailored pants showed off his long legs and above-average height. The white dress shirt fit like a custom glove, outlining his broad shoulders. He'd lost the power tie he'd worn to the funeral. The top two buttons of his shirt lay open, and he'd rolled the sleeves to his elbows, showing off powerful forearms.

His coppery-blond hair curled over his collar and fell over his high forehead. A trimmed ginger-colored goatee hid the scar on his chin from a riding accident. The green ice of his eyes captured her gaze and made her heart race.

He gestured toward the pasture with a tall glass of what looked and smelled like whiskey. "I saw you and Mike. So, what happened? I thought you two would be together forever."

She shrugged and turned away from him as he took a long sip from the glass. "I don't see how that's any of your damned business."

A board in the floor creaked as he approached. She looked over her shoulder. He was so close. Her heart stuttered over a beat or two and something warm curled in her belly. How could he still affect her after everything he'd done to her?

He smiled, but it never reached his eyes. They remained two stormy seas ready to devour her in their relentless waves. "Oh, but I think it is very much my business. I want to see my daughter, Abigail."

"You lost that right when you drove away that night." She fisted her hands and faced him. "You lost that right when you let another man take your place in her life."

He narrowed his eyes and leaned closer. His breath reeked from the whiskey. She wrinkled her nose at the painful memories of her father's addiction to alcohol as much as from the stench.

"You know why I had to leave. It was my one and only chance. Goddamn it, you didn't give me any other option."

She snorted and squared her shoulders. "You had fame and fortune to chase. I'm glad you achieved your dreams. But it came with a price."

"I told you I'd be back. But when I returned you were married to my best friend."

"You were gone for seven months!" She gritted her teeth against the old hurt. "You never called or wrote, but I watched that damned talent show every week and cheered you on. Then the next thing I heard, you were dating Amanda Lang from the show. I figured you made your choice. You wanted no part of me or my baby. So, I made mine."

"Amanda and I were and are just friends. The media blew that whole duet thing out of proportion. It wasn't until I found out you were married and gave away my little girl that we became friends with benefits."

The memory of watching them together on the show churned inside her. Maybe the media had taken an innocent friendship of two teenagers and attached a connotation that wasn't there. Still, he couldn't deny he and the blond, green-eyed pop star started dating two weeks after he returned to Nashville after his winning the show and had been in an on again-off again relationship for years.

He looked into his glass of whiskey. "I'm sorry I didn't call or write. I was eighteen and scared shitless. I had to concentrate on winning, but the whole time I was thinking about you."

She laughed, but instead of coming out bitter, it scratched and resounded with too much raw pain. "You were scared? What the hell do you think I was? I was seventeen and pregnant. My father was dying with a brain tumor, and I had a ranch to run."

He grabbed her arm when she spun away. "I had to sing in that competition. Otherwise, it would've taken ten years to get to the kind of success I got from winning *America's Rising Star*. If I ever got that chance again. My mother never did. This place killed her. I couldn't let that happen to me. Or to you and our baby."

She swallowed but couldn't work her constricted throat.

"I wanted you to come with me." His voice dipped low enough it might have been on the verge of cracking. "I wanted you and our baby, Abigail. You are the one who turned your back on me. You're the one who couldn't wait to fall into bed with my best friend."

Oh, how she wished she could tell him the truth about her and Mike, but she wouldn't. She glared at his hand on her upper arm, then at him. "You're drunk. Let go, now."

He stepped back, letting go. She was amazed at how calm she'd sounded, because inside her a twister had taken up residence. Her heart raced and her jaw and hands ached from clenching tightly. "You knew why I couldn't run off to Nashville with you and live on dreams and fairytales. Mike understood, and he was here when I needed him. He gave me what you wouldn't."

But neither of them knew the real reason she didn't go with Seth.

When she reached the grass again, she turned toward him and folded her arms in front of her. "If you're thinking about staying here, you can forget it. I don't want you around. My being divorced has nothing to do with you. Mike is still Emily's father, and that's how it's going to stay."

She blinked against the burn in her eyes. Damn, if she didn't soon get out of here, she'd start bawling. "Go back to your fast cars and even faster women. Go back to your stadiums full of groupies and your high life as a Grammy-winning superstar. McAllister, Texas, has nothing for you. It never has."